PRAISE FOR *AWAY TO STAY*

"*Away to Stay* is sinuous and zizzy, cinematic and beguiling. Mary Kuryla brings us news of our shared precarity, our brutal and borrowed world."

— Noy Holland, author of *Bird*

"*Away to Stay* is a tense, propulsive, and thrillingly subjective coming-of-age story, with gorgeous prose and slippery characters that will stick with you."

— J. Ryan Stradal, author of *The Lager Queen of Minnesota*

"Kuryla has an unflinching eye for the dark strangeness of domestic life and her ravishing prose only deepens the provocation. A powerful and stunningly original book."

— Lexi Freiman, author of *Inappropriation*

110645251

AWAY TO STAY

Mary Kuryla

Regal House Publishing

Published by
Regal House Publishing, LLC
Raleigh, NC 27587
All rights reserved

ISBN -13 (paperback): 9781646030729
ISBN -13 (epub): 9781646030972
Library of Congress Control Number: 2020952065

All efforts were made to determine the copyright holders and obtain
their permissions in any circumstance where copyrighted material was
used. The publisher apologizes if any errors were made during this
process, or if any omissions occurred. If noted, please contact the
publisher and all efforts will be made to incorporate permissions in
future editions.

Interior and cover design by Lafayette & Greene
Cover images © by C. B. Royal

Regal House Publishing, LLC
https://regalhousepublishing.com

Printed in the United States of America

To Eugene, to stay.

RIVERSIDE, CALIFORNIA. 2006

1

This may be a good house, but it is single-story and wanting. What the house does not want in yard or in fence, it wants in room. Still it is three o'clock in the morning and what is a knock on the front door when there is so much room for this house in me? Mom says I am the one who wants, the one who stays, so the knocking must come of my flesh. My knuckles float over the wood as a low growl heats up the other side of the door.

The porch light flicks on. The house rumbles from someone stomping up. The door swings wide and before I let go a word, a big dog busts through the screen. It is rude and surprising and sporty. This dog about knocks me flat.

"Stop the dog!" A man in a camouflage jacket barrels out the door after the dog.

The dog comes short under the orange nose of the cab—the driver is keeping Mom in his pumpkin until someone pays. Mom palms the passenger window, telling me to stay, while the man in camouflage pivots on the dim street to look both ways for his dog that might have gone either. He calls for his dog. It sounds like "brrrrr."

Mom opens the cab door. "Hello!" She waves to the man tugging now at the hem of his checkered pajama hooked on his heel. "Do you mind, Jack? Somebody must pay a driver."

So this Jack, Mom's long-lost cousin Jack, the owner-of-the-house Jack, stares at Mom, considering, but soon he is back to calling for his dog with both hands cupped at his mouth. Even from here on the stoop, in the middle of the night, it is clear as daylight that the reason this Jack is not pulling for his wallet is because he is a lot more interested in what got out of his house than what wants in.

Mom has a remedy for this. She is a nurse and nurses think

with their feet. She tosses her high heels on the driveway then stretches out a leg to loop a heel on her toe, turning to see if Jack looks. Jack's head swings so fast to Mom's leg, his hands cup air not mouth. He catches himself and his hands drop. He shoves them into his pockets, so nothing happened. But he has made his choice. Whether he knows it or not, she has won; he has chosen Mom now.

She rises up out of the cab, shifting her skimpy hips to tug down her skirt, and Jack shakes his head and Jack smiles. Maybe I was wrong. Maybe he knew all along that he would choose her, but the way he takes a last glance over his shoulder for his runaway dog is going to cost him. If Mom notices, she is not showing. She pokes at the bun pinned high on her head. Jack jogs up the driveway to Mom and wraps long arms around her. She goes up easy, light and fine.

They walk across the lawn, Mom carrying one suitcase and Jack the other, knocking into each other like teenagers, as the cab driver backs out, reckless with his pay. The driver never asked Mom why we were living in our car. He did not ask what had gone down in the park. The driver never even looked at her stepping around the gashed tires, broken window glass sprouting in the tufts of grass. He did not ask as Mom hauled suitcases from the trunk of our car and dropped them in his. But as the driver cruised out of the lot in Griffith Park, he looked at me in the rearview mirror, his eyes small and sad, until they got studious. I stopped looking back before his eyes got mean.

"That is Olya," Mom says to Jack as they come alongside me.

"Don't you know not to let dogs out," he says, "Olya?" Jack wheels around and stomps back inside his house.

I follow but Mom swings my suitcase like a gate between the door and me. "You not allowed in."

"Funny, Mom."

She points at the holed-up screen hanging open. "You heard him. You let out dog." She rolls her eyes and shoots her eyebrows up and down and, in case I am not getting it, screws her index finger at her temple to say he is crazy.

I start in anyway, but she holds my arm.

"No, this is not the best way now. It's me. I will do it. I will make so he invites you in, so he begs." Mom sets down her suitcase and feels for the zipper. A sweater appears in her hands. "Sit," she says. She tucks the arms of the sweater around my legs. Standing on the threshold, she frowns at the houses across the street. "Don't talk to strangers," she says and backs inside his house.

I do not talk to strangers. Talking is not something pretty I do. But I cannot worry about pretty. I am going to talk my way into a place to stay. I have not had that, something regular to come home to, and I will soon be a teenager and so will roam. I should prepare a few remarks, make my case for why Jack should welcome me in, but my feet have already taken me back to his door and the only thing that comes into my head is how painting blood on the door was never enough to keep out the Angel of Death. Specifically, the lintel had to be soaked in lamb's blood, or else goodbye firstborn. I do not know where the lintel is on a door, but I am my mother's firstborn so maybe I am better off without a house. If there is no door to pass through, there is no sacrifice.

The door hangs slightly ajar, and Mom stands with her back to it. She says, "Olya has no place."

"What does she know?" Jack steps up close behind Mom.

"What do you care? That dog is what you care for." Mom looks over her shoulder, sees me on the other side of the door, and latches it again. The door quakes against the jamb.

I stand here, stupid, before a house.

Jack's dog paces the sidewalk, his yellow eyes on me. "What do you know?" I say.

The dog's nose scrunches. Its lips draw up to the gums, showing teeth. Do dogs smile or is this one fixing to bite?

Now a lanky black dog saunters up out of the suburban blue to sniff at the open garbage can on the street. The black dog's greasy coat has never seen a brush. It is all ribs, ugly, nothing like Jack's dog, whose fur swirls over his shoulders, whose glossy coat only hints at black like sunlight hints at shade.

The black dog leaps up and topples the garbage can onto the curb. He works his nose into the junk, coming up with a paper sack from some homey mom-and-pop BBQ joint. He shakes the bag until the bottom rips open and charred bones scissor out. Jack's dog stands very still beside the black dog gnawing at the bones. Until he pounces on the black's spine. The black yelps, ducks and runs. Jack's dog watches the lanky black go out of sight. From the tail of his eye he throws me a look and he, too, glides up the street but in the other direction. He never once looked at the bones.

Jack's dog is going away, and it might be he has gone to stay. He had that air about him. Not exactly disloyal so much as not bothering anyone with the hurt. Dogs cannot be much different than people when it comes to feelings. Whether or not he comes home is nothing to me, but it is probably a big something for Jack, and since Mom's cousin is not kneeling on the threshold begging yet, it comes down to the dog. My fault the dog escaped. If I can get the dog back into the house, there is a chance I can get in too.

The rocks fit okay in my pockets. Jack's dog is rounding the street corner. I whistle. The dog looks back.

"Here, boy."

The rest of him turns to me now. His tail swings. He pads towards me, curious and cautious, each paw lifting the blacktop like tar. Jack's dog hits the curb. I dodge around to the street and pitch rocks at him. He growls. The rocks are a surprise. Hit, his hind flinches, his leg buckles. It occurs to me now that throwing rocks at a dog to make him stay makes no sense. But the dog springs off the curb and on up Jack's driveway to the open gate. I guess Jack's dog has no more sense than I do.

I empty my pockets on the dog. He is halfway through the gate, shoulders caved, nose twisted, offended, when he freezes. He whirls around to me. I stumble back. What is he after? The dog drops on his front paws, tail waving, haunches pitched. His eyes switch from me to the rock in my hand. I draw my hand back, breathe in, but not out. The rock trembles in my palm. I toss the rock to him and he leaps in the air, supple dancer, and stops the rock with his teeth.

Hinds swaying to the wag of his tail, the dog trots back down the driveway to screw his wet nose into my hand. I do not move, but the last rocks slip from my fingers. My legs wobble so I sit on the curb, tense against what the dog will do next. Jack's dog lies at my feet.

The front door swings wide. Jack fires down the walkway. From the door, Mom hollers, "So what? Dogs run away!" She is not paying attention, or she would see his dog here beside me.

Jack makes it to his truck before his dog rises on jittery legs. He stops cold to stare at his dog. He studies it. Though I do not want to, I reach out and quickly pat the dog's head. It does not object. In fact, the dog lies back down at my feet. He noses a rock at my shoe.

Jack looks from the dog to me. I look right back at Jack. I smile.

Jack slow whistles. The dog tilts its head at the sound, instinctive and without interest. Jack says, "Well, what do you know?"

2

Irina, I…uh…don't get a lot of guests." Jack shifts a bag of dog food farther down the sofa to make room for us. "You know?"

Mom sits erect and proper on the cracked green leather. She pats a cushion for me to sit. I draw my heels right up to the sofa as I do. The furniture in a vacancy does not wear out like Jack's sofa—nobody sits long in a vacancy.

Jack picks up a video game console from the coffee table and sits. "You familiar with dogs, Olya?" His forearms palm his thighs like he might leap.

I look at Mom.

"Is she?" he says.

Mom shrugs. "Dogs do not exactly bite her."

"No, ah, not like that. Bird, I mean, he responded to the girl."

"Luck," says Mom.

Jack smiles. "Bird won't have anything to do with luck." He turns to me, his irises sparking. "How'd you do that? Get him to come?"

"What about hello? What about nice to meet you?" Mom says. "That is how talk to guests, Jack."

He looks at Mom, nods, turns back to me. "Just for the record, ever worked professionally with canines?"

"This is Olya. You see her?" Mom says.

"What?" he says. "What?" He gives Mom a double take, like men do when they first lay eyes on her. "Look at you," he says. "Look at you."

"Look at her."

But Jack cannot seem to look at me, except to frown, like he is solving a tricky equation. Instead he rises up with the dog food, carries it a few steps, squats and shakes the bag over a bowl. Kibbles plink into metal. The meat and cereal smell rush out of the bag, mixing with the other dog smells in the house and the smells of sweat and leather. Naming smells sounds worse than the smell of them. At least there is no scent of air freshener or bleach to cover up the odor of the former occupant of a vacancy. Jack props the bag against the gnawed leg of a piano. "I bet you had a dog, huh, Olya?"

"No dogs," Mom says. "Not us."

Bowl in hand, Jack stands over me. "But you like dogs, Olya?" he says.

"No, she does not like."

"Bird likes her," Jack says. "Maybe what Bird needs is a little friend."

"So get him little friend," Mom says.

Jack sticks the dog bowl at me. "Go give Bird some chow."

"No," Mom says, "not allowed."

What Mom means to say is that I am not to give food to the dog. Mom does not always add the preposition that the verb needs to do its job because the language she grew up with, Russian, does not trouble with them. Things can get pretty interesting when her dropping the last word makes a sentence more of a game than it already is. In this case she is inventing a rule, which she will do sometimes when she wants things to go her way. But a rule like this one is headed in the wrong direction. The fastest way to this man's heart is through his dog. I take the bowl from Jack.

"Great," he says and points down the hallway. "Out back. Great. Great."

The light in the hallway is poor but good enough to see my reflection framed in the glass pictures I pass. All things considered, my eye is not swelling too bad. In these pictures Jack wears a police uniform and stands in green fields beside his dog. Jack is a very good dog trainer by the looks of the framed awards, first place, every time. In another picture, Jack kneels, wincing into the sun, yellow dust smearing his grin, his camouflage, the dog beside him. Nobody could argue with the joy in Jack's face. The same dog is in all the pictures, the same dog that busted a hole through the screen door, the same dog that turned my rocks into a game, the same dog that sits now on the other side of the glass door at the end of the hallway, his eyes on the chow I hold in my hand.

"How'd she get the shiner?" Jack's voice carries from the parlor.

"I told you."

"You told me someone broke into your car. Were you in the car?"

"Olya was."

"Why come here?"

"She needs a home, Jack."

"She needs the cops."

Mom says, "You are not a cop?"

"The girl must be examined. Reports need to be filed. Procedures followed."

"They will say it's neglect," Mom says fast, fast.

"Irina," he says, "you familiar with the K-9 training principle that a dog only performs something unpleasant in order to keep something more unpleasant from happening?"

"No," Mom says, "I am not familiar with this dog principle."

"Maybe not the principle, but you get the idea. Otherwise, you wouldn't be here."

The long tail wags on the other side of the door. The dog paws the ground. It cannot wait to eat Jack's chow.

"She *had* to stay in the car," Mom shouts. "I had no money."

"Money?" Jack says. "I'd have given you that."

"Give her home," Mom says.

"This house is no place for her," Jack says.

The dog's nose steams the spaces between my fingers pressed at the glass. It does not look at the bowl of chow anymore. The dog looks at me.

"Olya?" Mom's reflection swells in the glass as she shimmers up the hallway, her heels nicking the boards. The dog's eyes shift to Mom. I lift my hand from the glass. The dog draws back. His snout fires up in song, *hi-huh-hi-huh-hi-huh*—like wind screaming through a house, this high-pitched sound.

"He always do this?" Mom asks Jack, who jogs up the hallway to his dog.

"It's new," Jack says.

"Is terrible sound. Put the dog away."

Jack looks at Mom and me like we dropped from the sky and made a bad hole. He looks over at his dog behind the glass. "This is his house."

Mom shrugs. "Come, Olya." Her hands find my shoulders and march me toward the other end of the hallway. Like a guy on the plains, Jack shades his eyes, watching us go. He picks up the chow and pushes out the back door to his dog.

Mom keeps on for the front door. We pass another hallway that leads to a mess of bedrooms. The doors are shut, but I can picture one room after another and how they square out to windows. I see the whole house, all its rooms: bedrooms and bathrooms, living room, parlor, kitchen, dining room. Just places in my head, until now, here, inside this house, his house, and oh, all of it, all along waiting for me.

Mom picks up her suitcase and hands me mine.

I do not take the suitcase. "You promised," I say. "At the park, you promised."

"I know, I promised. But what can I do? You heard him. We can't stay. We will go to a motel."

"No. It has to be a house. *This* house."

Mom's eyes travel around the walls before settling back on me. "Some house." She blinks a couple times, tearing up. Mom takes rejection of any kind very personally. That is probably why she has never mentioned her cousin before tonight. She knew how things would come out.

What she did not know was me.

I reach for my suitcase but just to set it back down. Mom goes to pick it back up but is stopped by a commotion behind us. A scramble of nails gaining traction on the boards.

Something bangs into my knees. Jack's dog dances round as I get my balance.

Jack rushes up the hallway, leash slung from his neck, to stop short before his dog leaning against my leg. Jack runs a hand through his buzzed-up hair. "Bird's never done that before."

"Sure, he's never run away from you," Mom says.

"No, I mean, run to someone else." Jack leashes up Bird quick but draws a slow hand down the dog's long spine. He gives a firm pat to the hind leg and looks up. He says, "I've got a nice bedroom for you." He stares into Mom, but he means me. "Last one down the hall." With the toe of his boot, Jack nudges my suitcase at me. "Put it there."

Mom's face goes white beneath her make up. Her eyes shift between Jack and me. "You go put Olya's suitcase in the nice bedroom, Jack," she says, backing out the front door with hers. "Show how hospitable you are."

Jack lunges for her suitcase. "You too, Irina," he says, coaxing. "It's cold. Come on. Time to come in."

Bit by bit Mom's hand slips off the handle, and her suitcase is his. She pivots and bolts out the door.

"Stay!" he says.

Mom freezes on the stoop.

"Come."

"Funny, Jack," she whispers. But after a while she does turn around and, like stepping between two curtains onto a stage, she glides back into the house. The dog backs out of her way, something like a gentleman. Jack kicks the door shut.

3

You are one hundred percent novelty to Bird. The obedience you elicited, don't get a swelled head. His submission to you was beginner's luck ," Jack says over breakfast, even though last night he told Mom that Bird would have nothing to do with luck. But why argue with a man who has set out before you a plate of pancakes and syrup, ruby in a glass maple leaf?

Jack clears our plates and strides to the sink. He swirls dish liquid into the running water and rolls up sleeves to elbows. His forearms are wiry, the veins circling the muscles like fighters in a ring. Mom appreciates veins. That is a nurse thinking with needles. Mom kissed me goodbye before she left this morning. Even the smell of pancakes could not keep her.

"Do you have any idea what it takes to train a dog?" Jack hollers over the running water. "It takes commitment. It takes a professional. It takes a lifetime. I'll show you what it takes."

He twists off the water and tosses a hand towel to me. "You know how to dry dishes, right? Meet you in the backyard at 800."

I figured out how to get Jack's dog back into the house last night but only so that I could get into the house myself. Retrieving Bird did not go beyond that. Mom is right. I do not like dogs. One visit with that foster family to the animal shelter, with cage after cage of sorry-faced canines, was enough. When it comes to a place to stay, dogs have no luck at all.

I walk to my room to perch on the bed and watch Mom's cousin through the window.

He stands arms akimbo in the generous shade of the backyard's only tree. Bird leashed tight to his leg, Jack looks square at me through the window. He thumbs over his shoulder, get out here.

"Unpack now," Jack said after setting my suitcase down in this room last night. He watched me open the suitcase, take out clothes and stuff them in the bureau drawers. He nodded and left. I pulled open the bureau, took out all my clothes and folded them back into the suitcase. The suitcase I kept safe in the closet. Only my Bible stayed out. I placed it in the drawer beside the bed—a drawer very much like where I found the book in a vacancy, tucked in the drawer, secret and knowing and red. The Bible has got the talk down. Somebody in the Old Testament starts talking and the book takes off. That somebody could talk his way into anything. I believe I have talked my way into a place to stay.

"Stop dragging your feet, Olya," Jack says, pulling open a rusted chair for me as I drag my feet into his backyard. "This canine requires work." Jack lets the leash unwind behind him as he steps away from his dog. "The 'come' is the most basic command. Learning to come is the most basic skill." Jack swivels round to the dog. "Come, Bird," he says. "Come." When Bird does not come, Jack yanks on the leash.

Bird's neck bends with the leash, but the dog does not come to Jack. With each yank, Jack wraps the leash around his hand and his elbow until the long leash is a short leash, and one good yank finally gets Bird moving in his direction.

Jack draws a bright white nylon pouch off his shoulder. He pulls out hunks of dry meat. "Come, Bird."

Bird comes for the meat, putting up with Jack's fingertips on his snout. Soon as the meat is eaten, Bird backs away. "Come, Bird." Jack's hand rustles inside the pouch.

His dog takes a step closer, a step all four legs do not take.

Jack rustles the pouch, saying he does not respect handlers who rely on treats to motivate their dog. So why treats now? If not for all those commendations stating Jack is a sure-fire trainer, I would say this guy does not know much about a dog's wants.

Jack keeps rustling inside the pouch, making the treats in there speak. His other hand joins in. The rustling turns into

slapping, and Jack's hands come out fighting. One hand yanks
the pouch from the other and throws the pouch at Bird. Bird
dodges the pouch, and the leash snaps out of Jack's hand.

"Come, Bird!" Jack shouts now. The leash trails Bird as he
trots along the fence to the other side of the yard to square off.
"Goddamn punk, come!"

Bird hesitates. He seems to object to how important his
obedience is to Jack, how it seems to go way beyond learning to
come. A little shiver runs through Bird. He looks at the ground
and back at Jack, his eyes wide and his brows strung as wet
laundry. All he seems to want is a good petting. His head starts
to shake. The rest of him follows. Turning, Bird runs to the
fence, rises on his hinds, clears it, gone.

Jack looks back at the pouch on the ground. He walks to the
pouch, past the basketball hoop facedown in the dirt, past the
red punching bag tangled with the chain, a platform pell mell
with rusted barbells. He counts out loud as he walks past an upright bicycle rutted on a flat, past a hand-painted sign nailed to
the warped planked door of a doghouse that reads, Ho Sweet
Ho. "Fifteen!" Jack screams. "Fifteen shitty feet. You couldn't
come." He laughs. He bends over laughing and sits in the dirt.

"Don't leave me alone with him," I told Mom this morning.

"You wanted a home," Mom said. "Give Jack a chance." She
folded into Jack's luxury Chevy and headed to the repair shop
where our car had been towed.

The low branches of the only tree in the yard spread over
Jack's head in umbrella spokes. His shoulders curve round a
cigarette as I walk up. "Did I tell you to come?" he says.

We both know that he is acting foolish. For something to do,
I grab a low branch of the tree to test for climbing.

"Bird isn't up there," Jacks says. "In spite of his name, Bird
isn't in any tree."

The branch is strong. It will hold.

"Not that he isn't capable of it."

I swing a leg over the branch as I pull myself up.

"See where Bird went?"

I point with my foot at the fence.

"After that?

I shrug.

"Keep your eyes on the dog. You can learn from that dog."

From up here, the view is pleasantly dull: fence, driveway, front lawn. No sign of Bird.

"Of course, the point is what can the dog learn from us? That requires practical intelligence, the ability to conform to the desire of the handler." The hair on Jack's head curls every which way. This is hair that does not conform to a comb.

"Bird doesn't want to come to you," I say.

Smoke balls out of Jack's mouth. "What, are you fucking kidding me? You for real?" He draws on the cigarette. "Fucking crazy, like your…" But after a while Jack says quietly, "I might as well be a stranger to that dog." He blows on the tip of his cigarette.

I could say that Jack has the looks of a cowboy, blue eyes gold from loads of sun off the horizon, or the looks of a soldier, a superhero, an altar boy, or someone just wicked. Take your pick. I have no muscle for description. Looking at someone enough to describe him is time I seem to never have before Mom and I are called upon to leave.

"Bird is full of temperament," Jack says. "That's what you want in a police dog. But he isn't pure Malinois. Sure, he's got the Shepherd's sense of duty. He's better looking. That's the Chesapeake Bay Retriever. His forehead and snout are Chessie. Those eyes could carve a hole in you. Chessies have got courage but they can get a little sharp. Self-preservation plays a role." Jack tilts his head at me. "Know what self-preservation is?"

I stare at Jack.

"Yeah, ah…well." He flicks his cigarette then snuffs it with a thick stone. "In the case of a dog, self-preservation is putting the self first, instead of protecting the packmate—the human—against attack. A self-preserving dog becomes unreliable. A dog like that, which also shows a lack of courage, tends to bite out of fear."

"Bird has courage," I say. "He fought another dog over food in your garbage."

"Who won?"

"Bird."

"Must have been worth fighting for."

"Not to Bird. He left the bones on the ground."

"You don't know anything about dogs."

I drop off the branch. "I know courage, mister."

"I reckon you do." He climbs to his feet. He says, "You probably think you know about a lot of things."

"I never said I knew about dogs—"

"I'm not talking about dogs. I'm talking about me, about your mom and me, even about you, how you figure in it all. You may think you know what's what, but you don't. Quit acting you do."

He does not wait for me to argue it. He says, "Even the Germans couldn't train the Chessie. Foreigners. You know what language Bird speaks?"

"Not yours," I say.

"How old are you? Twelve, thirteen? Not a pretty year in a girl's life."

"What year is pretty?"

"How old's your mother?" He lights another cigarette. "At your age I was heavy into search and rescue. That's right, baby." He stomps up to the yellow doghouse, punting the clutter in his path. "Two kinds of dogs in search and rescue, the air-sniffing dogs and those that track on a lead. The sniffers run off leash, leave you way behind, and put out racket when they pick up a scent. The ones on the lead you must stick to for the duration. They will run your ass off." On every word, his fist knocks the roof of the doghouse. "Through creek, through thicket, down fallen trees, you keep up with the dog, and the strain either splits your bones or gets you in fit for the military. I just liked to see the dogs work." Jack cups a hand at his ear, making fun of his talk, but I cannot say I minded.

On the other side of the fence, a couple of girls walk haltered ponies past Jack's yard. The girls wear their hair in braids and their ponies' tails are plaited too. One pony's tail lifts, roping dung onto the pavement. This is just some old cowboy town. The houses all around have flat yards with wagon wheels and some western décor or other. Crummy stuff, but homey. Next door a man cares for his roses. Bird lounges in the street, sniffing dung.

Jack wraps an arm around the roof of the doghouse like they are old buddies. "The best training you can give a dog is in locating its master. It could take Pop's dog a week to track Pop down. That man knew how to get lost."

"You had a dad," I say.

He looks over at me. "Nobody gets out of that honor."

I pull my eyes out from under his stare and look back over the fence. The neighbor sprays his roses in the face. The roses drain petals. One of Mom's admirers flew in from Tbilisi with dozens of roses every time she performed in the Kirov. Rare roses only to be found in the south. Her admirer's front-row seat was reserved a year in advance so he could throw the rare roses at her feet and the petals could leap across the stage to her. When I asked if that man was my father, if he was the one, she said yes, you are our love child. But the man with rare roses was not her only admirer. I have asked this question about all of them. She always says yes. Some might think it careless of a child's feelings, this answer that is not one. But whatever Jack says about knowing, I do know Mom is not very happy no man has stepped up to claim me.

"Your mom tells me that when there's no place else, you sleep in her car—"

"A car is no place to stay," I say. "It's all windows and seats. Seats make bad beds if you want to lie beside your mom. A car is better than the shelter, though. Tents are the best. Mom makes them nice with pink lanterns, and the bugs tap to the light. You can roast marshmallows from a tent. When we have money, we sleep in a vacancy."

"What's a vacancy?"

"A motel, you know, with a vacancy."

"So you're basically homeless."

"We don't sleep on cement, mister."

"Ah, okay," Jack says. "Thanks for clearing that up." He pops to his feet and strides to the fence. Bird is still in the street. His nose points at Jack as he rises to uncertain feet.

"That dog," Jack says, "is not the smartest dog, but once he does learn a command, he has the ability to unlearn it. That shows adaptive intelligence." He looks at me. "French," he says. "Our dogs are trained by the French, in the language of love. Tell him to attack in French, he ought to do it."

"Tell him to come," I say, "in French."

He looks at me. "Is that how you got him to come back last night, talking in French?"

"I do not know the language of love," I say.

4

Bodies clunked against the door. Bodies clunked and flesh stuck in wet leaves to the window. Rocking, really. Really, it was more of a rocking, how the man and the woman propped themselves against our car to kiss. His thick braid smeared the glass. Our car was for their bodies only. If they had known I was in the car, known I watched from inside, it might have reminded them of not having somewhere better to be. What they wouldn't do then.

They did not look inside the car. They did not even look at each other. Once I thought our eyes met, the woman's and mine, but her eyes went soft and the lids closed. I drew my jacket closer around me. Maybe she was okay with using our car like it was hers. Maybe the car felt natural. That was the thing with being on the streets. Everything out there belongs to you and any place is as good as another for private doings.

The lot in Griffith Park was dim. Streetlights dripped milky over cookout grills, where the coyotes gathered, ashes poofing around their sharp snouts. In twos and threes, the coyotes slinked out of the woods to the edges of the lot. Mom had gone downtown by bus, but I stayed in our car in Griffith Park. She called me from the bus. "Don't leave the car," Mom said. "It will not take long to convince Misha." Mom planned to ask the great dancer Mikhail Baryshnikov for help with getting into a dance company, and he would do this because of Vaganova Ballet Academy in Russia. Graduates of Vaganova's do for each other.

After Mom left, I made it look like she was sleeping in the backseat in case anyone spied inside our car. I made Mom with a bed sheet and a lank leather belt stretched tight over a duffle bag. Then I got under my jacket and tucked inside the front seat floorboard to wait. I might have slept. But bodies clunked against the door.

The man peeled the woman off him and stuffed her against the window. Now she was his pillow. *Abstain from blood, and from things strangled...* The Bible says such things of the doings of a man and a woman. Not for my eyes. Her cheek buttered the glass. Little bubbles popped on her lips. He was grunting and rubbing her with his hundred hands. His eyes rolled up white. He set his face against hers until his eyes fixed. He pushed her out of the way. He dropped a hand on the glass, raised the other to shade his eyes, and peered in, like he had to see past his own image to make out the other pair of eyes inside. The man drew away, yanking the woman with him, but the woman stuck to the glass, squinting in. "Somebody in there?" Twisting in his arms, she hollered, "She saw us!" Fist pounding the window above my head. "Saw us!"

Pounding and pointing at me. "You like to watch?"

"Did you know laundry takes all day?" Mom stands in the doorway, her arms full of clean bedsheets. She flies a sheet across the wide mattress and tucks the sheet under; quick, how she does things. Next the top sheet, pulled tight. No time to smooth the blanket flat, so the bedcover, too, is rumpled. My job is setting the pillows, a thing better done before you are done. Mom regards the lumpy bed. "I want to make it like at the motels. What is trick?" Without waiting for an answer, she says, "I prefer to unmake." She hauls back the bedcover, the blanket, the sheet. She is getting in. "Come, Olya!"

Yesssssssssss. The sheets are heavy. Her arms wrap around me, the fabric of her shirt thick between my fingers.

"What is better? Bed you made or bed that is made for you?"

"One that you made," I say.

Mom's eyes wander to the window, tracking the sound of a car driving by the house. The window opens onto a little hill, where Jack's dog sits and watches in. Bird never stops watching. "Your presence in this house disturbs the delicate balance

between canine and handler," Jack said when I brought in Bird
from the street after he could not. "No problems when it was
just us."

Mom's arm rests on my shoulder. Her eyes close. She sighs.
"All we need is this bed."

In Jack's house the bed is the thing. Old time ivy curling up
the iron headboard, the bed sits high. Jack says the bed needs
to go; he has been meaning to make a donation to the Veteran's
Association, and he will tomorrow. I do not speak of this to
Mom, even to joke. I do not move, even to breathe. Living in
one place gets Mom down. "A dancer only requires what fits in
the trunk of a car," Mom said when she sold everything but our
bedding and the clothes in our suitcases in preparation for the
time when she stopped being a nurse and took up her dream
of becoming a great ballerina. Until last night, bedding was all
I needed to make it look like Mom was asleep in the backseat
when she was not.

"What happened in the parking lot?" Mom says. She knows
I have not told her everything.

When I do not answer, Mom says, "I should not have left
you alone."

"I was not alone." Her eyes slide toward me. "Coyotes," I
say. "They live in the park."

"That makes me feel better? Coyotes protect you?" She pulls
her arm out from under my head and sits up. "Why you not call
me right away?"

"Because a little light in a car is just what they look for."

She touches my cheekbone. "Why get out?" Here we go. "I
told you always stay in car," she says. "You are safe in car."

"I was not supposed to be there," I say.

"Sure. No one should be alone in car. But you know I was
hoping to talk to Misha."

"I'm sorry, Mom."

"Is okay. I will talk to him some other time maybe." She
makes a smile. "Thanks god you are not alone now. You are safe
here. In this house and is very nice."

"Don't you want a home, Mom?"

She rises off the bed, dragging the blanket with her. "I don't know. I am not good at making beds."

"You can learn."

"Oh, Olya," she says and stretches her arms above her head. "How can I explain about home? If I wanted to be a ballerina, the only home was a stage." It is not the first time Mom has told me this. Once she even said the ballet is the only family a ballerina is permitted. For Mom, ballet was an improvement on her own family. Her family lived in Dubna, which was built by political prisoners from a nearby forced labor camp. So many prisoners died building Dubna that Mom said that the city was built on bones. Scared to end up in a camp, Mom's family only whispered in their shoebox apartment. So much could not be said in her home, Mom took to dancing those silences and got good at it. Mom's grandma claimed her own child would turn her over to the cops on a slip of the tongue. Mom's mom was not much different and not much more of a mother. That was how family went in Russia.

The door to my bedroom swings open. Jack steps in, his eyes on Mom.

"You have nice linens," she says, "you old bachelor."

"Thirty-one is old?" Jack thrusts up his arms and starts doing drills, pumping an imaginary rifle over his head.

"Old," she says, "old, old."

His arms lower. He stares at the floor. When he looks back up, he looks for something to get mad about. "Why's she doing that?"

Mom leans across the bed and knocks my hand out of my mouth. I spit out the fingernail I was chewing.

"Isn't that a little odd?" he says.

Mom says, "Cousin Jack thinks you are little odd, Olya."

She means to be funny, but what is funny to Mom does not always translate. Russian humor throws a shadow, even at high noon, which is where the sun is in most American jokes. She keeps on anyway, saying I am a little odd. Like she wants me to give him odd. It does not matter that I do not want to give odd. That in fact what I want is for Jack to think I am all right, no trouble, an okay roommate. Someone to feed the dog and lock doors at night. But she keeps saying how I am a little odd, until odd feels like a code word for Mom and me against him. I follow the code. My tongue drops out. It lolls between my lips. My head follows my tongue, swinging, saying no, no, no.

"Why's she doing that?" Jack says. "Talks funny too."

"Pwetty," I say.

Mom laughs. The laugh rings with winning.

"All right," Jack says, like he is wearing that uniform in the pictures.

"I tawk pwetty, mister!"

"Give me a break." Jack turns and walks out. Before he clears the doorway, Mom clocks him with a pillow. The pillow goes soft onto its side before Jack turns around. He frowns then squats down, eyes on Mom, and picks up the pillow, rises and runs at us. Mom squeals and scrambles back in bed, pulling bedcovers up. Jack yanks them off and raises the pillow over her, staring down at her stretched out before him. "What the fuck is with that neck of yours?" He tosses the pillow aside.

Mom's long neck is something you notice.

Jack climbs onto the bed. The headboard is about as far as I can get from him. His knees straddle Mom and his hand covers her throat. His other hand rubs along the tendons of her neck. "This neck is wrong, Ira, all wrong. It lays a man low."

She coughs and raises her head from the pillow, eyes fixed on Jack.

"Let go of her, mister," I say.

His eyes stay on Mom, pressing. "Olya," he says, "life makes for a lot of chaos but on a rare occasion the elements assemble to make a female that is perfect on the eye." Mom glares at Jack but like this is a sport, like she cannot wait to see what he will do. "Don't be fooled," he says. "Chaos built your mother."

Mom and Jack are cousins. Maybe this is how they played as kids. Mom put up with a lot of this kind of play when she was in Russia. Every day on her way home from elementary school, a big kid played a punching game right in the raw between her shoulder blades, but she never told anybody until she told me. She reminds me of this punching game when I complain over starting at another school. Jack's choking is just another game.

I will stay out of this game. If I want to stay.

The corner of a pillow sneaks into my fist and I swing the pillow up against Jack's head. Really more of a wallop.

Jack lets Mom go to snatch the pillow and swipe it back at me, his eyes hot. The pillow must have hurt some. Mom grabs another pillow and swings at what she can get. She gets me good. I go down. Above me, between them, the pillows swing. In between feathers high on the air, Jack and Mom, inside just seconds, hold me here.

Glass rattles in the window frame. Bird slams against the glass, teeth barred. Jack springs off the bed and frowns at his dog. The pillow drops from his hand.

I crawl to the window and press my fingers at the glass. Bird quiets.

"Look at that." Mom's eyebrows fly up. "The dog is guarding Olya."

"All I've trained that dog to do," Jack says, "is disobey me."

"So? Is not a good dog. Get new one." Mom can make you feel stupid for not thinking of this stuff yourself.

"There are some in K-9 who say he's no use to anybody," Jack says. "It's too late for this dog. He's seen too much."

"Are you sure they mean the dog?"

"I'll make him obey," Jack says. He turns and walks, mad, out of the room and down the hall. The back door bangs open. Jack calls for his dog. Jack calls and calls.

For long minutes we listen to him call.

Thwap, thwap, thwap. Faint but close by. Bird is not at the window now. Not in the backyard, either. *Thwap, thwap, thwap.* The slap of a dog's tail. Bird is in the room with Mom and me. Or not exactly in the room but above us, like those rats that galloped across the eaves in the converted garage Mom rented when she had good credit. Or Bird is between the walls, like the bats that tumbled in at dawn in the otherwise unoccupied house where we spent last summer before the caretaker caught us. No, this sound is not in the walls. This sound comes from below.

"What you crawling under there for, Olya?" Mom asks.

The bed frame vibrates above me as she tosses pillows back across the mattress. I press my ear to the floorboards. I hear the slap of Bird's tail beneath the boards. Houses have cellars. Is that where Bird has gone?

From out back, Jack calls for Bird, louder, madder. The tail beneath me goes still. I imagine I can hear the soft suck of Bird's mouth dropping open, the panting. Jack can call all the way to the moon. That dog is staying under the house.

The back door cracks open as Jack stomps through the kitchen and back up the hallway. Swinging wide the bedroom door, he catches me halfway out from under the bed. "Is that where you're hiding him?"

Jack drops on his haunches beside me and eases onto his hands for a look under the bed. When he does not see his dog, he shouts at me, "Let go of my dog!"

Mom squats beside Jack. "What dog?" She waves at his face. "Do you see dog?"

"No. But that doesn't mean she ain't got him."

"How can Olya have a dog?"

"I don't know. By…by putting a spell on him," Jack says. "Exercising black magic. Holding Bird hostage. Some explanation. Was she like this before?" He is eyeing me.

"Like what?"

"Weird…uh…witchy."

There is not an answer in Mom. She does not know what he is talking about. What can she know what others mean by me?

She touches her throat. "What is problem with you, Jack?"

"Problem? What problem? I'm the guy who went to Afghanistan to protect this great country," he says. "Got a problem with that?" He grasps the bedpost to drag up to his feet. "I've got a job to do. It's this dog. You don't like it—"

"I don't like it. Not dog. Not you. Especially not how you talk to my kid."

"Then go," Jack says, heading through the door but not going. His hand clings to the frame. His back is to us as he says, "Forget it. I don't mean anything by it, Ira."

Then Jack is gone.

Mom looks sideways at me. She protects her packmate against attack.

"How do you know each other?" I say. "You don't act like cousins."

Mom smiles. "How do cousins act?"

"Tell me," I say.

"Depends on family. With us it was best friends at first sight. When later I came to America, Jack said he want to be my *garant*. U.S. requires this for refugees. Jack guaranteed a financial support in case I could not make a success on my own. Good thing I could nurse. Since Jack went to army."

"Is Jack my father?" I ask though I doubt it is legal to have a kid with your cousin.

"Yes," she says. "He is your father." She says this like my question is nothing, a nuisance, like I asked to borrow her toothbrush. A yes, no different than all the yeses to all the other men I have ever asked about. Mom is very open about her secret.

"What about the other ones?"

"There are no others."

"The roses from Tbilsi—"

"You like a rich father? Or maybe you prefer *danseur*? Or maybe you think now that your father is Jack, then all this time you had a home. Okay, sure, Jack, vet of a war so shitty even Russia don't want, this is your father. He has such a fine house. Jack is your father. That what you want? He is father. Jack."

"Okay, okay."

"Happy now?"

"I am happy he is not my father." And really—I already have a starry-eyed mom.

"You so sure?" Mom says.

5

"You," Jack says, "eat at the counter."

Jack ladles stew into a bowl. He sets the bowl before me as I ease onto a wood stool. I fold my hands together and bow my head. "Bless us our Lord for these thy gifts—"

"Grace, huh?" Jack picks up a knife and tosses a tomato in the air, spears it dead center. "Why not wait on your mom for that? Save grace for her." He wipes the knife on his ruffled apron.

Bird scratches the kitchen door then noses a stick at the glass. "Work first," Jack hollers over his shoulder at the dog. "Then play."

"Tomorrow I'll train Bird to stay," he tells me, tossing an avocado over his shoulder and catching behind his back. He tosses the avocado back over his shoulder.

"Don't you first have to train Bird to come?"

Jack fumbles the avocado. "That's a mistake," he says, "to assume a dog's got to master one command before moving to the next. Training Squadron at the AFB will tell you, 'You're not teaching commands. You're building drives.' The dog they teamed me with at the base…Daed, he was crackerjack. Daed didn't need to be told what to do. Strong drive, that was Daed."

This talk about the crackerjack dog, this Daed, does not sit right on my ear. Not so much what Jack says about the dog, but how he says it, like he is not telling the whole story. Like he came up with the dog's name on the spot. Why would Jack make up a name for a dog I will never meet, or want to?

Jack watches me spoon up stew. "You like dogs," he says. "Sure," he says, "kids like dogs." His eyes follow as I take the empty bowl to the sink. "How's my stew?"

"It's cooked," I say, "at home."

"Yeah, sure, I hear you. A home-cooked meal," he says.

"That ought to make your mom stay. What do you think? Will home-cooked meals do it?"

Now Mom has Jack worried. That is a thing with Mom. She sets you on edge, especially if she is the one asking the favor.

In the window of the microwave, Jack combs his hair with his fingers, but there is not much he can do with hair that short. After a while, he stops combing and swats his forehead in frustration. His eyes catch mine and he says, "Dessert's there in the drawer."

I open the drawer beside me. Flashlights and batteries roll over a flattened pack of chewing gum. I pick out a stick of gum.

He nods. "Kids like dessert."

I peel off the paper and fold the stick against my tongue.

"You don't talk much," he says. "What's on your mind? C'mon, talk away."

"I don't know what to say, mister."

"Call him Jack," Mom says. She stands in the kitchen doorway, dressed in nursing scrubs. "He is cousin, after all."

"Did your parents come to the U.S. when you were little?" I ask Jack.

"What?" He stares at Mom. "What's with the get up?" He sashays over, clasps Mom's waist, tangos her to the kitchen table, where candles teeter inside ill-sized stems. "C'mon, nursey. See what's cooking."

"You don't sound Russian to her," Mom says, looking over her shoulder at me. "That what you mean, Olya?"

"What?" Jack's hands fall away from Mom.

"Jack, tell Olya how my parents were born in U.S., same as your parents, and how my mom and dad moved to Russia."

Jack smiles at her but it is not friendly. "Because Russia is such a great place to raise kids?"

This is the first I have heard of Mom's parents not being born in Russia. "Are your parents really from the U.S.?" I say. "Where, Mom?"

Mom stares at me. "They are from lots of places. Not just America."

"Like where?"

She shrugs. "Paris, Peru, Israel, Disneyland," she says.

I do not bother asking more questions about Mom's parents. Her answers will just go the same direction as her answers about who my dad is—yes to everything and to nothing. Or maybe she is playing down the family history to keep from ruffling Jack's feathers. Whatever it is, Mom is moving on.

Jack pulls out a chair for her to sit.

"Sorry," Mom says.

"Got to eat." Jack draws a narrow metal box from his apron pocket, thumbs the hinged lid, and kicks up a flame. He lights both candles. "Olya's got to say grace."

"I cannot," she says.

"You don't like grace?"

"Have dinner without me. Get to know Olya. She is smart. You won't believe how smart. Last three schools, they put her in gifted program—"

His hand flies up, silencing her. He drops the lighter back into the pocket of his apron and steps to the cutting board, and tilts it into the trash. The cut vegetables slop off the wood. He knocks the blade against the board until the last tomato slice leaps. He does not look at her. "That wasn't the deal, Ira."

"They say is going to storm. I don't like to drive that. Can I borrow car?"

"The kid!" Jack says.

Mom looks at me. "You didn't like food? Jack is good cook," she says, pulling out the kitchen drawers, feeling around for keys. She finds the chewing gum and pockets the rest of the pack.

Jack points to the keys hanging from a hook by the door. Mom reaches for them. "A job opened in ER," she says. "First chance in a while. Olya will stay here, safe. That is only way I can concentrate on getting place of my own." She jangles the keys once and closes her fingers around them.

"Is that what this is about," Jack says, tugging at the knot on his apron, "a place of your own?"

"First you don't want us here then you don't want us to go."
She steps behind Jack and neatly unties the knot on his apron.
"You are crazy," she says.

Jack follows her into the hallway, but she heads out the front
door, light and fast, the way she goes. "If I'm so crazy," he
shouts after her, "why dump your kid with me?"

Mouth on a wet stick, Bird steams up the glass door. His yellow
eyes lunge up his skull in the slow wide swing of his tail. Now is
a good time to make myself useful. If I help with the dog, Jack
will mind less that I am here.

Bird drops the stick at my feet as I step out the door. I throw
the stick. Bird returns the stick in wizard time. I throw the stick
again into the darkening yard, and the stick swivels up into a
patch of lighter sky. So, this is fetch. So boring. The dog cannot
get enough. But a house sturdy at my back feels all right. This
is what a home gives you, something reliable, a little boring, a
soggy stick.

"What's your game?" Jack stands now on the back steps. The
wind snaps at his words. "Bird could eat you whole."

I want to say that a dog taking a liking to me is no game. It
comes of offering a little consideration to another living being,
but how would that sound to someone listening with Jack's ears?

Bird drops the stick at my feet then backs up, ready, ready.
I only pretend to throw, and Bird falls for the trick and shoots
off. Jack laughs. Bird trots back up. The way his eyes flick between the stick and me says this time he will pay attention.

Rain specks my cheeks as I lob the stick. The wind carries
the stick to the fence. Thunder booms. Bird's eyes swivel up in
alarm. Tail tucked, he scoots as if kicked across the yard.

Jack jogs after Bird, but the dog bolts and scrambles around
the side of the house.

I find Jack on the north side of the house, beside his truck,
which is parked before the closed gate. He stands like a cop,
legs spread, arms folded across his chest. Lightening throws
him in silhouette. No sign of Bird.

"Ah, tell me, Olya, where'd he go?"

I shrug. "Guess Bird doesn't like thunder."

"A little weather and poof! Bird disappears. Ira disappears. What will it take, I wonder," Jack says, "to make you go away?"

The sky opens up. I look straight into the rain at Jack. "A lot more, mister, than a little weather."

Jack's eyes drop to the concrete. He nods. "Kids like rain." He says it in that soft bright way people do when they have spoken in anger. He cranks open the door on his truck, pulls out an umbrella, and pops it open. "Your mom won't like it if you catch cold." The umbrella is Jack's way of saying sorry. I step under and we run inside.

6

Today is training the stay. Stay, dog. Stay no matter what. Stay when Jack comes, when quail stir in the brush, when wind blows, when guns fire, stay when Jack goes. Jack has skill. He says, "I can make that dog sprout wings."

"Will wings make him stay?" I say.

"Someone in your situation," Jack says, "ought to know when to zip it."

Jack is testy. Bird was still missing in the morning. No matter how hard Jack called for his dog, Bird would not come out. Worse, Jack knew Bird was hiding close by. He could hear him whining.

What Jack did not know was that Bird was under the house. His whines were fingers feeling under the floor for me. "Shush-shush," I said, squeezing under the bed, quieting him with shushes and hushes, floorboards only wood between us. I pictured Bird crammed into a hole dug out under the floor. Or maybe he was wriggled into a cellar walled up in cement. Jack's dog was staying the only way he knew how, out of harm's way. "'When you lie down, they will watch over you,'" I sang to Bird from Proverbs, "'when you lie down, your sleep shall be sweet.'"

While Jack walked the neighborhood hollering for his dog, I headed out. Jack had left a box of glazed donuts on the kitchen counter. I took the donuts to the yard. Grass, hedge, and garden hose, all were still and still a little damp, except for a slight quiver of red berries dangling from a bush on the north side of the house. Something underneath the bush was shaking those berries. I knelt beside the bush and craned around the stems, patting the ground. My hand slid into the mouth of a hole. A gap at the foundation, one big enough for a dog to squeeze down.

The box of donuts fit okay under the bush. Dogs liked sweets. Soon Bird would crawl out from the hole for a donut. But he had better do it quick. Any minute now Jack would give up calling and come 'round stomping. If Jack figured out Bird was under the house, there would be trouble. If he figured out that Bird's hideout was right under my bedroom, more trouble. He would say it was all my doing.

Pebbles shifted at the edge of the hole. Bird's nose peeked out from the dark. His nostrils flared on whiffs of donut. I stayed patient. Stayed calm. Bird clawed out a few inches under the bush and set the berries swinging.

Bang! Bang! Muffler fire echoed from the street. The sound startled Bird. He whimpered and fell back into the hole.

I ran to the fence to see what had scared Jack's dog. A wide brown lowrider drifted up the street like a log dragging a current. The dude behind the wheel fingered the neck of a guitar that was not there. His other hand held a cigarette at his mouth. The car seemed to steer itself. Bang! Bang! Smoke shot out the rear of the car. The tires bumped off the curb as the lowrider knocked around the corner out of sight.

The red berries were still on the bush. The donuts lined up in the box, good soldiers, all accounted for. The muffler on that lowrider had scared Bird right back under. Thunder, lightning, loud mufflers, Bird was easily spooked.

The lowrider came putt putt up the street again. The dude's long bony arm dangled over the door. Out of his index and middle fingers he shaped a V and pointed the V at his eyes then swiveled his hand around and pointed the V at me.

I saw you too, buddy. Not a pretty sight.

I waved my hands at the dude to get him to shove off.

He did a thing with his tongue you would expect from a dude like that. Bang! Bang! He screeched off. Hopefully, the last of him.

I knelt again before the bush and gave the donut box a soft shake. Nothing. Bird was not coming out. The sound of Bird's panting was faint but companionable, and my breath eased in rhythm. The yard, soon the whole neighborhood, opened into the quiet now that the lowrider was gone. I picked a donut from the box and scooted it up to the hole. A long pink tongue shot out and swiped the donut. But the next instant, Bird spit the donut out on a bark. He burst up out of the hole, cut through the bush, barking to rip us in two. I dove to the side.

Bird leapt the fence, landing in the front yard. Something had gotten that dog out from under the house, but it was no donut.

I slammed open the gate, chasing after Bird. On hind legs, Bird was pitching at the front of the house, trying to scramble up the trellis beside my bedroom window. He was barking at someone teetering on the roof of Jack's house. It was the dude who had been driving the lowrider.

The dude waved at me from the roof. He pointed over his shoulder. "Your chimney needs inspection," he said.

I grabbed Bird's collar and went down on one knee. Bird sat, chest pumping, eyes stuck on the dude who perched on the roof like a mantis.

"This house doesn't have a chimney," I said.

"Whose fault is that?" he said.

"Come down. I got the dog."

His straight brown hair covered one eye. The other eye inched over me. "You come up, babe."

"What do I want with a roof?"

"New vistas. Yonder is a road lined with sweet California sycamore. Over there's a footpath into the hills. Not to mention the cutest little freeway onramp you ever saw."

"What's so great about a couple of roads?"

"Every single one," he said, "leads out of this hole. Don't laugh," he said. "You'll be wanting a road out sooner than you know." He said, "The elevator broke. Start climbing." He said, "Don't worry, I won't let you fall. I'll hold you so tight—"

"How old are you?" I said.

"Just turned sixteen."

"How come you're not in school?"

He shrugged and picked at a hole in the knee of his jeans. He said, "Why aren't you?"

The front door flew open. Jack lugged a rifle as long as his leg. Bird scooted behind me. Jack marched up to the dude.

"On my roof now?" Jack said. "I'll thank you to get off."

"Thank your dog, not me," the dude said. "You really ought to train that animal. Vicious."

Jack raised the rifle.

The dude rose up so quick he slipped on a shingle but recovered. He threw up his fists at Jack. "Want a fight? Huh? Come on up. Mano a mano."

Jack cocked the rifle.

"Gun pussy." The dude extended his arms and leapt off the roof. He soared, clearing the eaves. Really, it was flight, until he landed wrongly with a thump. Face down in the dead grass. Bird growled. I looked at Jack. The dude pushed onto his knee and limped over the lawn to his lowrider parked at the curb.

Without looking at me, Jack said, "Go in. Get your coat. You're coming to the park."

"What for?"

"Watch me train Bird."

"Don't be such a cop," I said.

"I don't want to be such a cop. I don't want to be a cop at all. But every couple of minutes you or your mom seem to compel one. That little hick on the roof? Earlier this morning, I caught him peeping in your window."

The park was walking distance, so I tagged after Jack and Bird. Did it feel okay to have Jack looking out for me? It surely did. Jack had proven himself trustworthy. Bird needed to learn that about Jack. If Bird would trust Jack, this could be a good home instead of a battlefield that burned up all the breathing air.

"Everybody wants in," Jack said, Bird leashed in tight at his thigh. "That hick, your mom, you. You think you can just waltz into my house, like it's guaranteed? Let me correct you there. There is no guarantee. I am a veteran and I own a house. That is a miracle. Miracle, you understand, not guarantee. Guys like me are sleeping on cement. But I got a house. Know why?" He stopped to look at me. "I don't let anybody in."

Jack pivoted sharp around a low western fence bordering a park where people ran their dogs on leashes and off. But before entering, Jack stopped at the window of an ice cream truck idling at the curb. "How'd you like an ice cream?" He handed me a chocolate cone. "Kids like ice cream." I hopped up on the fence with my cone as Jack staked out a corner in the park and knelt gently before his quaking dog. The next minute, a very tall Black guy pulling his dog's leash accidentally backed into Jack, which caused Jack's ice cream to slam into his shirt. Jack pushed the guy off. The Black guy stumbled forward, tangling in his leash. "Sorry," he said. "Didn't see you."

Jack wiped his shirt with a paper napkin before throwing the guy a napkin. The guy caught the napkin and stared at Jack. Jack stared back until the guy tugged his leash to guide the crook-eared dog away.

"Catahoula Cur," Jack said, coming alongside me at the fence. He studied the guy's dog. "Herder. Hard-headed. Watch what happens when his master says to sit."

The guy had staked out his own area beside a sapling. He began to run commands with his Catahoula Cur. He told the dog to sit. The dog refused until the man's wide hands pushed the dog's hips down into a sit. The guy was kind and not impatient.

"Now he'll try the stay." Each command failed, just as Jack said it would. All the guy's attempts to correct his dog also went bust.

Jack tied Bird to the fence and pushed off. He stepped up to the guy. "May I?"

The guy looked sideways at Jack then at his Cur that strained toward a passing shepherd. He handed Jack the dog's leash. "All yours."

Jack squatted before the young dog. He clapped his hands sharp before its snout. The dog glanced vaguely around before swinging back toward the shepherd. Jack placed his palm against the dog's snout and drew the snout toward his own nose. A wire formed between them. Every time the Cur dodged, Jack's hand caught the snout and drew it back to his nose. Jack stared at the dog until the dog looked back, eyes lowering every blink. Now Jack slowly rose to his feet. He lowered his other hand, palm down. Following the direction of Jack's hand, the dog sat. Still holding the dog's snout against his palm, Jack made a stop sign. His hand slid off the snout, and he backed away from the Cur until he came alongside its owner. The dog's eyes did not stray from Jack. Neither did mine. This dog would do anything for him. Sprout wings for Jack. It was Bird that would not do for Jack.

"What the fuck magic is this, man?" the owner said, smiling at his pet.

"Sign language. Your dog is predominately deaf."

"Can't hear?" The guy said, like how come nobody told me?

"Tell him to stay with your hands," Jack said.

The guy made a stop sign with his hand.

Jack nodded and stepped back to watch.

The minute Jack did, the guy rushed to his dog. The dog licked his master's face, the leash went slack while the guy pet with one hand and made a stop sign with the other. The Cur did not know what to focus on so noticed a walker tangled up with a half-dozen dogs. The Cur shot after them. The frustrated owner snatched up the leash and yanked. The Cur whirligigged, head over paws.

"Poughkeepsie!" Jack said. "What I tell you about yanking?"

The guy frowned at Jack. "Sorry? Uh, no Poughkeepsie here." He turned to his dog and made hand signals, glancing at Jack, trying for approval.

Jack was not giving it. Hands in fists, he scanned the park. His gaze gone long and wayward, as though the park had lost its boundary fence and opened onto some vast sandy plain. Any moment a tank would roll through.

"Let's go, Jack," I said. "He'll get the idea."

Jack might as well have gone deaf too. When the Catahoula

Cur swung out, the owner yanked the leash again. Jack stormed. He ripped the leash from the guy's hand. "Shred your brains, Poughkeepsie?"

The Black guy was taller than Jack and bigger but, unlike Jack, he was reasonable. His hands came up, he stepped back, he said, "Uh, at ease, brother."

Jack nodded. He smiled then he shoved the guy. The guy stumbled back, like he did not see it coming. Jack took advantage and backed the guy to the fence. "You going to pound your Cur he disobeys? In the head? In the head?" Jack said, slapping the side of his own head.

The guy pushed Jack off. Jack pushed back. The guy rebounded off the fence, the Cur nipping at their legs. Bird started to howl. People stared. Shouted. Some guys playing basketball ran straight at Jack and knocked him to the ground. The whole place shook.

After the basketball players tossed Jack around, after the owner of the Cur asked Jack what infantry he had served in, after he told Jack that was no excuse, after Jack mouthed an apology, after the cops showed up, after they asked the owner if he wanted to press charges, after he said he would think about it, we walked out of the park. Though both our lips were buttoned and my heart never dropped from my throat, at least it felt like Jack again beside me.

I imagined what Mom would say if she had witnessed this. "Go to doctors at VA, Jack. They give drugs for this kind of traumatics."

But Mom's prescription would be way off. No doctor could fix Jack's behavior. By my reckoning, Jack was in a head-on collision with the holy.

♾

Jack's truck backs down the driveway now. Bird's snout pokes at the window crack. Jack is relocating Bird's training session to the Loomis Shooting Range. A shooting range cannot be good, for Bird or for Jack. But Jack is ignited by what went down in the park, fired up with faith he can now make Bird stay around guns.

Jack is a man possessed. Maybe he has come under some malign influence from this house. What this house needs is a good clearing. Some folks clear by burning sage, others shift furniture; at one time I might have even turned to the Good Book. But such methods will not appease the household spirits that Jack has riled up. This house needs *The Perilous Hearth*. Last year, Sister Hedge at St. Anne's Elementary taught us that the people of the Middle Ages understood the seriousness of taking up in a dwelling and offered thanks for the privilege. Sister Hedge read aloud of rituals for appeasing the wrathful spirits of the domain. She never said if the rituals worked to appease the spirits. But maybe they did work. I could mention a couple rituals to Jack when he gets back from the shooting range. Who knows, maybe it is wrathful spirits that bedevil him and Bird. Appeasement is worth a try.

Meantime, I am to stay inside, doors locked, blinds drawn, safe from peepers.

◈

The bed whimpers, cries slice through the floorboards, pink smears the walls and ceiling. I snap up the window blind. Outside the trees are red. Jack's truck is not in the driveway. "Jack?"

No answer.

Jack is not back from teaching his dog the stay.

His dog is.

In the yard, the shovel's wooden handle is worn and pockmarked. I smack it old like that against the bushes, scattering red berries and snapping little branches to bits. Between spider webs and clipped leaves muddied onto stems, Bird crawls out from under the house and into my open hands. His coat red in the sunset. My fingers weave red into wet fur. The wet is blood.

Bird backs out from between my fingers and sits, butt hovering above the ground, tail slapping the dirt, saying sorry for being so cut up. Don't mind me. No trouble at all. My hands make a basket for his snout. Those eyes look up at me sleepy, his head rests in my palms. Bird's eyes shift toward something behind me.

An ambulance is pulling into the driveway. Swirling lights flash without sound. Two men get out of the ambulance. The younger man pulls open the rear doors and hops inside to guide a wheelchair onto the tailgate. The guy sitting in the wheelchair is Jack.

Jack's chin lifts as the tailgate lowers. He points at the dog beside me.

Bird's tail sweeps dirt.

Jack pushes up out of the wheelchair to come after Bird, but the wheelchair stays with Jack, buckled in at his waist. Now the wheelchair is on his back and the wheels spin in the air. Jack is as flipped over as an old tortoise. The men crank the wheelchair onto its wheels again, and Jack slams back into the chair. The younger man wheels it up the walkway to the front door, one hand on the chair, one hand on Jack's shoulder keeping him down.

The older man waves me over to the ambulance.

Bird stays in at my heels.

"I need a signature to release him," the man says as we come up. "Jack Marea, age thirty-one. Is an adult in residence?"

"My mom's at work."

"I'll make a note of that. You the closest relative?"

"I don't think he's close to any family."

The man laughs. "It sounds like you're related enough." He gives me the paper, pointing at a line, and I write my name there. Beside my name, the man scrawls, *minor*. He flips over a second sheet. "We were heading him to the hospital, but he rerouted us here. That needs initials there."

The younger man steers the empty wheelchair back along the walkway. He says, "Tell him if he wants his shotgun to ask Riverside PD for it."

"Did he kill somebody?" I say.

The older man frowns. "Certainly shooting," he says. "That he didn't kill somebody is just luck."

The young man squats before Bird, who draws back into my leg. "Poor pup. What happened?"

"He needs a vet," I say. "You've got to take him."

"I can put in a call to animal control." The young man looks up at me. "But it could complicate getting the dog back."

The heat from Bird's spine fires up my leg. He needs stitches. The way he breathes, every inch of him must ache. Someone has to look after this dog. "No, Jack will take care of him," I say. "He's good with dogs." Do not interfere. The best way to stay here is to stay out of it.

"Over at the firing range they said he was shooting at some dog," the older man says as he climbs into the van. "He wanted the dog."

The younger man looks back at Bird then smiles at me. "The dog will be all right."

A call comes in on the radio. They drive out, and the words *Riverside Emergency* glide past. I watch the ambulance go until it leaves the street empty. No point staying out here waiting for Mom to come back from work. Now is something Mom's good at staying away from.

Inside, the house is silent. To kill a little time, I count citations. Eleven before the parlor door, not including medals. Jack is a professional. He knows dogs. Something unexpected must have come up at the shooting range, an accident, nobody's fault.

Clank-clank. Around the corner, Jack, on hands and knees, clanks a gun, another gun, one no bigger than his hand. Jack clanks the gun on the floorboards. Each time Jack clanks the barrel against the boards, the seam of his coat sleeve splits a little more.

"Don't hurt Bird," I say.

"I don't hurt dogs," he says.

"He's bleeding," I say.

"Dogs hurt themselves," he says.

The skin under Jack's eye is purpling. Red scabs crisscross his forehead. He says, "You been having a nice day?"

"Swell. You?"

"Look," he says, "don't get huffy. I didn't mean to leave you by yourself. It's just that training 'the stay' takes focus."

He opens the gun so the cylinder waves out round. He holds the gun up to his good eye. His lips form an O and he blows down the barrel. He touches his tongue to the gun's inside. A shake of the wrist and the cylinder snaps shut. "Where'd the dog go?" he says. "He was there beside you."

"Someplace safe."

Jack starts up, like he is coming after me. "You okay?"

"Are you?"

"No, I mean, you seem a little jumpy." He follows my eyes to the gun in his hand. "What, this? This is nothing. This is show. This is *safe*." He rubs his purpling eye with the heel of his hand and winces. "Here's what you need to understand. It's not about building the dog's trust in you so much as building your trust in the dog to tell you what it knows." He shifts into a squat. "My dad's dogs taught me that. Those dogs were little mothers to me. You just had to let them put you in your place. If you allowed that—because the dog is telling you, oh so subtle, abandon yourself to the greater good of the pack—you'll glean it. That's trust."

"You should start trusting Bird."

Jack stares at me, and this little grin gets going that says I have it all wrong. "It's the other handlers that don't trust," he says. "It's the Poughkeepsies. They second guess. They screw up their dogs. Next thing you know, Poughkeepsie's dog screws up your dog, like an infection, like a foxtail or a burr, it stuffs the nose with the wrong scents. Before Poughkeepsie showed up on the base, your dog believed only in the wisdom of your hand." He points the barrel of the gun at his hand. "Your dog lived for your hand. Your hand was the blessing it yearned for." Jack's hand switches side to side, the barrel of the gun switching in time, signaling directions to a dog that is not there. Jack goes on about Poughkeepsie who, it turns out, was a handler at the base where Jack was deployed. Poughkeepsie took over a dog named Daisy. "Instead of waiting for Daisy to show him what she knew," Jack says, "the *fucker* stopped trusting and started tugging. After days of tugging, Daisy was distressed. Your own dog notices. Your dog, that only had eyes for your hand, now has eyes for Daisy, a dog that has lost the ability to trust her nose because of Poughkeepsie's tugging; she is unmoored; she has lost purpose. Worse, your dog gets interested. Your dog gets ideas. Your dog's sole concern is no longer for explosives, for soldiers torn into more than anybody's got mind to collect."

The hallway has settled into pitch. Below us somewhere is Bird, also in the dark. Would Jack keep talking talking talking about trust if he knew that under his feet Bird is hurting? Is that the kind of handler he is talking about? One who requires absolute trust from his canine and does not trouble to mend the dog's wounds when it bleeds?

"Is he under here?" Jack says. Before I can say, Jack is up and running to the back door, calling, "Bird!"

I find Jack in the backyard pointing his gun at a bush. "I know where you go, Bird," he says to the bush. He looks at me. "You got him coming under there at night."

Jack lays the gun on the ground to dig around the bush with the shovel. Dirt flies over his shoulder. "Look under there," he says, "for his hole."

I crawl around the bush and look for a hole I know is not there.

"See anything?" he says. "Keep looking," he says. "How else you think he gets under the house?"

Jack's two big hands squeeze the neck of the bush as he tries to yank it out, the roots fighting back like roosters. Finally he says, "Fuck it," and kicks the bush. He picks up his gun, turns around and stomps back into the house. Who can know how helpless a man will behave at the disobedience of his own dog?

A little ways from where I stand, red berries quiver on another bush. Bird scrabbles to the edge of the hole and his eyes blink out from the dark. This is as far as he will come.

Pop! Pop! Gunfire. My throat leaps.

A yap. Bone cold panic. Bird swings round and plows back down his hole.

"No, Bird. Get out!" I shout. "Trust me!"

Pop! Pop! Jack fires again and again. Bullets thunk through the floor over Bird's head. The faint jitter of cartridges bouncing along the boards.

Bird's not coming out. Not alive.

"He's still there, isn't he?" Jack says, one eye pressed to the hole he just bulleted in the floorboard. He drops against the wall, his eyes switching from my bedroom to me standing now at the end of the hallway, covering my nose against the stink of gunpowder floating up. "Bird's in there with you, under you, I mean, in the bedroom you are in temporary occupation of."

Through the open door, I watch him shift my bed and point the gun at the boards. All this roughing up my bed bugs me. A minor point, considering the gun.

"Jack," I say. "Killing your dog won't make him stay."

Jack looks over his shoulder at me, smiles. "I'm not shooting at Bird. I'm shooting him out."

"I thought you guys would rather shoot yourself than shoot your dog."

"Damn right. I'd shoot myself all day long before harming a hair on Bird. But this is the only thing that gets him moving. You think I haven't tried every other way? You think I want it this way? That what you think?" Jack shoots. Splinters fly and a hole leaps up from the floor. The terrible sound of something scramming around below.

"Jack!" I scream.

Startled, he fires again, missing the floor but blowing a hole in the bathroom door. Jack swings around to me. "Don't scream," he says, pointing at the bathroom door. "Scared the whit out of me!"

"There is another way," I say. "Let me get Bird."

Bird is out already, sitting in the yard. Jack's shooting got him out after all.

Jack is right at my heels. Bird rises to all fours. Jack tells me to go back in the house but does not make me. He grabs hold of Bird's collar. Gun aimed at the tree branches, he shoots. Leaves burst a hole in the canopy, and Bird flies off his feet, bucking.

"Stay," Jack says. "Stay, Bird!" He shoots again. A tree branch snaps and drops, skims Jack's shoulder.

Jack fires again. "Stay, Bird." His hand tightens on the collar. The collar cuts Bird's neck. This dog would rather lose his head than stay.

"You got to learn," Jack says, "to stay."

Jack fires again into the tree. The blast echoes round my skull. A neighbor hollers from some other porch. Dogs in other yards pitch in yowling. Someone somewhere is tooting a car horn, someone is shouting, whoo-hoo, shouting, bang-bang! Jack fires again, opening dry stars in the branch-crossed ceiling overhead. Jack fires, his eyes bright and frightened.

He-uh, he-uh, Bird's chest heaves, a sharp weird wind sound.

Stay out of this if you want to stay. This dog is nothing to you.

I get between Jack and Bird and work the buckle on the collar. Jack tries to wedge my hands off with the barrel of his gun, the leather tight around Bird's windpipe. His yellow eyes roll white. No song. The clogged tongue. The whole of him dropping dead off the collar.

Jack tries to kick me, but I dodge most of his boot. It is not hard. Neither are his kicks. Too much of Jack is tied up with not letting his dog go.

"Hold on," I whisper to Bird, and in this still second, this brief stop, I undo the buckle.

Bird is free.

Only a collar in Jack's hand.

"Stay!" Jack shouts after a dog already flown.

7

Mom is halfway up the walk before I can say, "Jack is unhinged."

"Jack is family." She drops a bag of groceries in my arms.

"He has a gun."

"Households have guns," she says.

"Do you know what kind of house this is?"

She backs up to take in the house. "I don't know. American house?"

"That's not—I mean *this* is the kind of house people leave in a coffin!"

"In a coffin? What talk. You sound like Jack." She disappears behind the hole in the screen door. I picture her walking along the hallway, the floorboard shot full of holes, one hole catching the high heel, the heel snapping, her ankle twisting, groceries rolling as she hits the boards. She screams for help, but nobody comes. Not Jack, who split to take Bird to the vet. Not I. How could I hope to stay in such a house and be happy?

Mom sticks her head through the screen. "Olya? Take bag to kitchen."

I set the grocery bag on the ground and kick it over. The grub rolls out.

What I am really after, what's starting to weigh on me, is the question of safety. I mean, why would a guy who handles dogs try to get his dog to stay so much that he would scare the dog off forever? How can wanting something as simple as a dog to stick around become so unsafe? There is only one option: wait in Mom's car until she admits Jack is one crazy mother and packs up and drives us out of here. The good news is she drove back in her own car even though she left in Jack's Chevy. The tires on her car are new and the window is fixed, like nothing happened. The bad news is something did happen in that car.

"Know where this goes?" Mom thrusts a can of tomato soup at me.

I slam the groceries down on the kitchen counter.

She puts food away in places nobody would look for it. "Got time to eat?"

"Do you? Where are we going?"

Instead of answering, Mom eats the sandwich she made, eats standing up, the rest of the food still in bags crowding her plate. She chews pell mell, swallowing down the dough. This is Mom in preparation for an exit. This is Mom eating her way out. She pinches up her empty plate and flies it like a Frisbee at the sink. The plate hits the inner wall and drops in the sink without a break.

"Luck," she says.

Jack says Bird won't have anything to do with luck. But not so Mom. Even though luck often runs on the other side of the road, she is known to cross the line to meet it.

She palms the crease in a brown bag and says, "I will not be gone long."

"You have another shift already? They must like you." I can hear how much I want this to be true.

"I am fired."

"Fired from the hospital? You just started." No matter how many times she is fired, it is always a surprise.

"Other nurses, they don't like someone works too hard. Makes them look bad. They want to sit around gossip and snack. So they take it out on the foreigner."

"I guess they can tell how much you don't want to be there," I say. "Why would you? You are a ballet dancer. You should be on stage."

Mom fixes her hair bun. Her feet are turned out, about to leap. "Instead I am stuck with nurses." She pivots and glides out of the kitchen. I follow her up the hallway into her bedroom, where she hauls her suitcase out of the closet to pitch in every little thing she brought into Jack's house. Snapping it closed, she looks up at me and says, "I don't mind about losing job. Really, no job is a gift. I am finally free now to dance. Finally! You have fine place to stay. We all have what we want. We can be happy. All of us!"

I grab her suitcase with both hands. She tugs it and me to the door. I could make a run for my own suitcase, which I keep packed because when we go, we go quick, but the time spent fetching is all the time she needs to get clear of me. She says, "Sorry, baby. You must let go." She drags us along the hallway, through the holed-up screen door and down the steps on to the front walk. But her suitcase gives up and snaps open. The things inside dump at her feet. She looks up and smiles, the nicest ever.

She is going.

She bends over to hug me, but I get her by the shirt buttons.

"Don't go, Mama."

"I thought you wanted a house," she says softly.

"I did. But not this. This is worse than a vacancy. This is wilderness."

"Home," she says, "is wilderness."

"Don't leave me here with him," I say. "Please," I say.

One by one she draws my fingers off the buttons of her blouse and presses my head into her chest, and I listen through the bones. "I have sacrificed enough. Sacrificed everything what I came to this country to do," she says. I must stay here so she can, once and for all, put her all into dance. Perhaps if she had talked with Baryshnikov the other night, but no matter. So long as I'm here with Jack, she will know I am safe. Jack is a K-9 cop. That is a secure job! Safer hands I could not be in.

"If he's so safe, how come his dog needs stitches? How come *Jack* needs stitches?"

"What stitches?"

"Jack wouldn't let go of the collar. Bird couldn't breathe. Choking—"

Mom's hand flies to her throat. "Shhhh," she says. Her arms drop down and her head too. "I knew it. Of course, you cannot stay here. What was I thinking?"

Her hair has come undone across her face. I draw a strand behind her ear.

"Where were you going?" I say.

"Does it matter? Get your suitcase. We go to motel. I will find another job." What that means is we will go back to living in her car. "Anyway," she says, "I hate to ask favor of Jack."

"You didn't ask him yet?"

"He would say no."

"Yeah, he would," I say. "Listen, I won't tell him you left."

"Impossible."

"Possible."

She looks up. "No—"

"But come back. Fast as you can—"

"Really, Olechka?"

Mom rises from the grass as though gravity has no hold on her. Walking backwards, kissing her hands and tossing the kisses at me, her things on the grass just something else to walk on, she says, "Thank you, Olya. You make me so happy. You will see how happy. What we both want. What we dream in. Olya. Do not make Jack mad. Do not provoke with smart talk. Just stay. Stay no matter what. Stay if he tells you to go. Stay if he shoots at dog. The dog is not us. We are the dream. The dream of ballet. If the house goes to pieces, stay. It is not up to you. It is up to Jack if you stay. Don't give him single reason not to."

She reaches the car, gets in. She rolls down the window. "Jack's Chevy is in lot at the repair shop. Same place as last time."

"What do you mean *last time*? You've used his car before?"

"No, never. Never mind. Tell him Franklin Motors. Tell him they will hold it until somebody pays."

The car heaves to a stop. She leans across the passenger seat and thrusts open the door. "This is nuts. Come with me."

"Will I have to stay in the car?"

"I will do my best?"

I step back from the car. No dice.

Mom studies me. She says, "You do not want to go back to sleeping in car? What else you not told me?" She points to my bruised eye.

Flushed with the faith that I can finally stop Mom from prying, I say that it is true, I have not told her everything about what happened when she left me in the car the other night. The truth is the two outside our car in Griffith Park were not people at all. They were coyotes and they took turns looking in through the windows, their canines dripping, eyes rising like mercury through their skulls, their tails lifted behind them as if strings from above drew them up. All I had to do was catch their eye, tell them what I wanted, and they would swing open the doors and together we would rise above the parking lot, the pine trees, the observatory on the hill, higher and higher, until the park was just a patch below us and the astronomer at his telescope would mistake us for a star.

"So nothing happened," Mom says.

"But it could have."

She nods and closes the passenger door. She says, "Jack may be something like a devil, but he is a devil that I know for long time and now you will know. Jack is little worse than he was before. Maybe from time in Afghanistan. But Jack is only devil about the dog. Only dog, not you. I promise. Perfect, no. But this is the safe I can get you."

❧

A mother's job is to know her child. Some mothers are better at this than others. Mom is perfect at her job. She is always right about those things held in secret. Mom knows that when I do not want to talk about something, I make a joke or invent a story. After all, I picked up the trick for hiding stuff from her, and she probably picked it up from her mom. I have not told her everything about Griffith Park, except that a man threw a rock at the passenger window. But I did not tell how it was the woman who reached through the broken glass to unlock the door, how the woman caught my ankle on my way out the other side. Screaming the whole time at the man to hold me. Climbing on top of me, the chains of her necklaces throbbing round her neck, her bracelets carving my bones as she pushed down my shoulders. The seat leather slippery beneath me. She smelled of ashes, the hot powder of her mouth shouting at my face, "Like to watch? You want in on this? You dirty little spy!"

He held my knees. The black strip of hair swinging in his eyes.

"Now you've done it," the woman whispered. "Now you'll have to pay."

"She's a fucking mustang," the woman told the man. "Hold her. That kick." How could he tolerate a dirty spy watching what they do? "Hurt her," she said. "Hurt the little pony." She fell out the door lunging at the man. He let go of my legs. His eyes tucked behind the black strip of hair. *He let go.*

Slam down the handle. Roll out the other door. Hit the blacktop. Silence sucked out. In this vacuum a damp hand closed around my shoulder. Might have been his. Or just the dark holding on. Never ran so fast. Wind drying the sweat I had not known I was soaked in, the park lights blinding. Did not see it coming. Smack, straight into a tree.

Mom figured right. The black eye came of making the man and lady angry. The sorry truth is, I wanted to look at them, wanted to get a really good look at what they were at. How can I tell Mom that instead of bolting from the car and running while I still had a chance, I stayed to watch?

8

A nts march over the things left on Jack's front lawn. They march across Mom's pantyhose. Ants scale the bristles of her hairbrush. There are no obstacles ants cannot find a way around.

A cruiser pulls into Jack's driveway. The letters K-9 flash gold in the industrious light as a lady cop slides out from behind the wheel. She adjusts the gun belt on her hips before walking across the lawn. She walks pretty fast for someone short.

"Hello," she says, going down on one knee before Mom's open suitcase. "Need a hand?"

I snatch Mom's pantyhose back from the lady cop, and the dog inside her cruiser flames into action. The window glass strings with saliva.

The lady does not look back at her barking dog. She rises and spreads her hands as if to say, *I won't touch a thing.* "Are you visiting Jack?"

It takes a minute, but I say it. I say, "Staying." The buckle on Mom's suitcase snaps shut under my fist.

"Looks more like you were running away."

The lady follows me inside the house, saying she'll wait for Jack. He won't mind. I put Mom's suitcase in her room, then head for the kitchen for that sandwich I made but did not eat. The lady is in there poking around.

"Food goes bad if left out," she says as she snatches a can of dog food from the counter and takes it with her to the kitchen table. The milk, the meat, and the frozen stuff thaw on the countertop.

The lady pats the chair beside her. "Sit." When I do, she says, "My name is Barbara. But you can call me Officer Ross." She laughs like it was a good joke. "What's yours?"

I tell her.

"How do you know Jack?"

"Mom and Jack are cousins."

"Ah, the suitcase belongs to your mother then? You do seem youngish for pantyhose." She bangs the can down on the table. "Do you like Jack's dog? Bird, right? What's he like?"

"Like your dog," I say, "only without that kind of attention."

"You mean Bird doesn't give Jack his full attention?" she says.

"I think that dog gives Jack what he's got."

She folds her hands over one of mine. "You seem special. What grade are you in?"

"Whatever they put me in."

She laughs. "Oh, come on."

"What?"

She studies me. "I don't know. Maybe it's just how you're small. Small-boned. I was the same. I still am petite, but nobody notices now." She makes out to be lifting weights.

The back door bangs shut as Jack steps into the kitchen. The lady's hands fall away. "Oh, Jack," she says, "look at you."

Jack's eye is swollen shut. He lifts a hand wrapped in gauze to scratch a cut at his cheekbone. His other hand grips a fast food bag. The greased window reads: *hot*. He looks at me, and then he looks at the bag.

"Get a plate," he says and limps to the table, lifting out chicken thighs from the bag and setting them on the plate. He hands me a napkin and, without a word to the lady, pulls out the seat next to hers. He says, "I thought you might be hungry, Olya."

Jack and the cop watch me eat. Bird shows up behind the glass door to watch me too. The lady tries to act like she does not notice but she is taking note of that dog.

Jack reaches into his coat pocket and pulls out Mom's hairbrush and pantyhose, her things on the grass that I would have put away if the lady cop had not shown up. He lays the pantyhose across his legs. The pantyhose looks happy, sitting on his lap like that.

Barbara takes one look at the pantyhose and squeals up out of her chair. Grabbing the packaged meat and the carton of milk warming on the counter, she shoves them in the fridge. "How can you stand so much out exposed?"

Jack brings the hairbrush up to his good eye and studies the trapped strands of hair—red, Mom's red, not black like mine, not black like his. The hairs snap and pop as he unwinds the bristles.

The cop lady slams the refrigerator door. "Jack," she says, "give me a break?"

Jack nods with approval at the chicken I pull from the bag. He goes back to laying each strand of hair alongside the pantyhose.

The lady cop snatches the hairbrush out of his hands and marches to the sink and tosses the hairbrush in. "Good idea, Babs," Jack says, and he grunts out of the chair to limp to the sink, setting the pantyhose on the counter so the legs dangle off. Jack fits a bar of soap between the bristles of the hairbrush.

The lady stands very still beside Jack. Each time her dark eyes shift to what he is doing, they flare, hot enough to torch things. "The wife of the fellow you messed with at the park, she understands. She had a brother in Iraq. But she's going to press charges anyway."

If Jack heard, he doesn't show.

"We've got your gun at the station," she says. "The report says you were shooting at your dog while at the Loomis Range. You've had quite a day."

"Shooting at the dog," Jack says. "What kind of sense would that make?"

She looks out at Bird, the bandage slung around his chest.

"He runs off like a rabbit when you fire. Straight through the brush. Chews him up."

"You're pretty chewed up," she says.

Jack shrugs. "I made a harness that lashed Bird to my chest. A mistake. When he spooked and ran, he took me with him."

"You said you liked working a dog on leash," I say.

Jack turns, looks at me, and smiles. He shakes water from the hairbrush and says, "I do like working on leash. But on my feet, not on my face."

"Anything broken?" The lady pokes a finger at his ribs, and he winces but laughs.

"Just my heart."

"Jack, you are the gosh darn Svengali of canines. You make eye contact, and the trained dog obeys." Her head tilts, her mouth opens like she is the dog waiting on her master's words. "When you walked into Riverside K-9 in those army fatigues, stinking of the desert and kabobs, the dogs lay down for you, scrapped their handlers for you, killed each other for you."

"Going a little far."

"They lost their heads over you." She wipes her eyes, but her hand touches only air. She grabs for him, but he ducks out of reach and sets the hairbrush to dry on a tea towel. The way this lady looks at Jack, it is not the first time I have seen such a thing. Mom gets that look from the men working the front desks at the vacancies. Their eyes longing and sore that all the special they did for her—letting us stay for free or slipping us coupons for breakfast—got no thanks. But this cop lady's face says maybe I had it wrong. Those guys working at the vacancies were not sore, just lonely over the trouble their hearts could get them into.

Jack thumbs over at Bird. "What's out there is a dog that requires training."

"Training for what?"

"To get on the force," Jack says.

"That dog's already on the force," she says.

"Soon as he's trained, we'll both be." Jack slumps against the counter.

"Jack, you know what a dog like that costs the force," the lady says, "about sixty thousand dollars, all in."

"What," says Jack, "do you think it has cost me?" He limps over to the door and stares through the glass at Bird, who stares right back.

"The force must recoup costs."

"Soon as Bird learns the stay, the force will recoup, and more."

"You keep pushing him, you'll end up without a face. Bird is out for number one," she says. "Give me Bird. He's not the dog for you. You need a dog that offers support."

"Yeah? What kind of support?"

"Like, emotional support," Barbara says, talking fast, selling Jack on the idea. "Emotional support dogs get very good results with veterans. They sense your triggers before you do. The dog stops in place. You have no choice but to stop too and ask yourself: hey, what's going on inside me?"

Jack nods, taking it in, but that all ends in a big laugh. "This thing between me and Bird is way beyond such puppy shit, Babs."

I slide the chicken bones into the bag. Jack says, "Had enough?"

"Yes, thank you."

"Bird will ruin you." The lady pounces on Mom's pantyhose dangling off the counter and stomps past me to Jack at the door. Her cropped wavy brown hair reaches his shoulder. "I looked the other way when you took Bird off police grounds to train at your personal residence," she says. "I've been covering for you since. Screwing with a stranger at the park is bad enough. But this incident at the firing range lifts the roof right off. We're both exposed. I'm getting reamed by IA. How do you expect me to protect you now?"

"I have never asked for your protection, Barbara," Jack says. His eyes stay on Bird.

"Because of this?" She flicks a leg of the pantyhose.

"Olya and her mother only came a couple days ago."

"You weren't pushing that dog so hard a couple days ago."

"According to the force, I was pushing too hard from day one."

She raises a hand to his face, touching it as if he were her own baby. "What do a couple canine guys at RPD know?"

Jack grabs the lady's forearm and drags it 'round her backside to drive her out of the kitchen. She puts up with this for a couple feet but this is a police officer. She yanks out of his hold and steps back to rub her shoulder where it hurts. "They terminated you, Jack, and you make off with their canine. Technically that's theft of police property."

"More like abduction," he says, "except I had your permission."

"Bird was on loan," she says, "until you blew it. I've risked it all for you."

She draws in her arm, checking how it sits in the socket, then throws it back at Jack, smacking her fist in his ribs. Something under Jack's belly flesh sounds a pop. He rears back, striking the counter, grabbing cupboard doors. Bird howls, paws whapping at glass.

Barbara's eyes go wide at what she has done, and her knees fold. She crumples beside Jack. "The dog's not worth it, Jack."

"Don't—" Jack sucks in breath. "Bird's worth all you goddamn people. You're just not worth him."

The lady drops back on her heels, rubs her nose, and gets to her feet. "I will give you one week to work that dog into shape."

"Two weeks."

The way the lady stands there, allowing her slow brown eyes to drag over Jack—love like that I have never seen in Mom.

"Olya," Jack says, "escort the officer out. See she leaves with only her own dog."

Jack breathes loud. He does not look good. I hesitate.

Jack glares at the cop lady. "See what you've done, Babs. Got Olya worried. Keep it up and she'll need one of your emotional dogs."

"Not your concern, Olya," she says. "I'll send someone to look after Jack."

"Not a nurse, you don't," Jack hollers. "I've got more nurse than I can handle."

The lady throws a last look at Jack, who gazes with awe at the can of tomato soup Mom could not find a place for.

"Watch yourself, Olya," he says without looking up. "She'll try to talk you into something. That's how she does."

⌁

Officer Ross folds into the front of the cruiser. Her canine's tongue shoots through the holes in the grate across the backseat. The lady sticks her head out the window. "You in school?" Before I can lie, she says, "Mind if I check?"

I shrug. She has got this little bully thing wound up and ready to strike.

"Your last name?"

"Volkova."

"Volkova. Look, Olya Volkova, when we come for Bird—"

"In two weeks—"

She makes a face, and I remember that Jack said two weeks, not her. "You'll help us. You know what's right for that dog."

"What do I know about that dog?"

But that is not what I want to say. I want to say, since when did Jack stop being a cop? Safer hands I could not be in, Mom said. And if Jack is not a cop but is going around acting like one, doesn't that make him closer to a criminal? Though it is a fact that Jack never said he was currently employed in police work. Mom said it, and maybe she really thought he was or at least hardly saw the gain in not knowing. I mean, leaving me with a not-cop does not offer the same level of reassurance.

"Help is on the way," the lady cop says as she backs down the driveway. "Jack cannot expect a child to fix his boo-boos."

On the other hand, at least with Jack you get what you see. That lady spiraling off in her cruiser is so deceived by her heart, she might not know if she will hurt or help from turn to turn.

The groceries are back out on the counter, even the items the lady cop put away. Jack has grouped them into displays like in a supermarket. He holds up an egg to his good eye, turning the egg this way and that.

"Perfection," he says. Eggs are nothing but perfection until he moves onto cans. "Tomato soup," he says, "speaks volumes.

When I think all this time she could have been shopping for me," he says, squinting at me over the can.

"My mom can't shop worth a damn," I say.

Jack may be nothing more than a *garant* to Mom, but Mom is something else to Jack. She is messages in canned foods to Jack. She is pantyhose.

"The little police gal?"

"Gone, not your dog."

"You are smart, aren't you? You know where Bird belongs," Jack says. "Good."

But I did not make sure Bird stayed for Jack's sake. I made sure *because* of Jack. Bird is for my protection. "The lady asked if I was in school."

He nods and points to a chair. "Sit down," he says. "Sit down." He swallows a lot, short and noisy. He uses the counter to hold his spine straight.

"You okay?"

"Nothing beats a punch to the kidney," he says.

"I thought ribs."

"This is kidney." He points to his lower back, not where the lady hit him but who can argue with another man's pain? "How come your mom bought so much?" he says.

"She does that when she works double shifts."

"Right." He stretches out the word to say he is not buying it, then picks up the hairbrush and waves it in my face. "What was this doing on my lawn?"

"I dropped it."

He nods.

I would like to ask Jack why Mom had needed to use his Chevy before, but now is not the time.

He says, "You're covering for her. I don't like people interfering," he says. "You unfastened Bird's collar. He got away."

"You were choking him."

"I was training the stay."

"I saved his life!"

"You what?" Jack laughs and winces. "Saved his life? You

can't save lives, his life or anybody's. Bird doesn't want to be saved. Most don't. Once you get into the business of saving lives, you learn that. That's the first lesson in search and rescue. Not the official lesson but the one that turns up pretty quick under the discard."

Jack shuffles out of the kitchen with the can of tomato soup. He gets as far as the parlor. The coils in the couch twang under the bulk of him. I picture him curled up and cradling the soup can against his heart.

✺

First, I draw down the blanket on the camp bed, where Mom slept when she slept here. Then I dig out old clothes from the metal locker rising up behind the bed. Nothing is put away in this room, not Jack's guitar with the hippy strap or the camouflage tent half collapsed on top of army boots. Mom said the room smelled like a barracks, but she did not object to the clutter, except for a dog crate listing to one side in the corner. Jack had to remove that before she would sleep here.

Next, I roll up the old clothes and lay them on Mom's camp bed until the rolled clothes shape out arms and legs, torso and head. When I made Mom in the backseat of our car, I used pillows. But rolling garments to shape out limbs is more lifelike. Last step: pull the blanket over what now looks a lot like Mom asleep there.

I step back from the camp bed. From the door, it is a view of Mom under heavy covers. I did not expect to have to make Mom again. Not after we stopped sleeping in cars. But now I see that living in a house just requires that you make a more convincing Mom. If Jack knows anything about a nurse's schedule, he will know nurses only come home to sleep and he will have enough sense to let her. Making Mom is good protection from Jack so long as it tricks him into thinking she is still around. I told Mom her dream was possible. Possible means tricking Jack.

9

Morning light nudges the window beside my bed, no different than the morning before, except this morning Bird is not watching from the hill in the backyard. Bird is here in my room. He sleeps on the rug beside my bed. Does Bird hear the battle drum of Jack's rise from the couch and stumble up the hall, the wheeze and curse of him? I scoot out of bed. Bird rises in one movement, but I tell the dog to stay. Though he teeters into action, he does obey.

Jack is leaning into the doorway to Mom's bedroom but turns sharp at my footsteps. "Shhhh," he whispers, "your mother's sleeping."

I lunge between Jack and the door to pull it shut, quietly, as if to say, *Yes, yes, let's make sure she keeps sleeping.*

Jack frowns. The man likes his frown. He steps around me and opens back up the door. He looks at the camp bed, lumped of someone sleeping there. He frowns a little meaner back at me. He releases the doorknob and shuffles and huffs into the room to the bed. Jack looks back at me one more time.

I shrug.

He pulls a fist of heavy covers and sweeps them back. He stares at the space that should be Mom but is clothing rolled up to look like her. Jack stares for so long, his chin droops to his chest. Could be he has fallen asleep. Then his knees collapse onto the bed, right on top of the rolled-up clothes.

"She put you up to this?" he says.

"It's what I do when she goes away. I make Mom."

Jack tugs out a sweater from under his knees. He snaps up arms and legs, he snaps up head and torso, shakes them out into a hang of clothes. All this gyrating looks like it hurts. "Where is she?"

"At work. Three-day shift."

"You are a child," he says, feeling in his pants pocket. "Children lie. I don't like lies." He finds his phone, but the thing is cracked and will not turn on. He throws it at the wall. "Damn you, Bird!"

We both stare at the phone on the floor as Bird trots up the hallway. He looks in at Jack. Jack glares back at his dog.

"Olya, get your mother on the phone. I want the truth about her shit on my lawn. There was some kind of hurry—"

"She was in a hurry to work—"

"She in or out—that's what I want to know? If she's out, you are too, Olya." I turn away. Bird follows. "Where you going?"

"To get my phone."

"Leave my goddamn dog."

"Stay, Bird."

Bird does not follow me. "What the hell you do to my dog?"

I swing round. "You told him to stay."

"No, you did."

I run for my room. Jack would probably come after me, if he could. Never know what ailment a man with a temper can overcome. He is working himself up in there, bad temper mixing with his bruises. I find the cell at the back of my suitcase. I text: *He's not a cop. Fired. He could do anything. Get me out of here. NOW.*

Before I hit send, the phone bleeps. A few texts burn through, all from Mom. *Got to San Francisco in time for last round audition. Made cut of course. Is finally happening. All I need you safe. Stay safe, Olechka.* I kill my text. Shove the phone back into my suitcase and punch shut the snaps. Better to kill the message than Mom's dreams.

Knocking on the front door.

"Answer the goddamn door," Jack hollers.

"It's your door! You—"

"Answer it!"

Jack lunges for me as I come out of my room. I pitch against the wall. Bird rushes between our legs, snarling. Jack trips over the dog. His hands flail for the wall but the wall skips away. He stumbles, rights, stumbles, is down.

I wait for Jack to get back up, but he can only grunt and shrug uselessly up the wall.

The front door pops open, knocking up against Jack's splayed legs. A woman squeezes through the partially open door into the hallway. Her yawning umbrella is not as easy to wedge through the door as she is. The woman sets a pharmacy bag and her umbrella beside the door. She squats before Jack, who has pulled himself to sitting against the wall.

"Mr. Marea?" she says.

He nods. She fits long fingers under his arms. "I am Nurse Fenton." Nurse Fenton is a small woman, not ungentle; this is her job. She lifts him.

"You're not the nurse *I* want," Jack says, finding his feet with her help, frowning at me over her shoulder, like I conjured another poor substitute for Mom.

The nurse smiles at me. "Hello. What is your name?"

"Olya."

"As in Olga but spelled O-l-*y*-a?" She looks back at Jack but says, "What's everybody so mad about, Olya?"

"Nobody's mad," Jack says, tugging her hands off him.

Behind Nurse Fenton, Bird rakes his paw against the front door. Startled, the nurse lets out a little cry and spins around to the dog. "Our Lord and Savior, why is he doing that?"

"Take Bird out back, Olya," Jack says, his voice still and feeble and deeply colluding. "Where he belongs. Where he can be leashed. Where he won't run."

I grab Bird's collar, grateful for an exit. Sure, Jack and I were fighting over Mom, but it was our battle. Now with Nurse Fenton looking us u-p and d-o-w-n, she acts like it is her business too. "See that Bird's fed," Jack hollers. "A fed dog trains best."

Bird is grateful to clear out too. His championship urination against the tree is proof. The last pee he dabs delicately on the lawn furniture. I gaze over the fence, half believing Mom's car will turn into the driveway.

A muffler fires off. The wide brown lowrider that was

tooling around Jack's neighborhood a couple days ago slinks to the street corner. The same dude sits behind the wheel, easing alongside two girls walking with pink hair. Morning sun flares in the rhinestones lining the girls' hides. The dude guns the engine. The girls look at each other to decide on a response. He flicks his cigarette onto the street and slams on the horn. *Hooooonk!* The girls pull a horror movie scream and dash up the street. The dude watches them go, then he turns his head and looks right at me.

He shoots his tongue out like before. But this time he fakes slow licks off an imaginary ice cream cone. The length of his tongue is wrong. On the other hand, the martyr Philosophus had a long tongue. When his doubters bound him hands and feet to a soft bed and ordered a harlot to wrap her legs upon him, Philosophus bit his tongue in half so as not to be tempted by the harlot.

This one in the lowrider is no Philosophus. Look at him. So easily tempted by all manner of indulgence. To think not long ago I was grateful to Jack for protecting me from the dude's prowling eyes. I duck out from the fence and listen for the low-rider to chug off. But it keeps idling at the curb. I slip to the side of the house, unlatch the gate, and step out, out of sight of the lowrider. I slink to the sidewalk. A dash and a slam, and I am up against a fat oak. The dude in the lowrider cannot see me, but I can see him. Or, at least, see his waist down to his Wranglers, the only part visible in the rearview mirror. I am not much shocked when his hand pulls down the zipper on his pants. I stay to watch the denim separate like the sea. His fingers flick and pull, luring the creature. His hand closes around, shoving and shoving it into that imaginary ice cream cone. Onan, sin, forbidden touch, the words of the Good Book rush over us. In a blush, I run from my spying spot behind the oak.

Nurse Fenton is with the coffee machine in the kitchen when I burst in. She digs her fists into her backside as she waits on the drip.

I set Bird's bowl on the counter and open the fridge, sticking my head in to cool off.

"When did you last eat?" she asks. "Why aren't you at school?"

I decide that I do not have to answer.

She lifts out the pot from the machine and pours into a cup round as a soup bowl. She walks to the counter and sets the cup down. "Where is your mom?" she says.

A good decision. Answering would not have stopped the interrogation. I consider a package of bologna. I put it back in the fridge.

Nurse Fenton shuffles to the fridge. She takes out the bologna, rips open the package with long fine fingers, and brings it to her nose. She hands it to me. "I'd eat it."

"Excuse me," I say, stepping up to the counter drawer blocked by her narrow torso. When she clears off, I pull the drawer and grab a stick of gum. Glad that Mom bought more.

"One for me?"

I hand it over. Her quick fingers flick aside the silver sides of wrapper and she picks out the stick and folds it against her tongue. We chew our gum silently.

"Who is Mr. Marea to you?"

"What's with the questions?"

She says, "I am an RN in the homecare network. I help families make the best of a situation. These are normal families. It's the situation that isn't. But this." She stops chewing. Her fingers extract the knot of gum off her tongue. "This family is not normal. That man in there can only talk about dog training. Training in his condition?"

Scratching sounds at the door. Fenton spins around. Bird stares in through the glass.

"Do you like the eyes on that dog?" Nurse Fenton asks.

"I forgot to feed him."

"Why did you do that?"

I lock my bedroom door and lie across the bed, setting on my

belly the yellowed prayer card that Sister Hedge gave me before
I left St. Anne's. On the card is a painting of helmeted guards
stretching Saint Philosophus's arms and legs across the scattered sheets of a soft pallet bed. His eyes glow and his mouth
holds about a cup of blood. The guilty harlot squirms in a
corner of the pallet. I imagine the harlot preparing herself to
bewitch Philosophus: she squats alone in a quiet room pouring
rosewater over her black hair. My hand moves up my shirt as
water drips to the floor. Now the harlot massages aromatic oils
into her breasts. She tugs on her nipples. But her artifices have
failed to lure the saint, and now she gapes at Philosophus's cut
tongue licking the long air over her head. A wide brown lowrider passes through the room. The dude is behind the wheel, and
the V of his fingers sees me for what I am at.

I wipe my hand on my pants. The prayer card falls facedown onto the floor. My empty legs follow over the side of the
bed. I hang over my thighs, a ragdoll of damnation. I recognize
Sister Hedge's handwriting on the back of the card. *Olya*, she
wrote, *I will always remember you standing on one leg beside my desk.
The sunlight spread across your face and lit your spirit. Such possibilities
in you.*

Sister Hedge wrote that last year when she offered to get me
a scholarship for middle school. On my behalf, she had spoken to a nice family, dear friends, big supporters of St. Anne's.
Their children had gone to St. Anne's but had since left for
college. The mother, Kitty Wand, longed for a child to fill her
empty home. Sister Hedge meant no disrespect to my mother
when she proposed that I live with the Wands and stay on at
St. Anne's. "You must see how happy Olya is here," she said
to Mom. "Once Olya enters high school, she can board at St.
Anne's. The Wand's home is a temporary measure." Mom said
she would consider it. But Mom lost her job at the hospital and
instead of the Wands, Mom and I moved to a new vacancy. My
education has been strictly public school since.

Sister Hedge said she and St. Anne's would always be there
for me. The school is in Arizona. Not far by bus. Changing

where I stay will not interfere with Mom's dream so long as I leave her out of it.

Someone knocks on my door. Nurse Fenton, her arms loaded with bedsheets. I put my back to her. "Jack's in the bath," she says. "Come. Help me make Jack's bed the hospital way."

"You make Jack's bed. I'm getting out of here. So long."

Nurse Fenton pauses. "So long," she says. The door closes.

The phone number for St. Anne's comes up on my cell. My hands shake as much as my voice. "I attended last year," I tell the receptionist. "Sister Hedge was my teacher."

"Is that Olya?" the receptionist says. "How are you doing? We miss you." I picture the bright gloss of her froggy smile. "Sister Hedge would of loved to say hello."

"Loved?"

"Sister Hedge has gone up with the Maryknoll Sisters." The school bell tolls behind the receptionist.

"When is she back?"

"Nigeria." A second bell echoes the line.

"She said she'd always be there," I say.

"Sister Hedge," the receptionist hollers over the racket of kids. "Doing for our Lord. Check the Maryknoll Sisters website for pictures!"

Fenton passes me standing in the doorway to Jack's room. "You still here?"

Jack is damp from the bath. She guides him onto the bed. "Give me the blanket," he says but the blanket stays over Fenton's arm.

She joins me in the doorway. "A bed is only as good as its corners," she says. "Look at that." Jack is a tight sheet with only the points of his toes and knees. He is as bound as St. Philosophus. Except I am the one who must bite my tongue.

Fenton says, "That is the hospital way. Now the patient will stay. He'll stay still, he'll stay quiet, he'll stay in bed, because he's held."

"Why can't Mom do it like this?"

"Olya's mother is crackerjack at making beds," Jack says, "and she doesn't begrudge a man his blanket, lady nurse."

"Zsa Zsa," Nurse Fenton says. "My preferred name."

Jack squints at her like he cannot connect the name with this small woman. Fenton spreads the blanket over Jack. "All settled. Doesn't that feel better?"

Not sure if she is talking to Jack or me.

Frying pan on a burner, plate of raw burgers, buns, tomato, onion: Nurse Fenton puts out the fixings. She peels off a patty from the stack and tosses it into the frying pan. She slices onion. She opens a bun on her plate. She hands me a plate and says, "Your turn."

"Not hungry." I set down the plate.

From the kitchen door Bird sends up a *hi-huh-hi-huh* at the stench of frying meat.

Fenton looks sideways at the singing dog then leans into a bottom cupboard. "Where does he hide the condiments?" The cruddy wooden door falls off its hinge to chop straight down onto Fenton's toes. She curses and folds to the ground to rub her foot. "This house is falling to bits," she says. "The dog's mouth has got too many teeth."

I give her a hand up. "Okay?"

Her head swivels round. "No, not okay. You aren't either, if you care to look." She hobbles back to her plate. Propping her no-belly against the counter, she takes a deep breath and lifts the hamburger with both hands. But she sets it back down without a bite and turns her eyes on me. "No wonder you got no appetite. On edge. Ready to fly."

She goes crabwise to the stove and twists on the burner knob, staring into the pan as it heats up. Her hamburger cools on the counter behind her. "Go ahead. Eat it," she says with some kind of eyes in the back of her head. She swings another patty onto the frying pan, mumbling to herself about putting in a call to the homecare agency if she cannot get to the bottom of this child's custody status.

I have eaten up Nurse Fenton's hamburger by the time she eases onto the stool beside me. She bites off big hunks from her burger the way thin people sometimes behave with food. Her mouth is packed as she says, "My mother worked as a nurse in the Philippines, and she kept on being a nurse after she married my father and came to this country. I took up nursing, same as my mother. A life in service to others has taught me a fundamental: When no one is looking out for you, then you ought to look after others."

"What *others?*"

"You should see your face," Nurse Fenton says.

10

They expect me to help around the house! That text ought to give Mom a laugh. She never talks about doing good, like Sister Hedge and Nurse Fenton do, do-gooders that never do you any good when you need them.

Mom texts back in about the next second. *Who is THEY?*

The nurse taking care of Jack.

If Jack needs nurse he needs help. You MUST help house By the way I am in final round if you are interested.

Pretty good I guess.

You bet pretty good for dancer kicked out from Vaganova's school.

I text: *Kicked out! Ha ha.*

No response.

Joke right?

Still nothing.

It had to be a joke. I mean, she graduated from Vaganova Academy of Russian Ballet, the best in the world. That is the whole point. That she did. Still a child when she gave up her mom to live at the Academy. The sacrifice! Made it through Vaganova's though. Not everybody does. But she did.

I text: *Kicked out? How come you never told me?*

Bird barks from the yard. The hallway reverberates with the broad echo of pounding wood. Someone is knocking at the front door.

I go to answer. The cell stays on my bed. Why wait for a reply that is not coming?

On the other side of the holed-up screen the lowrider dude balances flat boxes on his skinny arms. Red sauce sweats through the cardboard. "Your pizza, ma'am." He shoves the boxes through the hole, and his narrow gray neck swells then deflates on the shove. I keep my eyes off his mouth in case he starts with the tongue.

I do not accept the pizzas from him. "You're not a delivery person," I say.

"Gainful employed," he says, "unlike some who spend every minute checking out dudes from their itty bitty window." He chins at the street. A lit delivery sign flickers crooked on the roof of his lowrider. This is not the only addition to his lowrider. People sit inside—a lady and a bearded man and a small girl, who waves at me.

He frowns. "Aren't you going to say hi to my little sister?"

"That's your sister?"

"Yep, and that's Moonbabes and Pap too. The whole family is riding along to celebrate my first day on the job." He shrugs. "I appreciate the moral support."

I do a quick wave at his sister and close the door.

But the dude blocks with the boxes. "Don't care for pizza? Me neither. Cheese stretching between your teeth, sauce lubricating your throat, slick, viscous, buttery stuff. Want me to eat the pizza for you? You can watch me. Let me in."

I cast my eyes to the floor. "I don't let anybody in."

"You don't?"

The bashful soft sound of his voice surprises me. I look up. His cheeks have gone red beneath his dirty curtains of brown hair. His nose is red too. It rises at the bridge and beaks from there. He is a red-faced, ugly young man, but then Judas, they say, was handsome.

He lowers the pizzas and cocks his head at the sound of Bird barking from the yard. "Is that your dog?" he asks. "He sounds very down. Pap works closely with misery. Happy Endings Animal Impoundment of Riverside. I'll go fetch Pap. He'll teach you to love that dog."

"No! Uh, thanks. No time. Because I am employed too. I mean that dog is my job."

The door draws back. Nurse Fenton stares out at the guy. He nods at her, drops the boxes in her arms, and hops off the porch.

Bird's torso quivers beneath the nubs of red rubber as I guide the brush down his scruff. His hind leg rotates like he might pedal off on a bike. This is called dog grooming. This is called needing something to do. Mom found something to do. Vaganova grad or not, she is trying out for the San Francisco ballet. That person with the pizza even found a way to get paid for cruising the neighborhood. This dog needs care. Who else will do it? Not Nurse Fenton. Dogs are not her thing.

"Have you no mercy?" Jack's roars echo along the hallway.

"Cut the ruckus," Fenton says. "A couple of cracked ribs aren't such a bother. This is stirred up pain. Where were you? Afghanistan? Iraq?"

Jack shuffles into the kitchen to stop dead at the sight of us. Bird ducks my brush but stays put. "Who told you that you could do that?"

I point the brush at *The Encyclopedia of Dog* spread open at my knees. I found the book beside the rubber brush on a shelf in Mom's room.

Jack grabs for the brush. Bird rears back. The sudden move cost Jack. His cursing is of a kind you find in the Bible.

Fenton scoots up behind him. "You like to go back to bed, mister?" Jack dodges her. He lowers himself into a chair like the chair might tip at any moment.

"Not the way to brush down a dog," he says. "Not even close."

The nurse instructs Jack in the raising of his arms, the flexing and stretching of his limbs. His eyes stay on my grooming. "Such a fuss," Jack says. "You will ruin him."

"Did your brothers-in-arms trust you to make the roads safe?" Nurse Fenton says, back to her questions. "I hear you dog handlers also sleep with them?"

"Locked in our brother's arms."

She slaps the back of Jack's head.

"What the fuck, lady?" Jack draws a pack of cigarettes out of the pocket of his robe and shakes one out of the pack.

Fur glides off the brush to spin along the linoleum like

damselflies. I net it up between my fingers so Jack won't belly-ache about the mess. On the kitchen table is a tube of ointment from the vet's. Before dabbing it on Bird's cuts, I catch Jack's eye. "Okay?" I say.

"You're the expert." He breathes smoke at me.

Nurse Fenton leans over and tugs the cigarette out from between Jack's fingers. "You want a hole in your lung?"

Jack glares at Fenton as she finishes smoking the cigarette. She places a few slices of pizza on a plate and sets it in front of Jack. But Jack's eyes are on Bird. "You're blowing ointment like a sailor with pox," he shouts at me.

The book says to inspect the dog's mouth for odor, inflammation, and debris. The toothbrush I found knocking around the bathroom drawer should do. Holding my breath, I draw up the skin over Bird's teeth.

"Stop right there," Jack says. "Do one more sissy-ass thing to that dog, and its balls will hit the floor."

Around midnight Mom answers my question about Vaganova's. Her answer is news: the auditions in San Francisco have come down to a choice between her and another dancer for the corps. This is Mom's way of saying that no dancer kicked out of Vaganova's goes so far. But her lie gets to me. Graduating from Vaganova's was a big part of my faith in her dance. If graduating was a lie, what else about our life is a lie? I do not know how to be about lies. Mom probably felt the same way about whispers in her home in Dubna. She learned to dance in the silences. Dancing is not my thing. But neither is sitting around, silent. I will start doing. Get busy, act with purpose, like Nurse Fenton said. All is in the doing. The first thing I do is my room.

In the morning I show Nurse Fenton the can of yellow paint I dug out from Jack's garage. "Don't you think it will cheer up the walls?"

"Don't know how the walls will feel about that yellow, but I do know how you will," she says. "Sometimes, you know, generic color is okay."

"Vacancies are generic."

She frowns. "Vacancies? You mean like motels? I never thought of that. But I know what you mean. Empty, empty rooms." She presses her fingers against her flat chest. "I have stayed in motels. It is no place like home."

Nurse Fenton flips through the paint chips samples I found inside an issue of a magazine called *Sunset.* The magazines were stacked beside the paint can. The colors of the sample wheel blur. "Over the rainbow," she says. She chooses paler shades of yellow and holds them against my bedroom wall. "Sunflower or butterscotch?"

Nurse Fenton explains how homeowners use the color wheel to decide how much *pizzazz* to give a room. For example, the hallway in Jack's house could be goldenrod for a warm feeling. The dining room tidal-wave blue. The kitchen walls green mist, the parlor hoop orange, relay red for the dining room. Military green for Jack's bedroom. "Or maybe denim blue to match those eyes," Fenton says and hands me the color wheel. "This is your home. You're making it work. The more you do, the more you stay."

Every day, Nurse Fenton walks with Jack around the yard. She has been here almost a week, and he is getting stronger. Today, I hold the color wheel to the walls of Jack's bedroom while they walk. In the morning light above Jack's bed, the military green paint chip glows yellow-bellied.

All at once the door slams shut behind me. I am trapped. The doorknob vibrates. Someone on the other side is fiddling. "Grab hold," Nurse Fenton says, back already from the yard. The door creaks from the weight of something tugging on it. Nurse Fenton likes to use doorknobs to anchor the exercise bands. "Grab hold!"

"These things don't do any good," Jack says. "Training my dog. That's all I need."

The door tenses and eases against the jamb with what must be Nurse Fenton making Jack pull the bands. He curses. I want to curse, too, but then they would know I am in here.

Fenton sighs. "Mr. Marea, the agency I work for has many capable nurses. Why don't I put in a request? I am not up to you." Her voice sounds a kind of tired I have not heard before.

"You lose interest if the gossip isn't going your way." He grunts and exhales noisy and in rhythm with tension on the bands. He says, "Bet you'd favor a dirty story?"

I tiptoe to the other side of the room, out of earshot. Against this wall, I hold up the denim blue paint chip. I hold up lime.

"Valentine's Day," Jack says, his voice still loud and clear. "Routine domestic violence call. This little beauty answers the door in see-through underthings. I am dickblinded."

Lemon yellow. Vibrant orange. Dangerous mauve. Not a color on this wheel will improve Jack's walls. I should climb out the window or lock myself in his bathroom. If I don't and they find me here, they will call it spying. Like the man and the woman against Mom's car in Griffith Park called it spying.

I tiptoe back to the door. To listen. *Dirty spy.*

"Wasn't much to her," Jack goes on, "thin as a foreign greyhound. Blood running down a split lip that her valentine sent her. She'd only been in the states a week. Veins popping out her feathery arms, and I'm thinking 'user.' I'm scanning for train tracks, but it's baby flesh, an underfed baby. I pictured pulling her onto my lap and feeding her spoonfuls of warmth, her hard little behind jabbing my thighs as the food went down. This little beauty stands all but naked in the doorway before a couple of cops and she has the temerity to slide her eyes down to my crotch. She wasn't likely to survive many more love letters from her valentine. My first day on the job and I about ran to the squad car, trousers ballooning."

The color wheel slips from my hand.

"The next day I get a message," Jack says. "It's from her. '*Save me.*'"

My neck prickles dangerous mauve. *Get out, get out.*

"This woman?" says Nurse Fenton. "Was she the child's mother?"

I grab the color wheel, turn the knob, push open the door.

The door swings through Jack's talk. The band snaps. Jack tumbles. Nurse Fenton's face pops behind the door. She fires a smile. I shoot one back and bolt down the hallway.

I chuck the color wheel into the yard. Bird scrambles to his feet and lopes after it, bringing the wheel back to me. His soft mouth gumming up the laminated strips as he fights biting down hard on the thing. Fancy that? Thinking I could run a few color ideas past Jack and together we would paint the house the colors of the rainbow.

I drop on the steps to pet Bird. That story Jack told Nurse Fenton made me think of Mom. Nurse Fenton thought so too. Jack said the woman in the door was thin and was a foreigner. It could have been Mom, it really could have. But if that was Mom, then it was the first time she and Jack met, which is impossible since they are cousins. Besides, the way he talked about her, I mean, he got pretty worked up, and cousins do not get worked up about each other, at least not in that way. So, I guess, that was not Mom standing almost unclothed in a doorway on Valentine's Day.

This is what you get for eavesdropping: a run-in with the darkness of your own soul. I am impelled to hear what is not for my ears, to see what is not for my eyes. In the low light of the parking lot in Griffith Park, I watched the two touch each other against our car, heard their kisses, the rub of skin. At those times the outer world seems to cloud my mind so that the nudges and thunks of the car feel like some far-gone vehicle on the road. A fever works over me, and I do not want to be like others, I want to touch this thing that is forbidden me. This thing that seems to hold the last missing part that will complete the image of the world that I alone can know. Something insists, though, some premonition calling me. Is it to know who my father is? Is that the missing part? Will I always be nothing but a spy?

Bird drops the color wheel before me. He sees I am not up for games and lies down at my feet. I am radiant with gratitude for this abiding soul.

"Throw for Bird." Bird backs off the steps as Jack lumbers

through the door, arms flung over Nurse Fenton. She helps him down the steps. Jack toes up a stick from the dirt. "He's got fat on your petting. Time to train. We don't got much time."

I snatch the stick out of the air, spin around and fling it across the yard. The stick flips like a weird baton. Bird flies after it.

We watch Bird pull the stick out of the air. Dogs need daily physical exercise. *The Encyclopedia of Dog* said to clear a space for the dog. Until this morning, the yard roared disorder. Nowhere for a dog to run without tripping over itself.

"Who resuscitated this piece of crap?" Jack says, slapping the arm of a hosed-down lawn chair on the patio.

"Your little friend," Fenton says, drawing a blanket over his legs. "She's been scouring and repairing all day." Bird runs the stick back to me. When I reach for it, Jack snaps, "No touching the stick while in the mouth! No tug-of-war games. This is a working animal."

"Mr. Marea," Fenton says, "what is with you and that dog?"

Bird drops the stick at my feet, eyes switching from the stick to me.

Routine exercise is necessary for routine muscle movement. Routine watering would save the rhododendron clinging to Jack's fence. I throw the stick at the few blooms. Bird leaps and snatches the air right out of the stick then ambles up to his doghouse to gulp water from the bowl.

Jack points at the doghouse. "What did you do to it?" Jack says. "Damn."

The yellow shouts caution now that the paint has dried. Nurse Fenton called that one right. "I put in a blanket," I say.

"Stop tarting up the joint," Jack says. "Take the blanket back where you found it."

What is all his complaining really about? Jack is nervous about getting Bird under his command before Officer Ross returns for the police department's dog. Two weeks was the deal he struck with her. Does he know that six days have already passed?

"Mr. Marea." Nurse Fenton pulls up a lawn chair alongside

Jack so she can rub cream on his bruised ribs. "What was your first dog? Was it an army dog?"

Jack looks back at the nurse like he has no idea who she is.

"Take it easy. Just a question," she says.

Jack's quiet, but Nurse Fenton's rubbing seems to move his mind off the yard. He eases in. "My first MWD picked me. He trotted up and started showing me around the base, like he knew the place. Only he didn't. That dog was a newbie, like me."

I throw the stick again and Bird chases. Throw-chase-return. The bees hover over the rhododendron. Newbies, like me.

"Telepathy," Jack says. "No need to teach him the stay. That dog wouldn't think of going without I tell him to. He was exceptional. He earned commendations. He told jokes."

I hurl the stick.

"What was his name?" Fenton says.

"Over there he went by a few names."

She laughs. "Top secret."

"I'll tell you a secret," Jack says. "That dog was the only thing I'd ever done completely right." He cranes around Fenton. "Come here, Olya," he says.

I step up onto the patio, obedient. When on the return Bird finds me here beside Jack, he freezes, ribs contracting, the stick vibrating in his mouth. Bird sets the stick at the lip of the patio.

"Until I did wrong," Jack says, swinging past Fenton to snatch up the stick.

Eyes hard on the dog, Jack draws his arm back. Bird spins round and scrabbles out across the lawn in anticipation. But Jack sets the stick on his plaid pajama pant.

Bird tiptoes back to us, his head lowered and his ears flattened, embarrassed that he fell for Jack's trick. I drop into a squat before Bird, and he wipes his tongue across my cheek. The puppy makes demands from its mother by licking her face, according to the book. *Adult dogs perpetuate this puppy form of comfort-seeking communication by jumping up on their owners and trying to reach their lips.* Not my lips. Not that mouth. I twist around to Jack. "Throw the stick already."

"Dogs don't screw up. People do," he says. "You're screwing up my dog."

I push Bird off and tell Jack, "Throw the damn stick."

"Shut your trap." He waves the stick in the air. Bird rises, muscles twitching. I grab the stick. But Jack holds to it. Neither of us lets go.

"Mr. Marea, give the child the stick." Nurse Fenton's voice is very quiet honey. "Put the energy into getting well."

Jack's eyes fog. He nods off. But some gray misbehaving shadow pushes against it. His eyes drain bright. Fingers tighten on the stick. He pulls back hard. The stick's broken bits poke my palm. Nearby, the bees buzz. Bird growls. Make no trouble. You promised Mom.

I let go of the stick.

Jack gazes down at the thick damp thing in his hand. His eyes wash up to mine. His arm draws back, the hand rising up, his eyes pitching the stick straight at my head, hovering there—

I glare back at him.

Nurse Fenton snatches the stick out of Jack's hand from behind.

"I wasn't going to throw it at her," he mumbles. He yawns. Nothing a nap won't cure.

Fenton scrapes the lawn chair 'round to face him. "Why are you so angry, Mr. Marea?"

Jack lunges for the stick in her hand but misses and falls off the chair onto his knees. Still, his hand snatches for the stick. She keeps the stick out of reach.

Head low, eyes following the stick in Nurse Fenton's hand, Bird slinks up the steps toward it.

"What in God's name is going on in this house?" Fenton says, backing to the edge of the patio as Jack crawls after her. "Why isn't Olya in school like other children? Why can't you parent Olya properly? Where is her mother?"

"None of your business, nursey." Jack rises up, unstable bear, and pounces—not for the stick. For her. Without a backward glance, Fenton lopes across the patio. Jack hurls headfirst off the edge into the yellow tufts of grass. He grunts and coils up.

Nurse Fenton steps down to kneel beside him. "Give me the phone number for Olya's mom." She jabs the stick at his ribs. He moans and shovels his face into the dirt.

"Leave him be," I say, pushing past Bird to Jack.

Fenton holds calm beside him. "I should leave him, Olya. I could lose my license for getting involved. But a person in my position has to know who needs the help. Sometimes that person is not your patient. Olya, does your mother know what goes on here?"

"She knows."

"Do not lie, Olya," Fenton says. "Leave lying to the adults."

"What do you know?"

"Lying is the only excuse for his behavior. Your parents lying to you. Maybe because they lie to themselves, I don't know."

Nurse Fenton has got it wrong about Jack being my dad, but no time to explain. Jack's arm has snaked round her waist. His hand plucks the stick out of her hand. By the time this registers with Fenton, Jack has her held from behind, the stick at her chest. Fenton's eyes go wide.

Bird leaps at them.

Fenton screams. Jack drops the stick, and Fenton ducks behind Jack.

Bird is stopped midair by Fenton's screams. He eyes the stick but does not touch.

"Take Bird inside," Jack tells me.

I take Bird to my room. Nurse Fenton is not far behind. She keeps her eyes off the dog. "Pack up," she says, fumbling with her umbrella. "We are going."

"You and I?"

She grabs my suitcase from the floor of the closet, looks up, surprised. "Heavy!"

"I never unpack."

Her eyes on Bird, she sets the suitcase beside me. "I'll get mine. We meet at my car." She moves out but stops to say, "Don't worry. I gave Jack a sedative. He won't hear a thing."

I walk the hallway. My suitcase knocks at my calf. Bird's nails clack against the boards. Before Jack's closed door, I pause. Not sure how to say goodbye. Not sure he would care to. But something in me sticks around, if only to say some words. Until I hear the distinct click of metal and mechanism on the other side. The picture of Jack's gun rising in his hand. I grab Bird's collar and race slide down the hallway to the exit.

We keep this up across the grass. I swing round to the rear of Fenton's silver hatchback that she has left open. I pat the balding carpet for Bird to hop in beside my suitcase. He hesitates, looks at me then at Jack's house. He hops in and circles out a spot. I shut the hatchback and stumble glad against the passenger door. Fenton does not look up from her cell as I fold in beside her. "Giving Officer Ross my notice," she says.

I will call Mom, too, soon as we reach Fenton's place. Mom will not like that I left Jack's, but I can probably stay with Fenton until Mom is officially accepted into the ballet. I will join her then in San Francisco.

Fenton's eyes rise up to me. She pats my hand but says nothing as she stores her phone in her purse and starts the car, adjusting the mirror before backing out. Her hand freezes on the rearview. Then drops to her lap like someone knocked it off. Her shoulders draw over her chest. She speaks to the wheel. "Get it out of here," she says, "go on."

"You said I could come."

"You can, you must." Her eyes shift to me. "You cannot stay another minute in your father's house. But that dog? Tried to kill me!"

She stares out the windscreen. I follow her gaze in time to see the parlor curtain shift. A figure swells out behind it. "Jack is not my dad."

"Whoever he is, he knows we are going." She throws the car in gear. "Say goodbye to the dog. Say it quick."

I look back at Bird. His tail alternates a steady side to side.

11

The fuck were you doing with my dog?" Jack uses the wall to hold himself up.

"Nothing." I let go of Bird and he trots to the kitchen. "We were saying so long to Nurse Fenton."

"You were leaving," Jack says. "Not enough that you got your mother staying away. Try to take my dog too."

"Nurse Fenton is afraid of dogs."

"That why you came back?"

I look at Jack now. I do not see him. "None of your goddamn business."

"Your mother doesn't like questions either. Answers pin her down." He turns up the hallway. His knees swing as if worked by strings. "Well, good riddance, Nurse Nosy. Go tell boss Barbara. She'll love hearing how I'm dicking around instead of working Bird." At his bedroom he says, "How about one of your famous sandwiches?"

I slap mayonnaise on the faces of the bread, picturing Nurse Fenton's silver hatchback motoring across the plains. Fenton once said, "Take it easy, people disappoint us. Heck, we disappoint ourselves." I did not think that meant her. Guess I should have seen it. I should see a lot of things. Like the wall in front of my face, or else I will keep walking into it. But what is so bad about walking into a wall? Even better, four walls. Four walls make a house. Most people think poorly of walls, as things that cramp you in or keep others out. But that is not how walls are to me. Walls are worth getting to know. Without knowing the four walls in front of your face, you end up knowing very little. Sure, you will think you know, but not in the way others who have had the benefit of growing tall inside four walls know. Knowledge of the simplest kind, like house and family, are hard to read without the four walls to teach you. This is not peanuts. This is not some fancy, some craze. I am talking about existence. How I inhabit my body. I cannot be all the way in without having first inhabited home. Those times when Mom and I squatted in abandoned houses, she warned me to keep away from walls with exposed wires. Could my senses be as exposed as those wires curling through rotted plasterboard? Is this why I come off to people in fits and starts? Already someone my age is looking for ways out of her four walls. But somebody only looks for ways out when she is already in. I am not in.

Jack sits up in bed when I come with the sandwich. He points at me. That long finger might as well be loaded. "Your mother home tonight?"

I say, "If the hospital can manage without her."

He nods. The smile he forms probably uses the same number of muscles to frown. "That's Irina, doing a bang-up job. Works herself to the bone for others. That accounts for why I haven't seen her. Nursing is really her thing, a calling, a mission. The woman is a saint," he says, "for others."

Jack's talk would irritate Mom. Though some of it is even true. Mom does work hard as a nurse. Yes, I think she probably does. Look what Nurse Fenton just put up with. What Jack really wants is for me to say that Mom is not at any hospital. I want to say it, and I would if there was any room in this house for the truth. So I say, "Mom has good qualities."

"Yes, yes. Many," Jack says, "qualities." He reaches for the sandwich, which he takes out in a couple of bites. "List them."

"Her qualities?" Jack balances Mom's hairbrush on the peaks of his knees. "Mom's hair is pretty."

He clasps the hairbrush and jabs the air like a saber. "Beauty is in the specifics."

"Fine hair," I say.

"Lustrous," he says.

"Is that shiny?"

"It is shiny." Jack closes his eyes. Probably conjuring an

image of Mom's shiny hair. He opens his eyes on me. "You don't want to talk about her. Nobody wants to talk about his mom. Nobody with any sense." He says, "And you've got sense. That's one thing I can say about you. No, not one thing. This, too: you can keep house, you can knock out a sandwich, and you are good to the dog." He smiles. "You probably figured you could rescue that dog."

Jack flips the sheet off his legs. Careful as a boy releasing a paper boat in a stream, Jack sets the hairbrush on the crest of bedding. His legs drop over the side. His ankles are deadly pale against the dark leg hair. He sits tense between arms extended at sharp angles, the fists punching the mattress.

"You can't rescue anyone, Olya," he says. "I know. I tried to rescue someone. She said my rescuing was killing her. She got a restraining order—against a cop! Not easy to come by. Takes money, lawyering, court time, disputation, money. Within a 100 yards. That's how far I was to keep from her."

His feet lift and fall in turn, pacing some invisible fence. "Come closer, Olya."

When I do not, he says, "I would have had to rescue by proxy if the paper held up. But paper didn't hold because the one person who could transgress the 100 yards was her. She snuck back into my house. She needed money. I'd give whatever she wanted." He lifts Mom's hairbrush. His quick thumbnail picks at the bristles. "She went back to her routine, coming and going. It was clear I'd have to teach her to stay. Now get this. All along this lady is chewing on her own leg to break out of this house. But here's the catch. She's chewing not on account of being kept, but on account of *being left*." He drops the hairbrush. His hands rise up. "She said that one day I'd give up, walk away on her, one day. We started going at each other like animals; me, trying to keep her alive; her, goading me into abandoning. I had my hands on her neck, that perfect sickening neck. Trying to just hold on."

His hands curve into claws, outlining a spider on the wall behind him. What color to paint his walls now? Ransom red?

"Thumbs on the windpipe," Jack says. "Eyes rolling back, but she's not making any noise, not anymore. Her hands slipped off mine, and I see what I am at."

He gapes at his clenched hands. The hands spring apart, and I scream. Jack's eyes bounce. From somewhere outside the house, a low growl rises like smoke.

Jack's fingers go slack against his thighs. He lets out a terrific yawn, fighting sleep. "If I'd rescued her one more minute, I'd have killed her. So I left, signed up and shipped off. She was right. I didn't stay." He looks over at me. He blinks and pushes a hand through his hair, says, "Is she gone, your mom? Hell, I know she's gone. Knew when I saw her items on the lawn. Only I wasn't in good health to do things about it. Besides, I don't want Barbara in my business. That's what she sent Nurse Nosy for. But it's been a while now, your mom gone. Must be serious." Jack lowers back onto the pillows. But changes his mind. His hand waves out. I catch it and set the hand on my shoulder. He uses my shoulder to rise off the bed again.

"Mom is pulling the favor of a lifetime," I say.

"Favor?" he whispers. "From whom?"

"Me…you."

With that, I duck out from his hand and shoot out of the room into the hallway. Bird barks at the back door. I make for my bedroom and lock the door behind me.

"Where did she go?" Jack hollers from the other side of my door.

"Go away."

A high-pitched *hi-huh-hi-huh* rings from my bedroom window. Bird's nails scrape the glass. I sit on the edge of the bed and hope the window will shatter.

Jack bangs my door with what must be his whole body. The top hinge rips from the frame. The door dips into the room. Jack's eye peers in. "You won't tell me," he says, "your phone will. Hand it over."

The door cannot hold. The window behind me is still.

Jack's fingers creep around, wedging the door open. He

works the hinge back and forth. His fist slams the wood, but the hinge holds. The door rebounds to slam him in the face. "Goddamn," he mumbles and vanishes from the doorway.

Farther off, the front door sends out a bang. Paws scrabble up the hallway.

"Bird—" Jack's at my door again. The back of his head pressed at the frame, his forearms thrust out before his face. "Off, Bird!" He elbows against Bird's teeth. "Off!"

The door twists and swings off the last hinge and collapses flat into my bedroom. Jack spread out on top of it, Bird on top of him. A gob of spit shoots out Jack's mouth. Blood leaks from under his hair. Is he breathing? Hard to say.

Maybe he is dead.

Teeth still sunk into Jack's forearm, Bird's eyes shoot up at me. I ease off the bed. "Let go, Bird," I say.

Bird's jaw drops open and Jack's arm slops out. Like all at once he cannot believe what he has done, Bird scrambles off Jack's chest and dashes out of the room.

Bird is halfway under the house when I get there. I duck behind the red berries until the dirt settles. I follow Bird down. Rock scrapes up my legs as I scoot feet first into the tunnel. Tight going. Until I drop into something roomy. All hard earth down here. More storage room than dugout, the ceiling so low only the four-legged would not complain. My kind does not fancy dens. Even Jesus did not stay long in his tomb.

Bird has hopped onto a small bed bordered by storage box-es. Not a dog bed, a bed that kids sleep in once they leave the crib. My head knocks the ceiling as I scoot beside Bird. Legs in the air, head upside down, the whites of Bird's eyes glow whacko in the brown light just lighter than darkness. Over our heads is the mess of holes Jack bulleted into the floor when he was gunning Bird out from under here. Now Jack is out cold somewhere over our heads too.

"You did that for me?" I say. "Oh, dog, not worth it." We are grinning fools.

A couple pats on Bird's belly, and I contemplate the passage into night in this strange place. This day does not know how to end, take a bow, drop the curtain. That is what Mom likes to say. A long night on stage could feel that way. And anyway, this house is something like a stage, someone either coming or going or going nuts, everyone going but me. I stay. What choice do I have?

"You have a choice," Mom would say. She once had a choice between two men. The first was a ballet fan, like the others, only this one proposed marriage. He was rich. The only catch — no wife of his would get pawed by other men on stage, or backstage. Once they were married, he pledged to wallop her for so much as a pirouette. Break her leg if she kept dancing. The other choice was a dude from Oakland, California. He told her the San Francisco Ballet was down the street, all his pals were in the corps, he'd set her up to dance the moment her slippered foot hit the Golden State. "Those men were my choice," Mom said. "Though I suppose when you want something, there is no choice." I never asked Mom if the American was my father because she said that his mouth only opened to tell a lie. His fist spoke the truth. She put up with the dude from Oakland until "Someone saved me." The saving was something like the story I heard Jack tell Nurse Fenton. Except Mom said getting saved is the worst bargain a woman can strike because it dulls desire. Of all of the men who could be my father, the rich guy was probably the one. Mom once joked that I reminded her of him, the breaker of legs.

Bird flips over and sniffs the air. A column of light burns up the tunnel passageway. The light rolls over Bird before swinging back out the hole. Blacker now with the passing. Outside the hole, people talk in whispers.

Bird growls.

Up the barrel of the tunnel, I can see beams of flashlights drawing distant lines across the backyard. More voices, speaking in whispers. Someone says, "Officer." Someone says, "Canine."

They soft smack the bushes, such little noise. Bird rises on all fours and hops off the bed to investigate, but I grab his leash.

"Stay."

If Bird wanted to, he could tear out of my hold. Low rumbles grind from his chest as the lights swing. All at once, the tunnel goes dark. Something stuffs it up, clawing the edges, whimpering, ripping it wide. The flashlights irradiate a dog's pelt. There are more dogs behind this one, squealing and snapping at each other's hinds. Dogs that look like Bird, police dogs, the whole K-9 crew, are fighting to get down the tunnel.

Bird's lips draw back in a snarl. I slap my hand over his snout. "Hush."

Yipping and straining at leashes, rimmed in flashlight, the dogs are bonkers for a find. Dirt sprays my cheeks. People yell in whispers. "Frigging rabbit hole," someone says, "all it is."

"Leave off." A woman's voice. Sounds like Officer Barbara is giving orders.

Tossing a few yelps of disbelief, the obedient canines back out the tunnel and go.

Bird stays with me. Like I wanted him to, like Jack said he should. The lady cop has come to take Bird from Jack, like she said she would, but Bird knew I knew best. I keep him better than Jack could ever keep him. Jack cannot do anything with his dog, except wear out his very soul.

Does Jack think he is the only one who gets to be angry and scary when Mom goes away? He once choked a lady, nearly killed her, said it himself. Might have done the same to Mom on my bed, or to Nurse Fenton. Go ahead, Jack, choke us to death, but you cannot make us obey.

Outside the tunnel, Officer Barbara Ross is whispering. Maybe she has concluded that Bird is no longer here, that Jack outsmarted her. But Barbara knows better. She maneuvered Jack into believing he had two weeks to train Bird when really he had only one.

The cops move on, smacking distant bushes. Here and there voices scold canines. Bird, my protector, is quiet beside me.

Bird has my back. He saved me from Jack. But can Bird save himself? Bird snuffles my cheek and I look into his abiding eyes.

I lift my hand off his collar and release him. I owe Bird that much.

On light feet, Bird folds into the tunnel. The hole goes dark with his passing and in the next moment he is gone, Jack's dog. Gone.

And then I am going too.

Something's got me by the foot—Bird's leash has wrapped around my ankle. I fly across the dirt toward the tunnel. I grope at the leash, but someone at the other end yanks it and I go up the tunnel, foot-first. Hands grab my legs and yank me out. Stupefied by beams of light, I tell myself: The old things pass away—behold, the new things have come!

Two police officers stare down at me. "Did we dig this up?"

I slap at the cop's hands trying to undo the leash that caught my ankle. By the light of their torches, I untie myself.

Barbara is telling the officers to subdue Jack's dog, which is demonstrating that it knows the command to come no better than to stay.

Bird shows teeth to the encircling pack of leashed canines. A string of cops forms a second circle around the first, looping rope from hand to hand as Barbara calls instructions. This is some ambush. The inner circle of canines tightens. They are free to snap at Bird, who stands still, his teeth shiny bones flashing in the swing of lights. Then in one movement, the cops haul back on their leashes as the outer circle swings in with rope to weave it around Bird. Bird rises on his hind legs, his head swinging at the noose, his hide throwing clots of sweat until he crashes to the dirt with a whap.

The wound at Bird's neck has started to run. His bandage hangs off a bush. The working dogs whistle through their muzzles. A couple of cops drag Bird to the front lawn where a wagon waits. Neighbors watch from their lawns.

I carry the old bandage to Bird. His eyes roll up to me.

"I knew you'd help." Barbara has come alongside us. "You know what's right."

"I don't know," I say. "But I don't think it is this."

"Oh, the restraints," she says. "A precaution. We've no way of evaluating the dog's regression from basic obedience." She lifts the bandage out of my hand. "We'll fix him good as new."

"Like you fixed Jack?" I want to tell her that taking away Bird is no victory. Jack would be out here fighting for his dog if he were not flat out on an unhinged door.

Headlights roll over the neighbors' bathrobes as the cruisers pull from the curb. The neighbors slip back into their homes. Not a curtain shifts on a window.

12

Morning and my bedroom is back. The door latched back on its hinges. Last night's blood wiped up. Like nothing happened, just another morning, breakfast cooking in the kitchen.

"Know the trick to pancakes?" Jack works the grill in his apron. Bacon curls under paper towel and maple syrup bubbles in a pot. "You won't learn standing all the way over there." Jack flips cakes fast. His torso twists to catch a cake. If it hurts, he keeps it to himself. "Try your hand at it," he tosses the spatula to me, "except it's all in the wrist."

I catch the spatula by the neck and set it beside the grill. Spare me the homey routine. Someone must hold you to account for your behavior last night. *For did not a mute donkey, speaking with the voice of man, restrain the madness of the prophet?* I go back to the safety of the doorway.

Jack picks up the spatula and looks at it. He looks at me.

His pancakes smoke on the grill. But Jack stays looking, his expression every bit as bamboozled as the faces of the cops who tugged me out from under his house.

Last night I popped into the night air kicking and screaming, something born. I passed from the darkness of the earth into flashlight. No Bird to protect me now. This newborn thing must protect herself from his crooked miles.

"Grubs up." Jack sits at the table with pancakes and bacon. I sit before the other plate piled high with his labors. For luck, I pat the letter folded in my shirt pocket. The letter is from Bird. Last night I sat with pencil and paper beside Jack, still out cold on the door. I was still scared of Jack and, it must be said, scared for him. He is a reckless and heart-sore army vet, after all.

Our forks and knives chime against the plates. The pancakes

taste fine, crispy at the edges and fluffy in the middle. Jack dips bacon into syrup. When he glances over his shoulder at the door, probably looking for Bird, I give dipping a try.

Jack pushes away his plate and exhales. Last night I held Mom's hand mirror to Jack's mouth to make sure he was still breathing.

"Olya," he says, "I'm sorry. My conduct has been poor."

His eyes drop before mine. Pink inches up his cheeks. He explains that he came awake in the middle of the night. Found me asleep on the floor beside him. He understood that I had sat vigil over him. He walked me to my bed then set the door back in place.

"Okay."

"Not okay," he says, slamming his fist on the tabletop. I hop out from my chair, but his arms fly up like somebody said, Hands up! "No, no, sorry. Please, Olya, sit."

Mom says apologies are rarer than hen's teeth, and we should accept them with grace. I sit back down.

"You're scared of me," Jack says.

I pull out the letter from Bird and set it beside my plate. "Not anymore."

He glances at the letter and frowns but he keeps on. "Of course you're not. No reason to be scared." He laughs. "Bird is besotted with you. He knocked me out for you."

Jack snatches his fork and touches the tines to his temple. A bead of syrup hovers there. "Bird knocked sense into me too," he says and springs to his feet, motoring plates to the sink, mess hall speed. "Time to suit up. It's training day." He yanks off the apron and strides out.

Jack's departure settles slow over the kitchen. The stove ticks and groans and goes dumb. The faucet quits dripping. The counter relaxes. After getting knocked flat by Bird, after hanging back up the door, after throwing together a big meal, Jack rolls out an apology. The man is operating strictly on adrenalin.

Jack shuffles back into the kitchen. His arms are halfway

up the jacket sleeves of his police uniform. Smoke curls out a sleeve. "Care to help a man?"

I grab the collar, and he shrugs the jacket over his shoulders, making little sounds that say it hurts. The wool smells scorched. The cigarette butt between his fingers flakes tobacco. "Before Afghanistan," he says, crushing the butt against a plate, "all I knew was search and rescue. But the minute my boots hit sand, I was locating IEDs with bomb dogs." He buttons the jacket. "Faced with that, you become a sure-fire trainer or you become dead. A dog never turned on me and none of my dogs, including Daed, turned on another soldier. It's Bird. That dog launched me out of my boots the day I showed up in the Riverside K-9 Unit."

"Was Bird with you in Afghanistan?"

Jack's hands freeze on a button. "Did you hear what I said? I met Bird stateside."

"I heard you."

"So why ask?"

"'Cause, like the Israelites, people who suffer together have strong bonds. You and Bird have that kind of bond."

"The Bible doesn't apply to dogs." Jack holes the last button and smooths down his jacket with both hands. I consider pressing the issue. If not for the untainted soul of a dog, there might be no Bible. But Jack is already at the kitchen door.

"Where are you going?"

"We still have a week," he says. "I could use, you know, that thing that you do for Bird."

"Use me?"

"Look, I am a practical man. That's why I'm effective. So, let's train him." He opens the door. "You *and* me."

"No."

Jack turns around and walks back to me. Now this walk he is doing is more like a falling. He stands over me, weak maybe, but listening too. "Is there a problem? I'd like to know. Because with you, girl, it's not easy to know."

"Yes," I say. "Yes, there is. You are too hard on Bird."

"Anymore observations?"

"No, just a few conditions. Quit yelling at Bird. Thank Bird instead. Welcome Bird. Stop making Bird feel like one wrong move and he's out on the street." It is crazy how good this feels.

"We talking about Bird or we talking about you?"

I look at him with nothing to say.

"Well," Jack says, clapping his hands. "Now that we've agreed, let's see how the old boy's doing."

I hand Jack the letter. He frowns but takes the letter, shakes it open, reading on his way through the door. The screen door closes on his back, ticking. He looks up, eyes scanning the yard then dropping back to the letter. He reads aloud: "'To Jack: I am writing to inform you that I do not like you. I do not like your long leashes or your short leashes, your scrawny treats of rawhide, your ho' sweet ho' sign above my doghouse. I am not your ho' and there is nothing sweet about your home. Why all that talk, talk, talk when a gentle wave of the hand would have done? I might have walked beside you had you let loose on the lead. I am certainly gun dog enough to put up with one if only you knew where to point a gun. But, no, even your bullets begrudged my tomb beneath your house. How can I stay in a home that is not one? I am leaving you. Goodbye.'"

Jack balls up the letter, opens his fist, and drops it on the ground. He pushes back through the screen door into the kitchen. "Bird didn't write that. Know how I know?"

"You don't...you don't know anything about Bird." I swallow, going for it. "Some dogs can write."

"Give me a break," he says. "Bird's got a much bigger score to settle with me than some adolescent girl soured on life could begin to confect." Jack tugs up the sleeve of his uniform. Puncture wounds dot his forearm. Bird's bite marks swell with blood and pus. Nausea blooms up my throat.

"See a doctor, Jack —"

"Boot prints and tire treads all over the yard. Was it Barbara? She come for Bird last night?"

"She said they would treat Bird better. None of you treat that dog okay."

"Did Irina put you up to it?" A shadow crosses his face at her name, but he waves a hand before his eyes, and the shadow is gone. "Your mother doesn't like Bird," he says, "how he has my attention. Bird is the one place in me she can't reach."

"Mom's not even here."

"That's what she put you in the house for. Her secret weapon. Next thing you know, her kid turns my dog over to the authorities. Mission accomplished."

"Turning over Bird had nothing to do with Mom."

He draws down the sleeve of his jacket, pulls out a chair from the table, and dumps himself into it. The chair just catches him. "Why then? You could have left already with that nosy nurse but you didn't. You stayed for Bird. Now you turn around and let him go. The one thing you seem to want in this world is a place to stay. Turning over Bird to the cops was the best thing you could have done to ensure you will not have one," he says, "at least with me. How do you explain a thing as stupid as that?" He folds the jacket lapels across his throat. "Do we have soup?" he mumbles. "I feel a chill coming on."

There is the tomato soup in the cupboard. I retrieve the can and set it before him on the table. "This is all we have."

"Tomato soup? All we have?" He pauses, his eyes on me like a push. "Yeah, so it is. We do not have Irina. We do not have Bird. We have tomato soup." He knocks the can off the table. I leap—but not quick enough. The can slams my leg. "Thanks, kid."

When Bird was under the house, it was a hole, dug up and dust-broke. Okay for a dog. But crawling back under the house now without Bird is a lament, not for the dead but for the living I had begun in Jack's home. A word like lament gets me into trouble with Mom. *Watch TV, game, text, anything anything, but quit with the Bible*, she says. Mom is right. Not about the Bible, but about home. No lamenting something that was never yours.

Spiders weave in the corners of this place. I do not mind such creatures. Bird had his share of bugs jumping the haystacks of his broomy coat. This space may be lined with dirt, but it is not dirty, not in the way a vacancy is. That is because nobody has occupied this space, except baby furniture. Furniture makes a room feel big, according to *Sunset* magazine. Even furniture as small as this stuff stacked up down here. I unscrew a mirror that was attached to a chest of small drawers and angle the mirror toward the tunnel. Tilted like this, the late afternoon sun lights the place up.

Then it goes dark. Gravel pitches down the tunnel. I duck behind a baby-changing table. Jack's misshapen shadow slides across the opening. On hands and knees, he cranes his head into the tunnel, his breath fast and shallow. "Four hours," he calls. "You've made your point. Come out of there."

"I know you're under there," he says. "I hear you moving stuff."

Cold, he says. Hungry, he says. Ill, he says. All these things I will become, he says, if I stay here.

Jack grunts and screws his shoulders further into the tunnel. He whispers, "I am not snapping another rib over you."

"Fine," he says. "Starve." The hole fills with sunlight. Jack is gone.

Mom said stay, even if the house blows away. Stay. Mom should know at what cost I have stayed. I pull out my cell and text: *SOS.*

While I wait on Mom, I flip through framed photos stored behind the changing table. The pink bow in a photo says girl, chubby-looking at two or three years old. No way Jack could be this child's dad, could be anyone's dad (even if Mom said, yes, Jack is my dad, like she says of all the others). But there must be something about the girl in the photos that Jack cannot give up. So maybe, just maybe, this baby stuff was once *my* baby stuff, I am that baby girl in the photo. The baby is me, it really could be, since Mom lost all of my baby pictures. My babyhood stored on a phone that got stolen some while ago.

Mom texts in: *What this SOS*
Save Our Souls.
Here is SOUL dancer jump too high and break her leg. She is out. Now is down to me again. And one other. Who is fat
Good luck, Mama.
How things?

Whoever these baby items belong to, they are mine now. Which kind of makes me the baby. On account of the low ceiling, I have to crawl on hands and knees like one. Soon I will manage this little bed, so the baby blankets stop slipping off.

Cozy.

Mom texts: *Not long now.*

The cold settles, just as Jack said it would. Creatures scurry along the walls. I suck the last bit of bacon I pinched until it pulps on my tongue. I did not think to bring water. It is now completely dark down here.

13

I am under my bedroom, maybe part of Jack's bedroom and into the hallway. Far from the kitchen but close enough to pick up the smell of roasted meat, onions glorying in oil, and sharp green scents of herbs at holidays. Overhead, furniture gets dragged around. Jack grunts and puffs. A chair creaks, like he is sitting. "Smell that? Love me tender," he says. "Love me mmmmmm." Jack chews loud enough for me to hear his teeth grind. A fork slides over a thick plate.

The edges of my mouth go fat with how good it must taste. By the time Mom and I eat the Thanksgiving Special under the diner heat lamps, the rosemary sprigs are skeleton spines across white dunes of meat.

"Start with a half lemon. Rosemary, sage, garlic. But just before the oven, I shove into the cavity three or four sweet Italian sausages. The fennel permeates the bird."

I sniff the air no different than a dog. If Jack gorging himself over my head were not so mean, it would be funny. What a man will do when he knows he is wrong.

"Daed was in the bunkhouse, hiding under a bed when we were first introduced," Jack says. "That dog would still be under that bed if not for my cooking. Daed was a rescue pup, of mixed descent. One soldier called him Yeller after *Old Yeller*, and he had a point. Daed could seem yellow-bellied on account of how he liked to hide under beds. I worked up a little something on KP duty and set the plate before the bed. He sniffed but no budge. Maybe Daed was yellow, like they said, so I fell to my own meal. And—*bang!*—that dog was at my side, salivating and teeth on my plate. I about shit my trousers."

A laugh blooms up my chest. Daed sounds just like Bird! I smother my mouth with both hands.

"You want to come on out of there, Olya? Eat some chow?"

Though I could eat a horse, though I am not scared of Jack, not anymore, though I cannot say why, I will not be tempted.

Quiet the rest of the day.

Rearrange furnishings. Again. Something to do against the cold. Start with the changing table. Could this be the centerpiece of my tomb? The table screams altar of sacrifice and offering. In medieval times, Christian people believed spirits lived in forests. Sister Hedge read aloud from *The Perilous Hearth* that when building a home on pristine land, one must sacrifice to the spirit of the site. Under the thresholds to medieval churches, they have excavated the bones of small children. Kind of like Jack's baby things. Were they placed down here for the sake of the spirit that once owned this ground? To transform the spirit into a protector? This house surely needs something, maybe it's protection.

I wrap my hands around the polished legs of the changing table and yank it from the wall. Cobwebs snap and glide. Behind the table, in the foundation, is a crack carved wide and deep as a smile. This crack is very wrong. Jagging the length of the southern wall, the upper portion juts like an overbite. Like someone snuck up from behind Jack's house and said boo. The whole house leapt. The crack runs straight, but the fissures that crisscross it shape letters in a foreign language. Could it be a message? Sister Hedge said God spoke in messages. "Be prepared for apparitions," she warned.

I touch my fingers to the crack, following the odd moist flows. Heat comes off the concrete and exhales into the quieting descent of this space.

I kneel before the crack. I set my forehead against the needling grit of the concrete. My lips brush the upper lip. I say softly out loud what my soul has come to shout. I say, "I don't want to stay anymore. I made a mistake. Please, God, get me out of here."

Beneath my lips, the crack trembles and beats. *Olya!*

I peel my lips from the wall and crumple onto my butt and

stare. The crack spoke my name? How can this be? The jagged lines seem to wait for my reply.

"Here I am," I whisper.

The crack murmurs without sound. It says, *Why here?*

I shake my head to wake up. Probably silly with hunger, thirst. "I'm going crazy."

You are not going anywhere, Olya. Not even crazy. You are staying here.

"I can't stay here!"

Your mother depends on you. She needs you to stay so she can do her work.

"I can't do this for her. Her dreams are nothing. I want to leave." I rise back up on my knees and set my lips against the crack. "Please help me leave."

Fine stone erupts from the crack, hot sand filling my mouth. *Too late.*

I spit out sand. "O God, I beg you, release me."

And I tell you endure the house and you will come home.

"To this? This isn't a home."

What is home?

"I don't know...That's what I mean. I should know."

What should you know?

"I should know about home, about family. But I don't. And in this house, family is so strange."

Is it so different in any family?

"Yes! So different! I guess."

Afraid you will have to stay to find out.

"Fine," I say. "But soon as Mom's back, we go. Her lies hurt less in a vacancy."

The lies that come with this house will knock you down. It is so. But you will rebuild. And anyway, the vacancies are filled. Overflowing.

"We'll find somewhere else to stay, better."

With foster parents, perhaps? Car, tent, cardboard box, the best you ever got was a vacancy. You have endured it all so as not to be parted from your mother. Now you must endure this. For I am testing you, Olya, your love of the hearth.

The crack stills, lips set together. Just a jagged line now. No heat. The wall shivers all the way to the ceiling. Beneath me the earth settles. Everything is still, absolutely still. The lids of my eyes droop closed.

The smell of roasted meat rouses me. I open my eyes and sit up, banging my head on the ceiling. Somehow, I am curled up in the little bed. Was I asleep? Dreaming? I am too parched to puzzle it out. My face stings like I dozed in the sun. The mirror ignites in the yard's last light. Is it true? Did I burn with the word of God? Jean D'Arc received messages from God, heard voices, talked to saints. Talking is not something pretty I do. Did Jean D'Arc worry about pretty when she talked to Him?

Reams of gold shine at the door of the tunnel. I reach up for it. Satiny stuff slides into my hands. A quilt of gold gentles around me, and I wrap it around. Never been so cold now that I get warm under this quilt. A plump pillow bumps down after the quilt. The pillowcase is loaded with sandwiches wrapped in plastic and bottles of water. I twist off a cap and drink and though it seeps out the corners and though it stings bitterly, the water honeys my tongue and throat.

I ease onto the little bed, wrapped in the golden quilt, pillow bunched under my head. Jack sent these things down. He does not sit right with things as they are. Surely this is a sign. God has instructed Jack in the ways of domestication.

Dawn settles on the tunnel like ash. I would check the time, but the cellphone is out of power. Time, its exactness, another thing surrendered in the occupation of this ground. The occasional car swipes by on the road, louder down here. Weirdly lulling, along with the sound of snoring overhead. A car slows up, scraping pavement as it rolls. The engine cuts. A door slams. A little later, someone walks through Jack's house, fast, tap-tap-tap. How come no knock before entering? This someone pauses along the hallway. Outside Jack's room? A drawer slides open, another drawer and another.

The burglar hurries into the room that used to be mine.

Money, coins by the sound of it, drop all over the floor, bouncing over my head.

My toes curl under the quilt Jack left me.

Someone says, "Damn!"

A snort stoppers Jack's breath.

"Jack?" a woman says. "Jack? What you doing in Olya's room?"

Mom. It is Mom.

"Look at you," Jack says.

"Look at *you*." The bed creaks above my head. "Why you sleep in cop uniform?" Now I am sorry for Jack. This is Mom when she comes back.

"Why you in Olya's bed?" she says.

"So I can hear if she makes a run for it."

"Makes a run?"

"You'd blame me if she wasn't here."

"What did you do —"

"But she knew you'd be back. That's why she didn't go."

"The only time I leave her—" Mom starts hitting maybe, slapping, and Jack is saying "ow" and "stop it" and he is laughing too.

She screams, "I'm turning you in—"

"I'm turning *you* in, Bolshevik, Russian spook."

The bed creaks louder. Sniffling and wet sounds.

"I am bad, Jack." Mom cries now. She does that after she comes back.

"How bad?" Jack says. He says, "Baby."

She says, "Let go, Jack." More coins drop.

He says, "Don't worry, keep the money. What's mine is yours. Yours is mine."

"No, Jack," Mom says. "No." Right above me, she talks in a dream. "Stop, Jack."

I would move so I won't have to listen, but the quilt tangles round my knees. This little bed is slippery beneath my back. I am a dirty spy.

"Shhh, she hears," Jack says. "Just a kid, Ira," he says.

14

Because she has come back; because she has run out of the house and into the backyard; because she is whacking bushes and calling my name; because I have waited for her; because she will stay now; because Jack won, a surprise; because she does not like surprises; because she screams my name down into the hole, *Olya! Olya!*; because I am under Jack's house; because she is not; because she said stay, stay no matter what; because I stayed because she did not, because I wanted her back; because God called my bluff; because the baby is coming on, the baby that comes on whenever she comes back; because chubby rolls over my belly, my face blowing up to a saucer, no neck, swelling to the size of a float pushing diapers in a chump street parade; because there is no room for such a baby to rise in this tomb; because everything baby is stored here out of sight; because she should not see her baby in such a place; because it will make her cry; because she is crying now; because she was gone; because she is back; because she cries, *Olya! Olya!*, I do not answer her call.

"Olya!"

The high planes of her face light up as she guides the beam down the tunnel. Her flashlight catches me like a pestilence burrowed into this little kid's bed. "Olya?"

"Turn it off," I say.

She does not turn the light off.

"You're shining it."

"You come out!"

"In my eyes."

She says, "I didn't believe when he say under house."

She curses in Russian. The light moves off my face at last.

Now she pulls through the hole, the flashlight pinched in her teeth. Her knees clear, and she loses grip and tumbles onto the ground. The flashlight spins across the floor to strike the wall and boomerang, beaming a column of light onto a missing ballet flat.

"Executed with grace and poise," I say.

Her back is to me and her shoulders start to shake. I think laughter until she lets out a sob.

I grab the flashlight and search her dark jeans for the darker red of blood. Cement dusts her leg. "You're going to be okay, Mom."

She raises her head and looks around. "I will never get out," she says. "This place is so bad, Olya."

"Try to get up."

"Just leave me here." Her body quakes. "Is what I deserve. I am without talent anyway."

"What happened? Tell me, Mama?"

"They choose the fat one."

"It's okay," I say, glad they did not choose her, that she has no reason to go now, that I do not have to tell her God is testing me, that we must stay.

"You let her down there?" Mom limps, her arm slung over my shoulder. Jack's outline wavers silent behind the rear screen door. Mom pushes off me and hops on one leg toward the door. "You kicked her out of the house?"

"I never," he says. "I'd never do that, kick her out. When I said she could stay, I meant it. I have given her food and shelter."

"This is shelter?" Mom is full of words for Jack. She says: "Olya could have died down there. Lucky the rats did not bite. Even rat will not live in that hole. Rat is too clean. Would you kill her? You!"

He is quiet when he says, "She went there of her own accord."

"So you sleep in her room?" Mom clings to the door frame.

"I staked out in her room to make sure she was all right. Your daughter is stubborn." He shrugs. "When she got hungry enough, she'd show up."

"You not feed?" Mom grabs her stomach like it hurts; my hunger is her hunger now.

"Easy," Jack says, "getting yourself all worked up."

"Is neglect. You criminal."

Jack bursts out, "Did Olya call you? Is that why you're back?"

Mom's foot, the hurt foot, lowers to the ground. Her face crumples from pain, but she keeps her foot down. Her hands rise to her hips, so narrow the fingers could touch. "Of course, she called," Mom says. "Why else you think I'm back?"

It is a lie so indignantly told that doubt pangs my chest. Did I call her?

"You tell me, Ira. You leave when it suits you. I reckon you show up to suit yourself too."

"Come out and say that to me," Mom says.

He turns from the door and heads up the hallway.

"You soldier?" Mom yells. "You police? You are coward," Mom yells. "Bully!"

Mom charges after him but stumbles on the first short step and goes down. Her ankle bleeds where the concrete sliced it. I kneel beside her, but the face she turns on me is so hot that I back off. Mom claws for the handle on the screen door. Jack stops at the sound of the door opening.

At the sight of Mom clinging to the door, he swings 'round and lurches toward her like that monster made of dead body parts. He drops onto one knee and thrusts his arms under hers and hauls them both to their feet. No easy thing with her little fists punching his ribs. Panting, Jack tries to support Mom while at the same time ducking her punches. His footwork is good. Until they both lose balance. Jack's boot clips her hurt leg and her fists fly, she is a hitting demon now. He yanks her to him to make her stop, and they freeze for a second. "What are you doing, Ira?"

They go down. Jack takes the fall so she lands safe on him. His face is a picture of unmended ribs. He holds her to him, feeling the length of her leg until his big hand finds the wound. He says, "Ought to look after these legs."

"What do I do now? I have rehearsal for ballet —"

"Ballet?"

"San Francisco Ballet."

"San Francisco? Congrats! That's a big deal —"

"Yes, it is big deal," Mom says quietly. "Olya, get your suit-case."

❧

Mom is in the supermarket while I wait in the car with our suitcases. Jack followed us far as his driveway, asking if we had money. "Hell with you," Mom said. "Hell with money. Olya must hide under your house. Does money fix this? Make you good guy?" The bumper on Mom's car scraped cement, she backed out his driveway so fast. Worry humped Jack's shoulders as he watched us go—but how could we possibly go? God said I must stay.

"Why did you tell Jack you had ballet rehearsal?" I said when Mom pulled into the supermarket lot.

"I don't know," she said. "Look, I'm all screwed up. I left you at Jack's and you starved."

"Jack made me sandwiches. He sent them down to me."

She just shook her head and took out her phone, dialing the number of a women's shelter in Riverside, but there were no beds tonight. She called another. All the shelters full tonight.

"Surprise!" Mom opens the door and folds back into the car, singing, "Marshmallow roast." She tosses a plastic bag on my lap.

Through the bag, I pinch the air from a marshmallow. "You can't roast marshmallows in a vacancy."

"You can under the stars."

❧

The lights of downtown Los Angeles crowd the stars above the top floor of the garage. Mom parks at the edge of the en-campment. "It's still here," I say, surprised the police have not rounded up and shoved off all the folks.

Mom turns off the engine and takes my hand in hers. "It's not for us, Olya, but is just for one night. Tomorrow we have

place in women's center." She points through the windscreen
at the far side of the encampment. "See, there's Darla and her
sister. They looked out for us before, remember? They'll be
happy to see you. C'mon, we can have fun."

Darla and her sister hold paper plates above their dogs that
circle on hind legs. "Olya?" Darla says as we walk up. "Don't
you look pretty."

"Tall," says her sister.

Darla makes room for us to set up beside them, but there is
no room. Space near the fires goes quick. Darla offers her own
crate to sit, but Mom says, "We'll come back."

I follow Mom along an aisle cramped between tents and
some homes of cardboard. Joey waves at us from the fires then
squirts lighter fluid into a yellow barrel chunked with garbage.
He throws in a match and the barrel rumbles up flames. "Put
some meat on you, Ira," he says. His eyes covering Mom. No
space in the central ring, so we step into the outer, where people sleep loosely, a lot without tents. The old woman still sits
at her school desk, writing on a sheet of paper leathered with
ink. This far from the fires, the cold comes on. Mom unrolls
the tent, and I slide the poles through the orange sleeves. She
stakes the asphalt. Mom is quiet, so I am. So much to tell and
nothing to say. My time at Jack's house shapes in words borne
of walls and rooms. How would they sound inside this tent we
can hardly see to set up?

"Mom, tie down the stakes."

"Look, there's Mr. Printz," she says, dropping her side of
the tent and walking away toward someone strumming a guitar
beyond the barrels. I set down the pole and follow her into the
music and the moving shapes, slow and easy, circling the sparks
that rise with the office buildings cooled and blue.

"I style you, Olya." Wood steps out of the dark with her
scissors. She pops a long T-shirt over my head and pulls my
arms through the sleeves, then snips at the collar, the sleeves,
the waist. Wood can scissor up the clothes she rummages better
than anything in shop windows. Mom blinks up at the light rain

falling. Joey tells us to eat already, hands us each a hotdog stuck
on a stick. The hotdog ignites and crisps to black over the fire.
"You out of practice," Joey says and takes my charred one. He
eats the hotdog, his lips smacking on the burn.

Wood spins me around. She scissors and rips, her head tilt-
ing side to side. I go arms akimbo, modeling. Darla and her
sister come up and I spin round to face them. "The cut doesn't
suit her, Wood," Darla says.

"No?" Wood clips fringe at the hem. She squints up at me.
"You change, Olya." Wood spins me around, then Darla spins
me, then Mom spins me too. I stretch out my arms and whirl,
the guitar strums faster, and the lights of the city fall over our
heads, all together, clap clap, stars.

The rain comes down hard, dousing two barrels.

"Want help with the tent?" Joey asks. "Or you got the car
for sleep?"

"Olya wants roast marshmallows," Mom says.

"Marshmallows!" I drop my arms and leap out of the circle,
tripping over people's bags as I run into the dark to the place
where we left the tent. Everything is huddled under the rain.
The orange of our tent glows farther away than where we left
it. Maybe the wind dragged it off. It lumps on the ground. Out
here outside the camp, the light from the office buildings is all
business. I reach under the orange nylon, thinking we should be
setting it up, forget marshmallows. I feel around in our collapsed
tent for the bag anyway. My fingers sink into something thick
and hot. A body roars out from under the tent. A man stumbles
up, red and yelling and fighting the nylon sacking his head. I
duck his swinging arms and scramble backwards, slipping on
soaked cardboard, knocking into the woman who clutches her
suitcase to her chest, who never lets go. She wails in horror at
me. Beside her a guy's legs jerk against the concrete, his face
bleeds. The rain stinks with urine.

Mom grabs me. "Olya?"

"We got to go."

Caped in our tent, the man falls over a loaded baby stroller.

Someone chases him, trying to cover his nakedness. He circles the flames, cape flapping, mouth on the bag of marshmallows, ripping it open. Marshmallows fly up into sparks.

"Take me away. Away."

"I knew it was wrong," Mom says. "We should not have come."

"Some nights better than others," Joey says, walking us to the car. "You picked a bad night."

Mom packs me into the front seat and throws a blanket over me. "No car!" I say. "Away."

"I have no money, Olya."

"To stay."

"Just car tonight. Shelter tomorrow—"

"No! Away to stay."

✍

The sky purples behind the thin line of sun above Jack's house as Mom pulls into the driveway. The front door swings open, and Jack hurries out to us. "Are you hungry?" he says, reaching for Mom's suitcase as we come up. Mom stops on the stoop. She looks at me. "You know," she says, "you are taller." She pushes past Jack into the house, shuffling up the hallway to her bedroom.

"I could eat," I say.

Jack ties the rose apron around his waist, opens the oven, and pulls out a plate of roast chicken, potatoes, and gravy. The heat of the oven ruffles the apron. He lifts a ceramic lid off a soft stick of butter. The gentle curve of the knife spreads over the bread. When he drops the slices beside the chicken, I grab the plate so fast the bread swooshes off.

"I was just going to set it on the table," he says, dropping to his heels to pick up the bread. He points to my lip, the blister there. "Want something for that?"

"I didn't get it from going downtown," I say.

"Downtown. Is that where you two went?"

I nod but that is all. A man who owns a home could never

imagine that marshmallows roast up fine over a street fire. They do roast up fine. Or they did, at one time.

Really what I would like to talk about is the crack in the foundation of his house, how the crack gave me the blister when it spoke, but Jack will never believe any part of a house can talk. Not sure I believe it, either. Instead, I ask if he built this house. Turns out, Jack bought it. Cheap. On account of the house being on a fault line. He says, "The foundation is shot. Needs a seismic retrofit. One solid quake and it will fall."

"Why'd you buy a damaged house?"

"It's the only one that would have me."

"Yeah," I say, wiping up gravy with the bread.

"Yeah," he says. "Hey, don't I owe you an ice cream cone?"

∾

"The chihuahua is cousin to the domestic wolf." Jack and I eat ice cream he has bought from the same truck at the dog park. "The pit bull is bred for fighting. Bonding with another organism is antithetical to this gladiator." Jack points his cone at a pit bull puppy getting a belly rub from a pregnant woman. "The human race is doing penance."

"What about that one?" I point out a curly yellow dog about Bird's size.

"Poodle mixed with a retriever. The best of each bred out of it. Labradoodle."

"No goodle?"

He looks at me and smiles. "Goodle."

In this park are gorgeous dogs and obedient dogs, dogs with swelled heads and simple-minded dogs. There are black dogs and white dogs, spotted and patched and speckled. Long-groomed hair and short-brushed fur the color of lavender gray and russet, orange and chocolate and seashore. Tongues lolling, tails wagging, noses lifted, haunches squatting, dirt flying, discs spinning, teeth in the air. Surely one among them will make a perfect family pet. But I already know that dog is not here because in all this park there is not one such as Bird.

Jack's hand is propped against the rail, chocolate dripping on

his knuckles. He looks up at me and this knowledge passes un-
spoken between us, and not without blame, but also something
rounder, an open frame.

Tattooed in the upper pink of Bird's ear was the letter Q
and some numbers. The Q maybe stood for quail. The number
was for how many quail he'd fetched up. Nobody ever said that
hunters used their dogs' ears to keep tally, but why else ink a
dog's ear? If Bird had been mine, I would have named him
Finder. Once he found blood going hard on his belly. Using his
snout and teeth, he worried little legs out of the blood. With
each lick, the legs shortened. His belly skin folded up around
the legs, a blue bruise in a ring of red.

Jack said you could learn from that dog, so I roll up the leg
of my jeans and use my eyes like a snout over my skin, every
inch, down to the birthmark at my anklebone. The birthmark is
a glob of brown lines curving around itself, a clump of letters
but never a word of its own. But as I squint my eyes, all at once
the letters form the word *DOG*. How does this reveal itself
now?

I show Jack the birthmark. "See what it says?"

He frowns at me then at my ankle. "That a birthmark?"

"Yes," I say. "It says dog. See?"

The sky in his eyes, astonished. "I didn't know."

"It took me a while to see it too."

He stares at me. "I didn't know you had a birthmark."

"D-O-G."

He clams up but not before he says, "Yeah. Okay. Dogs are
plugged into the sublime."

Mom limps into the kitchen. She wears a worn pink leotard,
but her smile is light and easy. Jack hauls up bundles in butcher
wrap from the fridge. He draws a mallet from a drawer and
pounds a slab of red meat. With each blow, every loose thing
on the countertop chimes and hops.

Mom shouts over the blows, "Where you two go, Olya?"

"To look at dogs," I say.

"Why?" Mom says it like the idea is the most mysterious thing that has happened so far.

"Bird?" I say.

"Bird?" She looks around. "Where did dog go?"

"Not your concern, Ira," Jack says.

She turns back to Jack, lands an arm on his shoulder. She says with such tenderness, such surprising tenderness, "C'mon, baby, what happened? Tell Ira."

Jack stops carving. He sets down the knife and looks up at me. "Nothing goodle," he says.

No helping it. I laugh out loud. Mom also tries for a laugh. But the green of her eyes has gone lonely. She stares at her feet, third position. "Some big friends now?"

15

Sunlight slides across the Bible balanced on my knees. Sunlight rounds the parlor sofa to the tips of Jack's shoes. And in between. I say, "I turn thirteen soon."

Jack pushes to his feet and shuffles out the door. He comes back with a lit cigarette and sits in his chair in the same way as before, the sun on his trousers now. "That's pretty old," he says, "for someone your age."

The cigarette spills ash on his shirt. He turns his eyes up to the ceiling, silent again.

"How does your Mom do your birthday?"

"She doesn't always remember. February 29th is a leap year."

"That makes you, what, like three. You like growing up slow?"

"I'm divided." The cigarette bobs on Jack's lips. "Teachers say I'm slow. But I can read," I say. "I just don't read what others do."

"The Scriptures," Jack says.

"Mom doesn't like the Bible."

"What your mother doesn't like," he says, "could fill this house."

"And the children of Israel said unto them, 'Would to God we had died by the hand of the Pharaoh in the land of Egypt, when we sat by the fleshpots, and when we did eat bread to the full; for ye have brought us forth to this wilderness, to kill this whole assembly with hunger.'"

Jack stares at me. He is nervous about Mom returning. So am I. She took Jack's wallet, drove to the market, promised to make the best beef stroganoff. "Hungry?" he asks.

The sun flames the sofa. Jack's face glows with bonfire. "Olya, you know why the Jews needed Commandments?"

"To build a covenant between God and his people."

"This house is in need of a covenant," Jack says, closing his eyes against the lowering sun. "A law-abiding home. You need to be in school."

"I can go to school," I say. "The one nearby. I could walk from home."

"Well, going to school is a hell of a lot better than making house out of someone else's house." He puts his hands over his eyes. "Ah, bullshit. What kind of bullshit am I getting in?"

"Why aren't you in school?" Jack says.

"I usually am. But we move a lot on account of Mom's work."

"Your mom's a nurse. Not an itinerant worker."

"She gets the night shift because of poor English."

"Once she proves her worth," he says, "can't she pull decent shifts?"

"The other nurses look lazy next to her," I say. "Someone gets her fired. Or a doctor gets fresh with her then *she* quits."

"Whatever your mother's excuses—and you do have them down—don't you find it peculiar that she would leave you on your own?"

"That's how she does it."

"What," he says, "be a mom?"

"How come there's baby furniture stored down there?"

"Your mother asked me to. I've been meaning to get rid of it. Unless you want it?"

It takes me a minute. "It's mine?"

Jack pushes off the couch and steps over to the upright piano. He flings aside the crocheted cover and plays a soft ditty. "Where did she go, Olya?"

"She told you, to join the San Francisco ballet. It's her time."

"What about the other times?"

"She attends the ballet or works at a hospital. But it is her time now."

"When isn't it her time?" He taps one key. "It's always her goddamn time." Jack holds down the key.

The chord dies out in a room gone dark. Jack cannot see my smile.

Someone whistles, long and low and not so faraway. "From the truth to a roof over your head, even I fail to grasp what all your mother has denied you." He says, "You should be furious."

I could be, but I am not. I am not even mad. I could stand up to Mom. I do not. Jack is no different. He wants to strike out at Mom for saying that Bird is through with him. Meanwhile, Mom fails to understand that Jack is not through with his dog.

White headlights roll up Jack's torso to his face, then out of the room. "I miss Bird too," I say.

Jack grunts. "Should have thought of that before."

Mom floats through the front door snapping on lights. In her arms she holds a puppy. She bends down to set it on the carpet.

"This will cheer up my two gloomies." Mom smiles down at the puppy. She looks pretty and full of life, full of life.

"Where'd that come from?" Jack is pointing at the puppy's hind leg that is shorter than the others, pulled up and cleavered as if by the butcher.

Mom scoops up the puppy and hands it to Jack. His hands do not come out for the puppy. "A pound," Mom says.

"There's a reason he was there," Jack says.

The puppy hangs in Mom's hands above Jack's lap. It paws the air. "Yes," Mom says, "so you could rescue. You like to rescue things."

"Lost cause."

Mom smiles. "You like lost causes."

He smiles back. "You're glad Bird is gone," he says and takes the puppy. To the puppy he says, "Welcome. Now crap up the house. Olya just started to set it right."

"You want clean house so much, have your clean house." Mom reaches for the puppy, but Jack grabs Mom before she can get away, grinning real wide up at her. "Welcome home, puppy." He draws the puppy's snout to his face and rubs the spongy black nose.

"Be gentle, Jack," Mom says, wriggling out of Jack's hold.

Jack sets the puppy on his lap and pets, fingers pulling deeply along the spine. The puppy's lids droop. Its legs flop around Jack's thigh. A deep breath and the puppy shudders, asleep.

"Don't do that, Jack. He doesn't like."

"Ira—"

"No, puppy is like baby. You are very bad with babies." She draws the puppy off Jack's leg and sets it on the ground. The puppy sits in a stupor. Jack snatches up the newspaper disarranged on the table and pores over an article.

"What should we call puppy?" Mom says. She looks at me.

I could think of a few.

No one offers a name, so Mom scoops up the puppy and hands it to me. "Happy birthday, Olya," she says. She glides out of the parlor.

"What about the groceries?" Jack calls after her. "They in the car?"

Mom pops her head back in and winks. "No groceries. I call for takeout. This is celebration!" She lingers some in the hallway, humming a tune.

I put the puppy back down. It wobbles around the rug, belly drooped, panting. In the little chest, a thumb-sized pulse. The puppy whimpers without direction, squats and pees on the rug. Jack rolls up the newspaper and thumps the puppy's butt. The puppy rolls onto its feet and waddles back to us. Jack looks at me.

Not the dog I would choose, either.

16

"e're going to be late, Irina," Jack calls down the hallway for her. He wears the rose apron over a dress shirt and tie and eats standing at the counter, balancing eggs on toast. The crust he saves to wipe up the yellow. Funny, we do it the same.

The puppy scratches on the screen and whines. Jack stomps over and closes the door. He looks at his watch.

Mom tiptoes into the kitchen. The bathrobe she wears is not hers. She says, "Go without me."

"I was going as your escort," Jack says.

"Tomorrow," she says.

Jack hunches his jacket on. Mom looks at him in his suit and his black eye. She says, "The school will not allow you through front door."

"Olya is currently not attending school. That is against the law. I'm not going to start breaking the law over you two."

"You know how I feel about school." Mom yawns and sits at the table. "Very important." She rests her head on her arms. "Why must puppy behave so like a puppy?"

"Huh?" Jack says, jiggling the car keys in his pocket.

"Puppy keep me up all night."

The puppy kept Mom up until she put the puppy in bed with me. *Keep it warm, Olya.*

"Where are you going?" I switched on the bedside light.

"To sleep." She tugged the shorts of a pajama set I had never seen. "Is only clean thing I have." She smiled and pulled tight the door behind her.

Mom lifts her head off her arms now and looks around the kitchen. "Where is puppy?"

"Making a mess. Someone finally cares to get this old place looking nice and you tote in a little crap factory."

"You hire maid?"

"I'm talking about your kid, Ira. Olya has taken an interest in the house."

Mom pitches back in her chair. "Sorry I am not good home-maker. I am not good at anything. Not ballet, for sure."

"Going a little far, aren't you? C'mon, puppies are a drag. Everyone knows that. You know that I like the puppy." Jack's arm slides around Mom's waist as he guides her out of the kitchen and down the hallway. He calls over his shoulder to me, "Olya, look after the puppy. Take it on a walk."

Jack talks softly to Mom about responsibility. Mom shows Jack how weak her leg is since crawling under the house. He calls her lazy, and she laughs because she managed to get Jack to say that he likes the puppy.

The puppy runs along like it has four good legs because puppies run with the whole of themselves, not just legs. The puppy runs past the fence that circles the middle school where Mom and Jack have gone to see about enrolling me. The puppy is slow, almost as slow as the wide brown lowrider that has come up behind me. The dude and his whole family ride in the car, the radio loud with talk of godly folk tiptoeing over this naughty world. The dude looks at the road, like roads are all he is good for. His dad sits the passenger seat. His red beard is long but trimmed, his head is shaved. The hair on his arm that hangs out the open window bunches through the holes of his sleeve.

"What happened to the leg?" Red Beard says, joggling his sports drink at the puppy that lags behind me.

I do not answer. Cars honk and swerve around the brown lowrider.

The little sister sits between the two in front. She says, "Oooowie" to the puppy.

The mom in the backseat says, "Dad," and Red Beard bends down between his legs and comes up with a can and opens it, and the spray hits the little girl on the cheek and she says, "Oooowie" again. He wipes his child's cheek and slides the beer over to his wife.

The puppy munches stringy droppings on the sidewalk. I have to drag him until he finds his feet.

"Where'd you come by it?" Red Beard says.

"Dog pound," I say.

"What, this one over here?" I shrug. "Well, I'll tell you what, baby, you didn't come by it at Happy Endings Animal Impoundment," he says. "I'd of seen it."

The mom says something about how they will be late, and Red Beard nods okay, okay. "I work at the pound," he says to me. "I got the job nobody wants."

I slow down but not to talk. The puppy is back to using just the three legs.

"Putting the dog to sleep, that's how nice people call it. The front office has got me doing it with injections and with a gasser. Mostly, I just bang a dog over the head."

The dude snickers and slaps the steering wheel.

Red Beard says, "What I'm good at is judging what the world needs more of and what it has no need of at all. If I paid an ear to instructions from the front office, there'd only be golding retrievers to adopt. Not on my watch. I let some real goners slide. You should see me. I might of let that little pup through. I'd of considered it."

"That's your job," I say.

"Why, you want it?" he says. This gets his son yucking.

"No," I say. "It sounds like you do your job."

"Sure, I do," he says, "with a little time off for driving while under the influence—"

"The influence of pussy," the dude behind the wheel says.

Red Beard throws his sports drink at the driver's head. "You talk like that?" The mom punches her honey's shoulder. Wincing from the thumping, Red Beard says, "I would take the pup off your hands, little darling, but we're on a family excursion. My chauffering son got his driver's license now. We are proud to have him behind the wheel. You have caught his eye, you have." His son grins at me. "What do you say about that?"

I take off up the sidewalk.

The lowrider hauls onto the sidewalk after me. I dodge and run across somebody's yard. The lowrider keeps coming. Their son is like to run me down. Red Beard drops both arms out the window. "Where you keep your pup?" he hollers. "Your house?"

Backing across the yard, I scoop up the stunned puppy and stuff it in my bag.

"He ain't house material." On hairless bowed legs Red Beard rises out of the still rolling car. He stumbles to his feet, then barrels across the yard at me, his arms extended toward the pup. "The pup is ill and ill begotten. Hand him over, little darling. Let Dad set things right."

An old lady pounds out her front door and down the front steps, waving a hanky at Red Beard and the lowrider tearing up her yard. I scram to the rear of the house, which backs up to a link fence. The puppy safe in my bag as I hop the fence. We land in an alley. At the other end of the alley the lowrider creeps along the street. Enough eyes in that car to spot me. I run to the cinder block wall across the alley. The lowrider shoots up the alley at me. I teeter at the top of the cinder wall just as the car rumbles under.

The puppy stays quiet when we hit the ground. I close my eyes to listen for the lowrider. No sound of an engine. All clear. I drop my hand in the bag to pat the puppy's head. But there is no puppy.

I pivot back to the wall, coming face to face with the dude. His spider thin fingers wrap around my mouth to smother my scream. He whispers, "Keep an eye, babe." In his other hand is the puppy, hanging by the scruff. The puppy is docile as salt meat. The guy plops the puppy back into my bag. "Pap's not himself since Animal Control canned his sad ass," he says.

I back away from the dude to leap back up the cinderblock wall. From there, I call down. "You got a name?"

"I do, my lady." He says, "The name is McFate."

⤙

I go up in his arms, held in the beat of his cage.

"She can walk, Jack." Mom hobbles down the hallway, tripping on nothing, giggling. She frowns back at me in Jack's arms.

Jack sets me on my feet. "You fell asleep," he tells me.

I follow Jack following Mom into the kitchen, where she pours a drink. Jack tells her to lay off the drink, so she pours him one.

"Hungry?" Jack sets a plate of leftover ribs before me. Mom fingertips the back of my hand. I turn my hand over, but her fingers dance away.

Jack pulls up a seat to the table. "We spoke to the administrator at the junior high," he says. "Knows his business. You'll meet him tomorrow, Olya."

I set down the last rib.

"Taste good?" Jack takes away the plate. "You'll want to make a good impression. Your mother and I have already made you a fine introduction."

"Who did you say you are?"

Jack looks at me, then at Mom, but she watches her feet move through positions.

"Who we are," Jack says. "How you say it is as important as *what* you say." Jack says, "For example, the administrator may ask about your interests. So what are your interests, Olya?"

I shrug.

"Not okay," Jack says. "I mean it's okay not to have any interests at your age. I have at best one or two interests at *my* age. But you can't let this on. This is America and in America we have interests. Interests direct our choices. But they don't need to do more than that. I mean, if your interest became a passion, well, that's still okay. It just means you'd collect more of whatever it is that holds your interest. But if it became something you might commit yourself to totally, at risk of injury, irresponsibility, even death, what good does that do? That goes way beyond what to buy."

"Excuse me?" Mom slams her drink on the table. "What kind of talk is this to my child?"

"I'm ensuring the girl makes a good impression."

"I want," I say, "to make a good impression."

"Good," Jack says. "What are your long-term goals?" He looks around. "What is anybody's? To be happy. But what will make you happy? For example, sometimes what makes you happy may not be what you want. What you want may not make you happy. What makes you happy may not always want you. It's not as easy an answer as it looks."

"You making that very clear." With both hands Mom lifts her hair off her neck. "Love. Is that what you talking about, Jack?"

"I am always talking about it, Ira. Always about love." He looks back at me and says, "Ah, what appeals to you about our school?"

Mom swings out of her chair. "I hear drugs pretty good."

"Have drugs been a problem with Olya?"

"Stop being a cop, Jack." Mom yawns and drops her head back against the wall. Her neck shines with tender light.

"You got a problem with education?"

Mom closes her eyes.

"Mom doesn't like how I like books," I say.

"Just one book," she says.

"Your mom is very proud of you. You should've heard her talk to the administrator." He looks at mom. "You got yourself educated," Jack says. "Ballet is an education."

Mom's head jerks up. She catches her reflection in the window and adjusts her posture. "So?"

"So, use it. I have a buddy whose wife is connected with the local ballet," he says. "Haven't spoken since Afghanistan. I'll give him a call."

"For what? Regional ballet? I was ballerina on biggest stage in St. Petersburg. I have talent. Great talent."

"Talent is overrated," he says. "Being great at something just makes you go bad."

"In Russia it makes you survive. Ballerinas survive."

"We do more than survive here in America, Ira."

"Do you?" Mom glides to the back door and opens it. The

puppy springs out of the darkness to snuffle at her feet. It whimpers. "He is hurt. Olya?"

"I did what you said. It was a walk."

She rubs the puppy's leafy ear against her lips. Jack watches her every move.

"I got him for you, Olya." Tears fill her eyes. "Probably you prefer *his* dog."

"That's enough, Ira." Jack swings an arm around Mom. She jerks out of his touch. "Go to bed, Olya," he says, glaring at Mom. "You've got to impress tomorrow."

"Impress? Who, bullies and bad students? They will laugh at her and they will abuse. She will not survive school."

"This isn't Russia, Ira," Jack says.

❧

Odor blooms. The puppy claws at our sheets. Mom piles blankets on me as she shifts over. The bed lurches and her body slams against the frame. "Olya," Mom whispers. "I slip."

I turn on the bedside light. Mom crawls to the puppy, her nightgown stretched from neck to knees. Across the back of Mom's nightgown, a wide black smear of puppy crap. Mom squats, lifting the puppy so its rear legs dangle down, crap pasting the tail. "Run bath, okay?" Mom says.

Water drips on my feet. I drop the wet towel on the floor to swab the crap. "You are good," Mom says. "You know how to clean. Think I don't notice? You wash this house so good I thought new paint." Mom stares at me, an eyelid fluttering. "You like Jack," she says.

I circle the crap with the towel. "Jack who?"

"Jack has passion, true, but he is like child, not always safe. He is not right for me. Ballet is right."

"Why do you talk like that about Jack? It's weird."

"You like him more than me, is that it?"

"C'mon, Mom."

"Promise you won't like him more."

I cover the crap. "I promise."

Moist bathroom tiles suck at our soles. Her nightgown swells as she kneels into the tub, the puppy she will not yield up settles into the bowl of her gown.

"Promise," she says, "that when I say is time to go, you will come away with me and you will be glad." Mom has never asked for a promise like this. It was always only 'promise you won't leave the motel until I'm back' or 'promise to stay in the car.' This is a promise about another person.

"You told me not to give Jack any trouble," I say. "I did what you said. Mostly."

"Did I say be best friends?" She lifts the puppy and hands it to me.

"Mom," I say, and I say it careful because this whole topic is a ticking bomb. "Jack is family."

"Family," she says, "is why you must promise." She shifts down until water covers her head.

17

Mom's foot rises. She props her leg against the door-frame and eases into the stretch. Trembles feather up her leg. Wood creaks against her weight. Her lifted leg bangs down against the anchored one. She looks at me. "Every day," she says, "the body obeys a little less."

A fat buttery smell of bacon blows in from the kitchen. Mom wrinkles her nose. "Olya," she says, "you will play." She strikes keys on the piano, foot tapping, singing, *dah-dah-dah-di-dah*. "Now you."

I ease onto the bench, creasing my slacks that Jack just washed and ironed. I tap the keys, thinking of the renovated garage Mom and I once lived in that also had an upright piano. Mom taught me scales so I could accompany her one-man show.

"No, no, no," Mom corrects. "A rest between. Try again. *Dah-dah-dah-di—*"

"Dah-dah-di-damn it. You're so good, do it yourself."

Mom steps back from me. "Olya?"

"I've got to get ready for school."

"School? You're not going to any school—"

"And you're not rehearsing for any San Francisco ballet."

Mom shrugs and walks on toe to the rear parlor wall that was lined with bags of dog food and rawhide until I found a place for them. She works her feet.

"From now on we will have a law-abiding household," Jack said yesterday. "Be a family like everybody else is family." I was to go to school, and Mom to work, but she would come home nightly for meals taken together. "Meantime," he said, 'I will continue to do what's required to get back on the force."

"You are not on police force?" Mom was pretty shocked to hear this. She went off on him for the lie. Jack said he never lied about his job. But Mom insisted he had lied and kept pressing for an apology until all that pushing her little weight around got to me.

"You're the one to say sorry, Mom," I said.

"To this guy?"

"To me. You left me with this guy."

Mom laughed and after that nobody said sorry to anybody.

I tap the keys and Mom's feet lift and drop, lift and drop. It is Mom who lies. Lies about prospects for the San Francisco ballet. Lies about going, lies about staying. "Why the lies?" I ask her.

Mom's feet go still. "Is not lies," she says mildly. "It is not accepting truth."

Jack stands at the parlor door, breakfast plates in hand. "Good to see you practicing, Ira."

"My leg does not hurt like it did."

"Well, it hurts just looking at you." Jack watches Mom the same way most men watch her. He sets a loaded plate on the piano, sliding it over so I can get to the eggs with my free hand. He spreads a napkin on my lap.

"We have recital," Mom says.

"She has to eat. She'll be late."

"And one, two, three…"

"Ah, listen," Jack says, "I talked to my buddy. The one with the ex-wife who's got connections to the local ballet?"

"*Local?*"

"Yeah, local. This *is* where you're living, isn't it? She said you can try out."

"Try out?" Mom's heels slam together. "For locals? Locals do not see talent if it dance on their eyeballs."

"You're not getting any younger," Jack says.

I snatch the plate off the piano before Mom slams down the lid.

"I am going to San Francisco. Day after tomorrow." She looks at me for a long moment before her eyes lower. "Director of ballet said stay in touch. Not stay here."

Jack leans across the front seat of his pickup as I step to the curb. "I'm getting the sutures pulled." He touches the back of his head. "Wait for me here."

"What's your number?" I pull out my cell.

"None of that. I'll be here at two. You be here too. That's how it works." He points to the orange brick school behind the cheerful lime fence. "Get in there. Don't be nervous."

"Should I be?" I say.

"It would be easier for you if you were." He reaches into his pocket. Change is what he hands me. "Something for the machines." Jack looks over at the puppy curled up in a square of sunlight on the narrow backseat.

Jack's pickup moves off down the street. The school entrance leads onto a field where kids in sports jerseys roll like marbles across the green. A whistle blows. Along the school's hallways, doors open onto rooms lined with short-legged desks and pictures crayoned when kids still think anything goes. No matter how many new schools I attend, there is nothing familiar about a single one, except the knowledge that the school was doing perfectly okay without me. Someone halloos from behind the door of the front office. I get on with it and step inside.

A man about Jack's age wipes paper towels across what looks like coffee dripping off a stack of files on his desk. When he glances at me, I say, "My mom made an appointment with the administrator?"

He adjusts his eyeglasses. "Have a seat."

"Administrator," he says, pitching the balled paper towel into a trash basket. "I like to think the word comes from the word ministry. What do you think?"

I smile and nod, agreeably.

He sits at his desk, legs hanging loose as he inspects his files for damage. "Have you ever been enrolled in this district?"

"What district?"

The administrator sets his files aside. He stands. "You know where you are? I mean, what state you're in, what city?"

I step casually over to the window beside the administrator's desk. The window opens onto a parking lot. One car parked there is a wide brown lowrider. The license plate is too banged up to read, but it is surely the same brown lowrider that the guy named McFate drives. I hope the dent running the length of it came from chasing me up the fence. "Riverside, California," I say. I go back to my chair. He nods. I am glad I got it right because sometimes I get the name of the town right, but the state wrong. The wrongness comes of never staying long enough to particularize a place. A home is how a place becomes known.

"Would you like to hear about my interests?"

"Why not?" he says. "Shoot."

"The Bible," I say, and by way of explanation for all the schools I have attended, I say, "I have been in Exodus."

He removes his eyeglasses, wipes the lenses, and sets them back on his nose. He squints at me. After a moment, he stretches his arm over a drawer, pulls it open, and lifts out a new folder.

"We've located about a dozen transcripts. Not even half." He looks up. "Olya, why Exodus?"

"I would like to have a home," I say.

"You don't have a home?"

"I'm trying to make it one."

He exhales. His pen taps his bottom lip. I have done it again, made one of these people in school offices wonder about me, but not in the way Jack wanted.

I sit up. I smile. I say, "I also have a long-term goal."

"Lay it on me," he says.

"Create houses," I say.

"Great!" This smile is real. This is something he can help with. "Did you know we're a visual arts magnet school? We have classes on design and architecture. I teach one. I studied to be an architect. My thesis was on stonework..." He drops his pencil and puts both hands to his mouth to cover up sudden laughter.

The door looks pretty good to me right now.

"No, no, Olya," he says. "I'm not laughing at you. It's your parents. They said you would need remediation—"

"Jack is not my dad," I say. Though I could also say that Jack would like to be my dad. Not for my sake. No. For Mom. Can cousins marry? If they can, why hasn't Jack asked her down the aisle?

"Okay," he says, "okay, right. Your mother wants you enrolled. It would have to be summer school, when all's said and done." He hands me a packet of forms. "Our summer school options."

A lady dressed in purple sportswear ducks into the administrator's office as I go out. She closes the door behind her, but I catch what the administrator says. "The parents, they're the ones," he says. "The most puerile—those two have arrested development."

This gets a big watercooler laugh out of the purple lady. Before I know my feet, I turn round, open the door and am in his office. "Excuse me, mister," I say, "why stones?"

He straightens and dabs his eyes with more paper toweling. "Stones?" he says. "Stones are to build."

"So why do you cast them?"

The administrator's eyebrows lever and he nods to the lady, who bows out. He reaches for my file, fiddling his eyeglasses before settling. "'Olya not only exhibits rare intelligence, even by measure of the gifted program, she is fierce in her ability to protect those weaker than she,'" he reads from the file. "This from the principal of Darrel C. Swope Middle School of Washoe County." He lowers his glasses. "Your reputation precedes you."

Two o'clock in the afternoon, but Jack is not waiting by the fence in front of the school. McFate is. He tugs out crud jammed in the chinks of the fence. A half block and a telephone pole are what I keep between us.

Squatting on new grass, McFate dumps out a load of bright fruit from his lunch pail. He saunters over to me with a peach balanced on his palm. "Crisp and sweet and rosy cheeks. Care to sink your teeth?" I make busy with my cell. He dangles grapes. "Plump enough for you?"

I can guess what he will say about the banana.

"No appetite?" His hand appears over my shoulder, the banana pointing at the school. "Ten minutes in that place can shrink the GI tract to a soda straw."

McFate jogs back to the fence and karate kicks the chain links. "Do you think I love this place so much I'm volunteering to wipe its wet ass?" From the back pocket of his Wranglers, he snags a long white rag and dips it into a bucket. Graffitied across the cement base of the fence is the phrase, *Some people never go crazy.* McFate rubs the damp rag at the phrase.

Jack's pickup swings to the curb.

McFate waves the rag at Jack. "Who's the tool behind the wheel?"

"Jack," I say. "He handled canines. In Afghanistan."

"Well, well, well," says McFate, stepping up to the passenger door and opening it for me. I fold into the front seat. McFate says, "I'd like to call on you, girlie. To whom do I ask permission, you or..." He looks at Jack. "Captain Canine?"

"Don't ask." I pull the door shut.

Jack gives me a look that says how little he thinks of this individual opening a door for me. He speeds from the curb.

"How'd it go with the administrator?"

"I tried to make a good impression," I say. "Like you said."

"I didn't say that," Jack says. "I don't talk that way, if you'd listen. It's your mom's concern, impressions. I'm just the driver here."

The back of Jack's head is still springy with red stitches, but the puppy is not in the backseat anymore. The puppy is not anywhere in Jack's truck.

"Well, did you?" Jack says. "Make a good impression?"

"Where's the puppy?"

"Puppy? Ah, yeah. You know, the damn thing ran off on me."

"What? You're a professional. How do you let a puppy run off?" Jack shrugs. "That was my birthday present," I say.

"Doesn't mean you deserved it." Jack hits the accelerator to speed through the light.

ॐ

Nothing is cooking in the kitchen when we get home. "We go out tonight," Mom says, tugging on a high heel.

Jack peers into the fridge. "Meat's got to be eaten or it'll go bad."

Mom says, "Let it go bad. That's what it wants."

You better take her, Jack.

Jack pulls out a wad of butcher paper and sets the package of meat on the carving board.

Mom crosses and uncrosses her legs under the table. An unstrapped shoe drops off her heel. She snaps it back on, then lets it slide off to dangle.

"How school, Olya?"

"I didn't go to school."

"Then what you two doing?" Mom says. "I could go stupid here."

Jack looks up from a wide stretch of marbled beef. "Tell that to your ballet director."

Mom smiles at Jack, the smile she gives strangers.

"I met with the administrator," I say. "He didn't know who you two were. I mean, who you are to each other," I say. "Were you kids?"

Jack sets down the knife, wipes his hands on the apron. They both stare at me.

"Sure," Mom says. "We were kids." She looks at Jack. "Kids together when you visit Russia."

"Huh?"

"You drove tractor on our farm," she says.

Jack starts remembering because he pulls off the apron and says, "Yeah, sure. Didn't you ride the hood, heels propped on the grill? Wore those cute white go-go boots Mother brought you from America."

"New boots from America melt on hot grill of Russian tractor," Mom says like she is reading a headline.

"You cried so hard about the go-go boots," Jack says, "I ran like crazy to the little ice cream hut. Two scoops to cheer you up."

"But you not come back. Next I see you, forget two scoops. You got two broke arms."

"Such a hurry to get to you," Jack says, "I tripped and busted them both."

"What happened to my ice cream cone?" Mom is laughing. I laugh along. Jack watches Mom with a big smile but when he looks at me, he frowns.

"That's enough, Ira," he says. Mom thumps round the kitchen like her whole body wears a cast. "Enough!"

Mom stops with a small leap. Her high cheeks shine. "Oh," she says, "you are no fun." But she is not mad, just kind of shy. She sits quickly back down.

Meat spits and flaps in the frying pan. Jack lights a cigarette, pokes the meat with a knife then reaches around to a cupboard. When he turns back, Mom points at his head.

Jack puts his hand to the stitches on the back of his head. "The clinic was closed." Smoke winds between his lips. Her eyebrow lifts. He stares back, drawing on the butt.

"Put out cigarette, Jack," she says. "I'm not die for you."

"Why not?" Jack says. "I'm dying for you."

Mom's head tilts like she hears something far off. "You have a puppy?"

Jack does not look at me. "He'll show up," he says. "Doesn't have enough character to stay away."

Mom rushes out of the kitchen, calling for the puppy. She shuffles back in, opens the back door and peers out. She calls for the puppy, her voice rolling across the flat backyard grass.

The puppy does not come.

Mom lowers herself into a chair. She could be balancing a book on her head, spine stacked tail to skull. She once told me the key to getting what you want is holding the body in perfect alignment when it longs to grab. Strength comes in resisting.

Jack yanks a mug out of the drying rack. He fills the mug with coffee brewed this morning and sits beside Mom. He reaches for her hand. "Ira, that puppy—"

"Is shit," she says. "Only Bird is important."

Jack lets go her hand. "Leave Bird out of this."

"Forgive me," she whispers. "We must not talk of the blessed Bird."

Jack studies her, all that warm color in his face flipping to the cool shades on the wheel. He lights a cigarette though one burns in the ashtray. "It clicked between Bird and me, give-give, win-win. This went way beyond the hunger two people have for each other. He was all with me."

"Until he wasn't," Mom says.

Jack's arms rest on his thighs. Inches from Mom, his smoke puffs against her chest. "If you had come in from the cold, baby, stayed put, it might have tempered—"

Mom rises and glides out the kitchen, down the hallway, to the front door. Jack bolts out of his chair after her. He grabs her neck before she clears the threshold. "You're not joining up with any ballet, hear?"

"Take hand off me," she says.

"You haven't practiced." His mouth at her ear. "Hardly lifted a leg." Her eyes shift as I inch up the hallway to her. She shakes her head the littlest bit at me. "You'll fail," Jack says.

"You'll quit me first!" She rips his hand off her neck. Red flares the long skin there.

"Hey!" I say. "What did you do to her?"

Jack looks at me without saying. He reaches for Mom's limp hand. "You want to go out on the town, baby?"

Mom's head hangs.

"Olya, put on a nice dress?" Jack says. "We'll go somewhere nice, where normal families go."

Mom's eyes lift. Something new in them for Jack. Though the feeling between them seems familiar enough. Call it vengefulness, like between siblings, Cain and Abel.

"What if the puppy shows up?" I ask.

"Yes!" Mom says. "Someone must wait for the puppy. Good Olechka."

᠅

Maybe someone has found the puppy, adopted, groomed, collared, tagged it. Maybe the puppy got lucky and will start acting like a dog somebody can spare affection for. It was not like that with Jack's dog. Such a dog is woven with spun gold. *He wore a robe, a majestic robe, an earthly robe that caught in its folds the glory of the heavens.* Such a dog comes down to earth only once. Arrayed in sunlight.

Come close. Lie beside me. Your snout a hand on my arm, muscling in. Leg punched, I am your springing board away. You stare up at me and I kneel before you. You might lick, sniff, sometimes nip. Can't be helped.

Jack could not keep you. One must know how to keep such a dog.

Rawhide sticks. Bird's favorite. I plunge my head into the bag in the kitchen closet and close my eyes, pretending rawhide is Bird's breath that I breathe. The smoked-meat scent gusting off the soft flaps of his lips. Bird is gone. Only this tall sack of rawhide stayed. I kick the sack and it pours over, rawhide roiling the linoleum.

Sunset magazine has a picture of a house with architectural plans to build it. All the walls are only windows. A split-level wilderness for nobody but the coyote to traverse. I build my house out of rawhide. A small handsaw loosened up from Jack's toolkit in the garage is good for shaping notches. *Thwick, thwick, thwick.* I work out the doorframe cuts, roof cuts, and the walls. A dab of water on the rawhide to stew it up gluey. I have a flare for home design. A house for me alone. No one leaves you when you live alone.

Bang! Something smacks Jack's front door. The walls shudder. I shoot out my chair, upsetting my model house. *Bang! Bang!*

More objects hurl against the door. Things flown or flung at high speed.

I ease open the door. A banana sprawls on the front stoop.

McFate's lowrider lurks under the streetlights flaring up. Out of the hole of his auto something flies at the front door. I duck. The pitch is long and strikes the casing. Grapes pour onto the stoop. Apples, cantaloupe, mango. McFate pitches fruit. Next time McFate rounds the corner, I am standing at the curb with a paper bag. He watches out the windshield, taking his sweet sweet time to pull alongside me. I swing open the passenger door and thrust in the fruit-loaded bag. "Bananas are good," I say, "for a monkey." I slip into the passenger seat beside the bag.

McFate's eyes go wide at me, here in his car. He punches the ceiling until dust sifts down. He whoopies. He pulls from the curb, hands on the horn. "She got in my car!"

"I need a good solid meal," I say.

He slows and pulls to the curb. His eyes never stray as he digs out a banana from the paper bag and peels. He says, "My family would welcome you at our table."

McFate's hair falls straight to his nose, which is most of his face. His hard muscles ball at the forearms and above the knees. He is that kind of skinny. That's what he is, poor. I have already seen what he has for family. He snaps the peel out the window. His tongue drops out his mouth and licks the flank of the banana propped between dirty nails.

"Such a nice invitation," I say to the white puppy figurine on the dashboard. The bobble head vibrates in the socket. The blurry eyes hold no judgment. "From a very nice family," I say. "Your mother, is she a good cook?"

"Is my moonbabes a good cook? Her pies win awards. Ribbons over the fireplace."

"Pies? Nice. I'm very committed to family, you know."

18

In McFate's house dinner is taken in the narrow yard. One side of the yard is lined with plastic dog crates stacked to the roof of the house. The lowering sun bursts so brightly against the crates' scrubbed white that McFate's dad instructs me to sit with my back to them. The opposite wall is a bramble of thorny vine, pinned by a single blackberry fattening like a drop of some prince's blood. The yard opens onto a shopping mall-sized area of stripped land, encircled by half-hearted barbed wire that dips and rolls. Might be tumbleweed. Beyond is a wood so green it could be black.

Everyone in McFate's family is dressed in uncomfortable grown-up clothes, which makes hunkering down on the heirloom macramé blanket spread out by McFate's mom, who he calls Moonbabes, quite a trick. McFate's moonbabes kneels to lift off the lid of what she calls tofu-turkey potpie. "Dad," she says, "offer gravy to our guest."

Dad's long red beard catches on a button of his Western suitcoat as his big freckled hands squeeze gravy from a tube. Beige gravy curls out toothpaste-wise along the crust of my slice of potpie. The other pie dishes are made of fruit. McFate's little sister Skinner has made a pie chart of her plate with slices of blueberry, strawberry and something she calls colaberry pie.

"Moonbabes, do get grace off your chest," says McFate.

"Why don't the girlie take a crack at grace?" says Dad. He stares at me.

They all do.

I smile and look out at the pies floating on the macramé to the sound of yellow jackets fiending off their crust. I fold my hands together, bow my head, and say, "Bless us, our Lord, for these thy gifts we are about to receive. For the sun that ripens the fruit on the trees. For this day and this family, Lord. For this yard beneath your great sky. Amen." This is the first grace I have completed since attending St. Anne's. Feels good.

"Ooowie," says Skinner, the rims of her lips dyed pie-berry blue. "Did the Lord say that grace?"

"Good question, Skinner," says McFate. He smiles at his little sister, then smiles at me. "Clever, like her brother."

"I guess the Lord did say that grace when He created the world," I say. "'I give you every seed-bearing plant on the face of the whole earth and every tree that has seed in it. They will be yours for food.'"

"Hogwash," says Dad. "Seeds are born of their own nature."

"Now, Dad," says McFate's moonbabes.

McFate's dad spurts gravy onto his son's turkey potpie. "The girl was born of an accident but she don't dig that. So she makes up God. Must hold someone responsible, hey, son?" He winks at McFate and scoops up a slice and pulls a colossal bite. "But I ask you, who then is responsible for giving up on that little pup?"

Nobody talks while Dad chews. McFate stares at his plate. His moonbabes lifts up her head and smiles at me.

I prod a leaky blueberry from under the legs of a yellow jacket. The insect buzzes at my fork. What does McFate's dad know about that puppy?

Dad looks around at the faces hung over plates, his own face turning orange with his beard. He throws his napkin onto his pie and all at once a small white sleepy dog wanders out from under the brambles.

It is the puppy Mom gave me for my birthday. Here, in their yard, tiptoeing over the macramé picnic.

"Finally! The party started!" McFate's moonbabes plucks American flag picks from her bra and spikes everyone's soda with a flag. "It's name day. Did our son tell you, dear?" she says. "Today we give our little dog a name." She looks around at the faces. "Open for suggestions."

"Um, that's my puppy," I say.

"Yeah?" says Dad. "What's his name?"

I stare at the puppy. "I hadn't decided yet."

"The pup was turned over to Happy Endings Animal Impoundment," says Dad. "He's ours now. Ours to name."

McFate's moonbabes sets down her knife and fork and pats my hand. McFate shifts closer to my side. The puppy sticks its stubby pink snout into the tofu potpie. It gags and grunts the stuff down. Now it gnaws out threads from the macramé blanket.

"I got a name for the pup. Homer. Homer had a few stories to tell," says Dad, eyeing me. He lifts his bottle. "A toast to Homer. You first, Skinner."

The girl lifts her soda pop. "Yay, uh, may Homer live a cute life."

"Cute life! Ha ha," says Dad, squeezing his daughter under his arm. He turns to McFate. "Kill it, son."

McFate nods, obedient, then glances at me. He hesitates. "Go, Dog, go?"

Dad's plump lips thin. He winces. But he says nothing. He raises his vast sports drink, says, "Though ill and ill begotten, Homer has nonetheless found redemption in the bosom of our humble home." He grabs up the puppy, which has fattened and now requires two hands. Its belly pours over Dad's thick fingers. "It's not just Homer who has been redeemed. This pup has supplied me a vision of myself as greater than Happy Endings Animal Impoundment. I am contemplating a career as a vet's assistant." Dad ignores his family's surprise at this announcement. He has me in his sights. "Tell me, girlie, why would you wash your hands of this wondrous item?"

McFate's arm shoots around me. "Pay no mind. Pap's just having a mess of fun."

"You asked me here to humiliate me," I whisper at McFate.

His arm slips off my shoulder. "Well, so, technically you asked yourself?"

"Oh," says McFate's moonbabes, picking up on our conversation. "If I'd known you were coming, dear, I'd of prepared a bag of party favors."

"Oooowie," says Skinner, bouncing up and down on her knees and clapping. "Party favors! Party favors! Party party party!"

"Was Homer renounced in the name of the Lord?" Dad asks, pressing his daughter onto her heels for a better view of me. "Folks never commit to evil so joyfully as when it's done in His name."

This is what McFate has for a father. Why did I think his family could be different than they had already shown themselves to be? Even in their debasement they cling to each other. They cling tight. No one can survive that clinging, can they?

"It's her turn to toast." Dad's eyes on me.

Just then the puppy circles out a spot on the macramé and squats. A thin line of urine jets over the weave. McFate and his family stare at the growing puddle. All at once they join hands together to clap, elbowing and winking at each other.

"He's getting the hang of it," says McFate.

McFate's moonbabes pats my knee. "That's why we dine al fresco. Homer's not quite house material. Let him tinkle under the sky."

Homer's urine seeps through the weave, inching toward my pants. And I can see the mad logic of accommodating the dog that is just obeying a call. Better than thumping him with a rolled newspaper. I am overcome with shame at how unkindly Homer was received in our home.

Dad eases up to a squat. Thighs wrapped in ironed denim splay before me. "You prepared to rise to the level of a dog?"

I scramble to my feet. Surprised how my knees rattle. "Well," I say. "Thank you for dinner. So fresh. I should go."

McFate grabs my hand before I can step away. "Pap, admit it, you had no love for Homer when you first laid eyes on him. Called it a goner."

"Don't you know not to talk a man's words back to him, son?" His father slams his fists on the macramé, sending a pie dish spinning. "It's this Lordlubber's fault. Filling our boy's head with churchified demons to disobey his parents!"

McFate's moonbabes hunches over her hands balled in her skirt. "Can't we just be a nice family?"

Lord, I think, forgive them for they know not what they do. I twist out of McFate's hold. The unexpected release sends McFate into the wall of crates. The crates shiver and quake with the impact. They topple. The family scrambles out from under, Homer mincing back beneath the brambles.

I see Dad scrape the air before his tear-filled eyes. On hands and knees, he digs out his son from the crates. Rescued, McFate flings long skinny arms around his dad's neck, his face bright with love and terror.

I head for the front door and might have cleared it if Skinner had not popped out of nowhere waving the same paper bag I used to return all of McFate's fruit. "Wait up. I rustled you all party favors." She holds open the bag before me. She points her middle finger at a bitty plastic window frame inside. "From my doll's house." She points at a crescent of metal and pink plastic embedded with teeth. "That's somebody's dentures dug up from the yard. A favor from Homer." I can guess who the American flag pick is from. The packet of seeds too. An airline liquor bottle drops into the bag, clonking against the dentures.

McFate fox-grins at me. "That bottle contains toenail clippings from Charles Bukowski," he says. "Those are actual relics."

I look down at the junk in the bag that Skinner holds out; I look up at the eager kind dazzled faces of the fruit-pie siblings, and I walk out, taking nothing.

The muffler blows open my ears long before the lowrider rolls into view. I could cut away from the sidewalk and race across lawns, but experience says this will not stop him.

McFate hits the gas and tears off, only to park at the end of the block. He nonchalantly shoulders a wide oak as I come abreast. He very deferentially hands me the paper bag I did not accept from his sister. I keep walking.

"You leave like that?" he calls after me. "You insult my family?"

"You call that family?" I turn around and walk to him, my index finger out until it hits his cage. "The first time your family and I met, they tried to run me over. Remember? You were driving. What are you trying to prove to them?"

"Family." He shrugs. "Requires compromise."

"Your family is compromised!"

He catches my index finger and bends it back on me. "Can't hack it? Don't have it in you for family? When the going got rough, you gave up the puppy."

"I didn't ask for that puppy. Mom got it from the pound. Jack must of given it back."

"Nothing to do with you?"

"Nothing."

"What about friends? Got friends, right? Where are all your girlfriends?"

"So many friends. It's just. Mom and I move a lot."

"So 'friends' are not your fault either."

Kids on bikes race past us. "It's just, when friends don't see you, they forget you."

"I wouldn't know. I attended the same schools since kindergarten. I have not forgotten a face," he says.

"They can't forget your face, either."

A slow smile stretches his mouth. "You know what I think? I think you sort of dig on the nomadic life. No putting up with, hanging in for, ashaming on anybody's account but your own sad self." He steps close and his beak could sever me in two. "Family is bad times and good."

"Oh, is that right? Family is bad times and good?"

"No fucking nomad, no, ma'am."

"I have committed one hundred percent to staying in Jack's house." I grab the paper bag.

"Baby, you ain't committed to shit." He heads for his car.

"Well, you sure are."

The high wheeling red of his cheeks is unsaid. He swings out a hip like the snottiest of girls. "On occasion they may be shit," he says, "but that shit is in plain sight. What's stinking up

Captain Canine's house? It is coming to light, girlie. You just try not to look."

A final shot of the muffler and McFate's wide brown lowrider is gone. Only then do I see myself as if from the high oak overhead. My elbow swung out on my hip, the snottiest of girls.

19

A woman shouts over loud canned music when I pick up the phone. "This is Officer Ross."

"Jack's not here." No one was when I got back. Just Officer Barbara, calling, calling.

"That you, Olya?" she says. "Good little Olya who helped Bird? Don't worry. Bird is going to be fine. That's not why I'm calling. You know if Jack's coming tonight?" Her voice pitches high.

"I couldn't say what Jack plans tonight."

"Off duty. Open bar. I invited Jack to my party. He didn't say."

"That ought to say something." I hang up, aware that I spread on Officer Barbara Ross some of the bad loaded up inside me. Doesn't mean I would fix it nohow.

A key turns in the front door. The door eases open and someone shuffles in.

I find Jack sitting in the parlor dark, elbows propped on knees and hands folded together prayer style, a narrow strip of white pressed between his palms.

I place on the coffee table a plate with the steak he fried earlier but nobody ate. Jack looks down at the steak. His eyebrows inch up. "How'd you know I haven't eaten?" His palms open up and the white strip drops onto the coffee table. I try not to look at it, to look at the motel key.

"Eden Motel!" I say. "Mom and I stayed there."

Jack's hands press the surface of the coffee table, like to leverage himself to standing. But he does not stand. He pinky-kicks the key. It spins on the table.

"A king-sized bed and a TV and a shower with bath, right?" He snorts.

"Brown carpet."

"What are the odds?"

"A painting of a dear little house and garden," I say, "hangs on the wall across from the bed."

Nothing from Jack now.

"That light from the wine store on the other side of the parking lot shines on the painting." What I do not say is how the store's light is the shape of a corkscrew. If you lie on the bed with the lights off waiting for Mom to come back, any minute she could, the corkscrew and the little house will appear as one. The corkscrew twisting, drilling down into the very bottom of this dear little house.

Plastic rattles along the floor. Jack, thrower of motel keys, is off the couch, unsettling the coffee table and launching the plate. As the meat sops onto the boards, Jack regards me from the doorway.

"All right," I say. "Where is Mom?"

"Your mother is driving all night for an a.m. rehearsal in San Francisco."

"She said she wouldn't go."

He shrugs. "She's gone and she's gone and she's gone."

"She'll come back. She always does."

"She'll come back," he says. "You always say." He walks toward me, reaches down, takes my hand, and pulls me to my feet. "Pack your suitcase. Get your coat. I'll be in the car."

"Where are we going?"

"You are going to San Francisco. I'm putting you on a bus."

I beat it to my bedroom for my suitcase that was never unpacked. Mom will not like me in San Francisco. The ballet audition was not going her way. She will need all she has to bring it around. I must stay here. God is testing me. McFate said I do not have what it takes to stay in a home, be part of a family, be a friend. I am my mother's daughter, never staying long in one place, except in my head, a place so much more reliable to occupy. Sister Hedge called it imagination. She said it gave me power over my classmates and that I must be careful how I use my power. This was on account of the nickname I made up on our field trip to the exhibit on the evolution of human shelter. Our chaperone mom wore a short skirt and glossy boots she crossed and uncrossed at the ankle the rowdier we got on the bus. I forgot my jacket. The chaperone mom was not around to ask so I ran back to the bus for it. I heard voices, but the driver was not around. The chaperone's legs stuck into the aisle, the glossy boots unzipped and spread open on her calves. The bus driver's head popped up over the seat and looked at me. I ran, but not before spying out a nickname for the chaperone. I found my classmates at a Neanderthal cave and I told them Hot Legs. "Hot Legs! Hot Legs!" my classmates shouted at the chaperone mom, who rode the bus home with a coat over her legs. That nickname got me a load of new friends, in case McFate was interested.

Abstain from blood, and from things strangled, and from sexual immorality. The Bible warns of the doings of a man and a woman. Such doings are wrong, but to spy upon the act is worse. I do not want to spy, but I spy away. What those two were doing on the bus, what Mom and Jack were doing at a motel when they'd gone for dinner, how can I wrap my mind around it with Jack hopping mad to put me on a bus?

Jack honks. The honks go long down his street until they don't. The front door bangs open. Jack storms up the hallway to my bedroom.

"You let me sit out like that?" He snatches the jacket from my hands, shakes it out, and stuffs my limp arms into the sleeves. One arm is still hung up when he buttons it. He says, "This the warmest you got?"

I shrug his hands off me. He picks up my suitcase. I remember the house model I built of rawhide and get it from the closet. When I turn around with the model, Jack frowns. I lift the house to give a better view. Jack leans in to inspect the model that I have mounted on a slightly warped piece of plywood. His finger runs the perimeter of the three-bedroom home, an open plan with no interior doors, lots of reading nooks and windows. He sniffs the log exterior. "Dog treats?"

"The rawhide is supposed to be wooden logs."

He looks up at me, mouth hung open.

"It's for when I start school," I say. "I could start, Jack," I say, "if I stay."

He rights himself but his eyes fix on the model. "School?"

"You know, I'm going to start summer school here." This is feeling good, like maybe I can fight this, like maybe Jack will listen because this is bigger than us, this is about mission, in other words, I need to prove that I can stay in a house.

"You go to school," says Jack, "and I, what, I join the PTA? I arrange carpool to soccer games and help you with home-work?"

"Won't need help. You'll see everything's easier when I'm busy with school. Busy on the weekends, too, with the house. This could be a nice home, Jack. If you'd let it, Jack. Maybe, you know, we could get a dog too. The right dog for this house."

"I had the right dog for this house." Jack's eyes heat up and rove the room until they settle on the model in my hands. "You toss out Bird and scavenge his stuff like he never was." His fist rises up, then slams down on the model. The wood support shudders as the house collapses in on itself. The whole thing hits the floor.

I drop to my knees to collect the pieces, to pull the halves of the house upright. Jack kneels beside me. On reflex, I scutter away from him. He will not look at me, but he puts his hand out to stay my hand.

"Of all the things to make it out of." He laughs as he picks up a loose rawhide stick. "I'm sorry I broke up the house." He stands, gently drawing me up with him, the model in pieces at our feet.

"I'm sorry too," I say. "Bird is the right dog for this house. He was always the right dog."

Jack nods. "Yeah, I've been thinking about paying Bird a visit." He waves the rawhide. "I believe he'd like to give one of these a chew."

"Visit Bird? When?"

"Now."

Air catches in my chest. My hands fly to my mouth. I breathe the rawhide on my fingertips. I inhale Bird. "Bird likes me, you know, Jack. Your visit could go better if you take me with you. Send me to Mom after."

Jack rolls the rawhide between his thumb and index finger. Light flashes in his eyes. He hands me my suitcase. "Put this back in the closet," he says, "for now."

"The bus?"

"You ride when we get back," he says.

"My model —"

"We'll fix it." He steps over the pieces.

He pushes me before him down the hall, like police probably do day in day out, through the door to the Chevy in the driveway. My joy at seeing Bird bangs up against this bullying.

"You forgot the uniform, Jack," I say, folding into the front seat. "Why not wear it? Acting like such a cop."

"What smart-ass talk is that?" He looks over at the house and he says, "Look, I'm going to go put it on. You got the right idea." He looks at me. "Stay?"

He only means in the car, of course. I nod.

He leaves the car running, the heat on. The keys in the ignition. Jack has left the keys because Jack is coming right back. The Chevy is a surprise. Usually he drives the truck that is all dents and time. This car is more Mom's thing—pearly white exterior and luxury seats. This Chevy is like any on the road. Maybe tonight Jack is after blending in.

Jack gets back in the car but not in a police uniform; he wears army fatigues. The pants pour into boots that lace at the ankles. In the rearview mirror, he adjusts the short visor on his cap. Then looks at me looking at the rifle in his hand. "I lost Bird once. Good and gone. Not going to happen again." He swivels the rifle and guides it over my head to lay it on the back seat. After a few miles he says, "Your mom says you sleep in the car sometimes when she works night shift. You sleep with the heat running?"

"She takes the keys."

"Jesus."

"I got this coat," I say.

Jack turns into the lot of a shopping mall.

Lawn mowers and tractors line green behind the mirror. The hood of the orange coat is bunched with wild dog fur. Jack zips up the coat, smoothes the shoulders. He tugs at the quilted material, roomy as a blanket. He runs his key down the arm. "It's thick, it's warm, it'll protect." He looks at the price. "Too much. Take it off."

Not pretty but this is a full-on coat, really something. I look good. Jack hands me others to try. Coats flashy with faux warmth. Might as well stick with the one I own. Mom bought my jacket at a discount fashion shop where everything got the rhinestone treatment. What the jackets at that shop lacked in warmth, they made up in their ability to startle. "Grow up in a place where the snow blinds pedestrians," Mom explained, "you know the importance of rhinestone. If you are seen, you survive." Mom and I compromised on a white satin jacket with no lining. Only now, with the warmth of the orange still in my blood, I know how chilly it is in satin.

Jack takes the orange coat to the register. "Happy Birthday," he says.

People stop to watch me go by in this coat. I did all right.

"A thanks won't kill you." Jack is driving again, fast now.

Without waiting for one, Jack starts in. "Dogs make good cops. They like feeling part of a group. Number two, any satisfactory dog will fight to get to the top. They do it by keeping the others down. A cop makes use of the feeling. He does it by setting up house with the dog in training. Dog and cop stay together through thick and thin. Now the other thing about a dog kicks in. Any satisfactory dog will protect what is his: your house, you.

"So what have we got? The cop and his dog that makes a

group. We got the dog trying to get to the top of that group, and the cop keeping him down. Ah, ah, everybody's happy. Then we got the dog ready to protect the cop, all cost, owing to the fact that the cop's become prized property. But what happens when the dog doesn't stay in the house with his cop? Because some won't."

Why does Jack talk like he is sharing something very personal when it is always only talk about dogs? Maybe talk of dogs makes Jack feel safe in the same way a dog curled at your feet makes you feel safe. Jack does not give off a lot of safety. What would it take for a man to talk past the subject that curls at his feet?

Jack drives into a parking lot where police cruisers line the cinderblock wall of a building alarmingly lit inside. Nobody around. Nothing has moved inside for a while, and you can tell that this is a place that people have left.

But the sound of barking. What a racket.

Jack parks the car to talk over it. "The dog that doesn't want to stay in a house, the loner, isn't necessarily a bad cop dog. A couple of the best have been loners. They have the spirit of the search and rescue dog, if not the soul. They're thinkers. Only in it for themselves, so it follows that they make judgments faster. They act on their judgments and don't ask for permission. Sometimes the dog's judgment is right on. So right, it goes way past what your average cop could assess. Are you getting this? These loners are perfectly servile and obedient on matters of course. They perform like any trained canine. But when it comes to a situation, I mean a *situation*, they fall back on their judgments. The problem is every now and then their judgment is off, and they don't take responsibility for it. I mean they take responsibility for themselves. They don't take responsibility for you. They're not making sure you're okay, all costs, before they act."

"What happens if you're attacked?" I say.

"Depends upon whether the dog thinks protecting you is the most effective way of managing the situation," Jack says. "See the problem? You're at the mercy of a dog thinking."

I say, "Are you talking about Bird?"

Jack turns off the ignition. Barks strike the windshield. "It's a beautiful sound," Jack says. "Their sense of right and wrong." He looks at me, at the orange coat. "You okay without the heat, 'cause the dogs will not shut up with this engine running?"

"This coat's warm."

"They'll cork it when they see me."

Shadows jump through fenced dogs paddling the ground. Jack strides up to them and, just as he said, the dogs do shut up. One keeps barking, stupid, until he hushes. Jack slips in and out of the dark between floodlights as he peers through the fence. I am starting to get an idea of what is on his mind.

Jack kicks the fence with his desert boot. He curses—at least his mouth flaps like it. He freezes, looks over at me, scrambles back to the car, piling in, yelling, "Bird's not the fuck here!"

He claps his hands over his ears; those barks could crack glass. "Think what they've done with him. Think. Think. Okay. Ah, who came for the dog?" He looks at me. "Olya? Do you happen to recall who you handed Bird over to?"

"Your partner," I say. Why bother saying I did not hand Bird over so much as Officer Ross took him? Maybe because I did not stop Bird from going. I did not stop the white puppy from going either.

"What?" he says.

I drag down one of his hands so he can hear.

"You sure it was her?" he says, driving again. "Yeah, sure it was. She thinks she's doing me a favor. Mother of God, that woman thinks too much and too goddamn much about me."

Jack's car jumps curbs—lurching forward and back; he thrusts his hand out in front of me every time he bangs to a stop. Where are the police with this kind of driving?

The answer comes on the next turn. Rows of parked cruisers line the street into a tidy cramped neighborhood. Cruisers jam fender deep up the driveway of a small stucco home. Some vehicles say K-9. Ears and noses behind windscreens track us as Jack slows across the street. Not a bark.

In the small stucco home, what *Sunset* magazine would call mid-century bungalow, the lights are up red and music pumps shots. A commotion of cops at the windows.

"Is this Officer Barbara's house?" I say.

"Shit," Jack says, "if there's grace and timing in this world, it ain't with me."

"She called. She wanted you at her party."

Jack raps his knuckles against the wheel. "Even better. Barbara's looking for me to show. Slipping in and out should be a snap." Jack squints at the house. "Fact is Bird can't live with anybody, not anymore. I mean, live inside a house. I conceded, accepted that we had to start from scratch. Got him the doghouse. But where did it get me? Bird crawls under my goddamn house, won't come out. I don't know if he was doing that before you came, do you?"

I look at him.

"Jesus," Jack says. "Better think sharp if I want to get us out alive." He looks at the house. "Bird will be in the backyard."

Jack drives the car down the block, backs up, and turns around. Now we are parked on the same side as Barbara's house. Reaching over my head to the backseat, Jack sets the rifle on his lap. "Operation Rescue. Hooah! Go get 'em."

I shake my head.

"I got you the goddamn coat," he says.

"Thank you," I say.

"That's not what I mean. I got you the coat so you could help me—"

"Happy birthday. That's what you said."

"I meant it," he says. "I don't want you to catch a chill from this."

"From what?"

He looks past the house, eyes darting in calculations. "Getting Bird back."

My head shakes. Side to side, faster. How can I explain this coat? The first thing I have received that served no purpose. Other than warm. Now he takes even that away.

"Wait." I touch his arm.

He sits back, scans the street, then looks at me. "What now?" You can hear the effort to stay patient.

"Why do you want Bird so much?"

"Why do you want a house? Look, when I took on Bird, it was for always. You don't go halfway into the fire."

I feel that fire. Jack's fire thins the air in the car. Jack is talking about commitment, no different than McFate's talk, and commitment burns up the oxygen. Bird is 'for always,' a creed that heats up beneath me fast and unknown and alluring.

"Look, baby," Jack says, cradling the rifle, "you take the dog away, you get the dog back." He points the rifle at me.

"Don't point that at me," I say. "I'm going. For Bird."

∞

Jack's hand squeezing my shoulder, we cross the street quiet, staying in the shadows of a gang of tall pines. We hit the driveway and the dogs in the cruisers go off. Bark-bark-bark, claws clacking glass. Jack stops, has to because I am not moving. They must hear us in the house.

"What?" Jack says. "Said it yourself. I got an invitation."

The music in the house gets louder.

His fingers tighten as he shoves me along. He trots us up the driveway, low and still but moving, desert stealth. Behind parted curtains, cops stuff up every bit of Barbara's house. Slipping his hand in mine, Jack draws me beside him, crouching us under the house windows all the way to the gate that spans the driveway. The gate rises higher than his head. He fiddles with the latch on the gate until the doors swing wide on their hinges.

In a pool of red light draining from a backroom window, Bird stands spraddle-legged. Eyes on us, reflecting red. Taut on his neck a threaded metal cable, also reflecting. The cable leash is anchored behind some cruddy doghouse. How lean Bird looks, flat and somehow hollowed. His eyes flick over me, and when they do, the eyelids spread, lowering. Soft dog, soft dog, come to me, nose my cheek, and forgive me for failing to rise to your level. You were always house material. I just wasn't quite yet.

"Hey, boy," Jack whispers. He takes a step. Bird growls at him. Bird launches. Does that dog go! Barking like he would be screaming if he could.

Jack slams me body and bones against the house. The window above rattles open, Jack flat beside me now. A cop slaps two hands on the frame, his big wide shadow falling out before him. The stink of beer pours out on the rap music.

"Shut up, dude," the cop says to Bird. "Never seen a cat before?"

Bird does not shut up so the cop shuts the window.

Jack whispers, "Cops are lazy." Pushes me at Bird. "Go to him, Olya."

Bird stops barking to lick my hand, to nuzzle. I swing my arms around him. His ribs jut. His coat hangs loose off his spine. What has Officer Barbara done to Bird? What did I do, letting him go?

Barking starts up from the dogs in the cruisers again but now the barking comes from the house too. That explains why some cruisers had no dogs. Those dogs got let in to party.

"Out of time. The dogs know. Undo Bird's leash," Jack says, "behind the doghouse."

Jack pivots the rifle at me.

"You don't have to use that on me."

"Who says it's for you." Jack eyes his dog.

The barks get louder indoors. Louder like the dogs are out, not in. The front door of the house opens. Collars rattle on barks. "They let 'em out," Jack says. "Ass behind doghouse. We've got a situation."

Jack slips silent to the gate. I hug the brick, Bird tucked at my heels. The music's *thunk-thunk-thunk* against us. Inside, feet stomp on boards. Jack knocks the bolt on the gate. *Bam!* Something slams into the other side. The gate vibrates. Claws scrape. Dogs growl, snap. Someone screams inside the house, but it winds up into laughs.

At the rear wall of the doghouse is a metal hook attached to the cable. If only the gyrating light would stand still, if only Bird would stop nosing my hands, if only I could see how to unhook the cable. It is hot in this coat.

"Hurry the fuck up," Jack says. I hold Bird's snout out of the way. Whimpers push the flaps of his mouth. I work the hook. What Jack and I are doing is not right, but neither is keeping a dog in this condition on a leash. I owe Bird. The cable releases. I pop up from the doghouse just as a canine claws over the top of the gate. Head caught tight as a hanger, teeth snapping at the butt of the rifle Jack uses to pry it off the gate.

"Leave off," Jack says quietly to the dog.

The dog's jaw snaps shut.

"Down."

The dog's claws retract. It drops behind the gate, out of sight.

Jack must read my surprise because he says, "This ain't entirely amateur hour."

Bark-bark-bark-bark! Bird spots another canine vaulting over the gate. He rips out of my hands. On hind legs, Bird tilts at the gate. He leaps, catching the invader mid-flight. Across the rail they are jaw on jaw, snarl, snap. Bird's hind legs scrabbling at the wood to stay on the dog.

Jack calls him off, but Bird is deaf. Something has my coat.

"Excuse me? What the fuck you doing?" Jack points the gun at a large rock near my foot. "Get me that rock."

"I'm stuck!" Both yelling now.

Inside the house, it is music, it is beer, it is red. It is my coat, caught on the cable that held Bird. Hooked and holed. My new coat, warm and sheltering as home. Might as well throw up.

Now it is dogs. The noise they make is blood.

Bird hauls the other dog to our side. Both hit the cement, heavy-backed, bone-dumped. The other dog's head fixed between Bird's teeth. Bird shakes the dog's head like a greasy paper bag. The dog's eyes knock at the lids as the teeth bump and stutter.

"Jesus," Jack says. "Look at that."

Jack grabs Bird's collar and yanks him off the dog. "Let go."

Bird withdraws, all his for once.

I turn back to my coat. "Leave it," he yells.

Another dog claws over the gate. Jack has Bird, so the dog clears it. Bird snorts and breaks from Jack to soar over the other canine hurling straight for me, teeth stretched red.

"Got your six."

A gunshot whistles. It pops. A dog drops. Could be snatched from below. Jack stands behind it, gun pointed. There is no sound. Dogs shut up. Music cuts. Red light blinking in a surging house gone still. In the silence Bird starts singing, a cry higher and finer than song. Hear it, this high, fine cry.

The fallen dog's flank is ripped open from the shot. Its belly convulses as it drags onto forelegs, only to crash on its snout at my knees.

Don't look. Look at the coat, where it is hooked. Now I see the coat is free.

"Fall in!" Jack reaches a hand to me. He kicks wide the gate, and we march through it, Bird trotting between us.

The cops come out of the house in threes and fours. They come stumbling and holding onto shoulders, fumbling for their holsters. They spread out across the grass, guns drawn. Some are dressed in party finery, some in uniform. Swaying and swerving with cups of beer, they spread out. Their dogs' cries amplified with duty.

Jack and Bird and I dart behind cruisers down the driveway. A little way up the street Jack shoves us under the low-hanging boughs of a spruce. We huddle in shadows of crossed branches. He hands me his rifle. "Stick it under your coat." I grab the stock before the rifle can slip down.

Flashlights skim by. Cops whistle across lawns. Two cops kiss against a tree. Someone giggles. A cop stumbles and spills onto the grass. The dogs in the cruisers are chomping nuts. No cop thinks to let out his dog.

A woman shrieks. Jack looks over.

"They found the dogs," I say. "The dead."

"You listening?" Jack says. "Pardon me, but are you listening?"

Bird's panting muffles under my coat.

Jack drops the car keys into the coat's pocket. "You walk to the Chevy with Bird. No big thing. You get him in the car. You drive home." Jack gives me a shove. "Now pop smoke."

"Where's home?"

Jack frowns at me. "It's like this—and fuck me if I've got it wrong—left, left, right. That's at the light. Drive up the freeway ramp. Head south. Exit in three. Take an immediate right, drive west five minutes. Look at the clock on the dash. You'll come to a major intersection. Go right, then you know the rest. It's where I live. Got it?"

I can only stare.

"Look," Jack says, "I'm telling it correctly. I drove to her place every morning for the past too many years. Carpool."

"You killed her dogs. What will you do?"

"Barbara said two weeks. She reneged. I owe her nothing." He tilts his head side to side like he has a kink. "I'll give it to you again."

"I can't drive."

"You telling me that all those nights she left you in the car you never took it for a spin?" His eyes lower. I do not need to remind him that she always took the keys. Jack says, "Throw the gun in the backseat. Now move."

"I'm scared."

Jack looks over his shoulder. They haven't seen us. In the driveway, cops huddle round the dead dogs. Others lay drunk on lawns. Jack looks back at me. What he does. He hugs me.

Bird growls.

"You did good." He turns me in the direction of his car. "And," he says, "we made a soup sandwich." He glances at the street and back at me. "Get in. Drive straight a half dozen blocks then pull over, that's it. Hide in the backseat with Bird. Wait for me."

Jack straightens, shakes out his fatigues, and flows out from between the branches of the spruce. Faint as a cat, he crosses lawns to Barbara's place, calling out to a cop prone on the grass, his flashlight tilted at the moon. Jack kicks the cop's boot. "What you assholes fuck up this time?"

No hope of seeing over the steering wheel of the Chevy. I shove my coat under me. Joggle the key—the starter turns over on a shriek. Dies. My foot finds the gas pedal, and I give the starter another go. Rage is the sound the car makes now. Alternate feet: left pedal, brake; right pedal, gas. I do this until my body acts automatic. If only I could do the same with my brain. Left pedal, brake; right pedal, gas. Right dog, dead; left dog, dead. Bird in the backseat, two dogs dead.

In the 3D *Outrun 'em* game at the arcade near our last vacancy, the trick was to keep your eyes locked on the distance. That boy at the arcade won lots of games. He tried to get me to play, and I never did because I never pictured myself outrunning anything except time, waiting on Mom to come back to me.

What Jack needs is a getaway driver. He needs McFate. Who'd think anyone other than the Lord Himself could find a use for McFate? "It's not how you drive," McFate would say, "it's whether you pull it off." Ready now, I step on the gas pedal. The Chevy plows into the car parked in front, heaving forward and lurching back before coughing out. Bird scrambles onto the seat he got knocked from. My forehead burns from banging the steering wheel. I restart the Chevy and pull it in reverse. The Chevy's front bumper is hooked on the rear of the other car. I stay on reverse until the Chevy's bumper drags off.

I cruise out 3D *Outrun 'em* style. The truck parked across the street leaps out at me. I spin the wheel. A couple of parked cars on this side trip me up and get sideswiped for their trouble.

Now that I know what I am doing, I give it gas. A white van speeding through the intersection lays on the horn. Now a cruiser's spotlight beams the eye of God. I pull over behind an orderly auto parked at the curb. I cut the ignition and scram into the backseat with Bird. We are any Chevy parked in any neighborhood. "Good boy," I whisper into Bird's ear. "You're not scared." I stroke his muzzle. I hold his collar fast. About to be busted. Bird pants hot into the long night. He licks and licks my knuckles. Bird is doing the feeling for both of us.

The spotlight pokes around the windows above our heads. I am ducked down in a car, hiding again, yes, but not alone. This time I have Bird. And, it must be said, I have this coat. The spotlight blinks off. The Chevy drenched in black.

Knocking. Siren. Kaleidoscope glass. *Open up! Torchlight!* He shouts, *Open up!* Halo falling onto seats. Black braid wiping glass. Black braid wrapping her neck. Dirty spy. *Open up!* Rrrrrrrrr. Hush, Bird. *Knock, knock.*

Like a curtain, the wall of the front seat opens up. Jack peers into the Chevy.

Jack.

He drops in behind the wheel, reaches for his dog. "Hey, boy," he says. "Hey, hey, hey."

Bird's eyes shift beneath Jack's hand.

Jack takes a deep breath and blows out. "Hooah." He adjusts the rearview mirror askew and slaps under the seat for the lever. Gives up. Makes thirsty sounds. "Got water?" His tongue is thick. Alcohol sweat dots his upper lip. He says, "Key?"

He lifts the key out of my palm. "Operation Rescue accomplished!" He swivels to the door and flings it open. He vomits. Bird sniffs the puked air, tail tucked. Jack sits upright and pulls the door, wiping his mouth on his sleeve. He looks back at me. "Key?"

"You have it."

He looks at his hand, where the car key dangles off his thumb, surprised to see it. He shakes his head to wake up. "Got to moto. My buddies can't be far behind." Extending his arm, circling the key like an airplane, he soars toward the starter when his head drops onto his chest and he slides sideways onto the seat.

Patrol lights from another cruiser bounce off the windows of parked cars a half block away. I pull Bird down into the well with me, clamping a hand on Jack's shoulder in case he comes to. The light beam leaves a slug trail over our seat rims and the dash. The cruiser passes. No telling when the next one will come. Only that it will. Bird leaps onto the front seat. "Back," I say.

Bird scoots to the backseat. "Sit," I say, and Bird does. I pat Jack's cheek until his eyes open. "I'm going to drive."

He blinks then smiles. "Roger that."

"You're in the seat."

He drops a heavy, damp arm over my shoulder, and I prop my knee against his hip to leverage him to sitting. He slides into the passenger seat. This time I manage to pull the car out okay. I have got the driving fundamentals down, except for stopping and going. Soon I will get the hang of turns.

Hoooooonk. The other car swerves just in time.

Jack gapes out the windscreen. "Put the lead in. Got to square Bird before they show up at the house. There's the ramp. See the ramp? Speed! Faster. Go, go, go!"

The rims scrape the curb onto the ramp. "Tell me sooner next time."

I lift my foot off the accelerator. The Chevy slows. A couple cars motor by, so it is okay to stop on the freeway. Jack snores into his camouflage jacket. What can be said to wake a man who takes out police dogs in a mission to get himself back on the force? Out here, in the last of five lanes, it hits me how little I know. About Jack, I know the least of all.

"Jack," I say, "why'd you do it?"

He raises his head. "We stall out?"

"No, I did. I need direction."

"'Cause you're being emotional. Losing it over dogs. Am I right?"

"You don't really want to get back on the police force."

He says, "Don't blame me. I may be the handler, but dogs still get themselves killed." Jack is full awake now. "Take Daisy.

Lee Poughkeepsie's canine. Before Daisy, dogs did not exist for Daed; he had eyes only for me, for the work and for the play. At an abandoned Taliban hub, Daed rooted around a cave. He came out and sat beside me, a sign the cave was stocked. The crew humped in for clean up. Then Daisy whines from the rocks overhead. She'd heard something. Daed bolted up the rock face to her. Next thing, we're in a shitstorm. Bullets plinking off rock when something dropped from the branches over my head. Daisy. Fell from a cypress, dead on impact. I was trying to figure how she'd managed to climb a tree, the physics of it, when more branches cracked overhead, and here comes Daed. He landed on Daisy. She broke his fall." Jack leans over and takes the steering wheel to guide us off an exit ramp.

"When Daed saw Daisy, he started singing. I got Daed to the truck and shoved him in the kennel. 'No singing,' I told him. 'You fell out of a tree and walked away. That sort of luck won't show up again. Stay put.'"

"Did he?" The more Jack talks about this Daed, the more I believe he is really talking about Bird.

"Know your way home from here?"

I scan the lawns without fences, the wagon wheels. I let him know that I do.

"The truck was ransacked. Daed's kennel empty. I cut out for him, but Poughkeepsie put a gun to my head. 'Daed's gone.' Not gone. Not your dog, you don't. You don't abandon that."

Jack knocks on the indicator. "I got Bird back," Jack says. "Because of you, Olya. You are the difference."

20

As *a dog returneth to his vomit, so a fool returneth to his folly.*
Knock-knock.
Who's there?

"Rise and shine," Jack yodels outside my bedroom door. "Give God your glory, glory!"

Wet nose, cold nose, Bird nudges my fingers up the whisks of his spine.

The door swings open.

Bird rises to his feet, and my bed tips. Jack claps his hands. "Enough," he says to his dog. "Enough is enough." Jack slips a choke collar around Bird's neck. Bird hauls back on the collar, and next thing, Jack is on the floor.

Jack draws up to sit cross-legged, coughing on the liquid back of the throat. "Goddamn parties," he says. "Smoking should be outlawed." He smiles at me. "You made it home. Only cost a bumper. How'd it go?"

"You came with me?"

He stares, face a blank. "Sure." Jack says. "Get ready for school, for Christ."

"What about San Francisco? I was taking the bus?"

"It's an open ticket."

"Open?"

"Yeah, you know, wide open." He climbs to his feet. "School was your idea. A good idea. Everybody wants to be a contributing member of society. School's the way to do that. Law-abiders have educations."

"You went to school," I say.

"Listen, miss. I'm feeling good. Things look bright. I got my dog back. I am a great canine cop. Watch me. I'll get this dog under, make him heel, make him stay. Then your mom will stay, and we'll get this thing together. I believe we can. Sure, the folks at Riverside PD know it was me who executed the canine abduction, but how, how? I was at the party, carousing with the best of them peace officers. Guess what, Olya, guess the fuck what? Fuck it! I'm back. Look at that and that and that." Jack kicks out a dance. "Hallelujah, kiss my ass, amen!"

Bird's leash wrapped around his wrist, not a breath between dog and man, Jack sets breakfast before me. He sits, stuffing Bird into the V of his legs.

"Barbara won't let Bird go easy," Jack says. "That her boys weren't waiting for us when we rolled in last night only means they were drunker than I was. They will sober. They will show."

My last bit of bacon fat vanishes with the bread crust. I hold out greasy fingers to Bird. His tongue probes my fingernails.

"He protected you last night," Jack says.

"Dogs protect," I say. "Like your hunting dog protected you, right?" He nods. "From what?"

"Dad." Jack squints through the tiny window he shapes with his fingers. "That sweet dog was wasted on me." He springs to his feet and opens the back door for me to go out. "Come. We are officially outlaws. Time to practice our aim. There's a firefight brewing."

Producing a pink Frisbee out of the morning sunlight, Jack spins the disc to me. He jogs to the other end of the backyard. He lobs the Frisbee in backhands and forehands. Bird leaps easily, lazily, into the air, a spitting, spinning dancer. Jack fires the Frisbee and I jump for it, but it soars between my fingers. I spin round and catch it and sail it back to Jack. He hooks the disc on his finger. He backhands it low, Bird stalking through the grass, but I snap the disc up from his jaws to fling it high on the air. Running backwards, colliding with the fence, Jack catches it, legs muddling beneath him. He is down. Bird snatches up the disc and runs it back to me. Play! Play! Don't stop the play. Outlaws, Jack and I are one in crime. This is our covenant. Soon Mom will come back, and what a joy of outlaws we will be.

I flydraw the Frisbee up and shoot it at Jack. The disc spins high over the fence. Jack sees where it lands. When he looks back at me, the fun is gone. He presses his index finger to lips thin and white. He waves me toward him, drawing a circle to indicate Bird should come too. Bird and I crouch up to the fence. Across the street sits a squad car, canine and cop staring out.

It is the broom closet now for Bird. Jack muzzles his dog's snout. Stuffing in a head that does not want to go, Jack snaps shut the door. He shakes a finger at me. "No sad eyes. Soon as the cop rolls off, Bird and I are going to hang out like a couple of old buddies, kick around the house, cuddle."

No scratching on the door, no crying, Bird is silent. Does he stare at the line of light under the door, behind him the two dead dogs faintly licking their wounds in the dark? "Leave on a light for him," I say.

"A light?" Jack says. "At this juncture you are a truant. The remedy is attendance at school. I'm not getting toted off to jail over you."

Jack needs to act like everything is normal. But there is nothing normal here and, all at once, I cannot follow another command without finding out just how not normal. "You went to that motel with Mom," I say. "What's going on between you and my mother?"

"Ah, not a whole hell of a lot since you showed up."

"Was something going on before?"

"Good," Jack says. "You're trying to figure things. Put two and two together. Tell you the truth, I thought there was something shut off in there." He points to my head. "But don't blame me if you don't like what you hear. If it beats the living dickens out of you. Ask away. I'll tell you what I know. But it won't be the worst of it. You'll need your mom for that." He looks over at the front door, like he hears the cop at it. "Only hurry."

I start to shape something of what made me question him in the first place.

But I do not know what I am asking.

Or no longer care to know.

If what Jack says is true, it will surely hurt to know, and didn't we just get Bird back? At last, I am happy—we are happy, Jack and me. We have that. Ask too many questions, this happiness might vanish. My mouth closes up shop.

"Then remain silent," Jack says, quietly. "The more you talk, the more you give yourself away. As any good cop knows. Get your coat. You'll wear it to school."

"But the administrator said not until summer school?"

"Hurry."

The coat is hooked over the top knob of the bureau. I grab it up, looking and not looking at the rawhide pieces of the house model I built scattered now on top of the bureau. Jack must have collected the bits last night and set them beside the party bag from McFate's family. I dump the party favors onto the bureau.

Jack is brown bagging a lunch for me when I come in. "What the hell took you so long?" When he sees the model in my hands, he looks away. "You rebuilt."

"Better." The house came back easy, thanks to rawhide and spit. But now it has a view from Skinner's window. At the center of the house is a hearth, with a grate of dentures and an eternal fire made of the red poppies pictured on the bag of seeds gifted by McFate's dad.

Jack flicks the American flag spiking the roof of the house. "Good prop. One of those overboard school projects." He points to the airline liquor bottle over the entrance. "How's that?"

I do not explain McFate's bottle of Bukowski's toenail clippings above the threshold because then I would have to explain McFate. Neither do I explain how the rawhide represents ancient spruce, or how the roof is raised from the walls with clipped Q-tips to allow in sky, or how the second floor is set at a 75-degree angle from the bottom floor so the occupants can move with the rotation of the sun.

Jack does not understand home design. Just look at his house. The administrator at the school will know what I am after, how the design holds open for wilderness. This is talk between architects.

Jack stuffs my lunch under my arm and says, "Let's moto."

The squad car plays it loose, staying just in sight of us all the way to the lime, high fence around the school. Jack pays no mind. He pulls in front of the fence and tugs the collar of my coat. "Pick you up at three." He shoves a twenty-dollar bill in the pocket of my coat, calling it emergency money. He runs a finger along the rawhide wall of my model. "Watch the dogs don't eat your homework."

Students check out my model as I pass in the hallway; probably, they wish they could live in such a home. Jealous, they whisper behind hands. Sorry, kids, this house has room for only one. Destroyed once, it has been made stronger, as any great architect knows.

The outer door to the administrator's office hangs open. He paces behind it, running a hand through his hair, hollering into a phone. I help myself to a chair in the outer room. The administrator *yous* into the phone: *you* said this, *you* don't understand, *you* don't care, *you you you.*

He passes his office door again. I position the model to give the best view. The phone crashes in the cradle, and the administrator swings through the door. His face says he did not expect anyone. His eyes track from my new coat to the home on my lap. He frowns. Neither did he expect something so original. I will remain open to his suggestions, his architectural know-how. The design is pushed, though flowing and inclusive. He will see that.

"You're early." The administrator talks like he talked to the person on the phone. "The summer school enrollment fair isn't for two weeks." He looks at the door to the hallway then back at me. "You'll be notified. Anything else I can help you with?"

I lift the model for him to view. "This is the house I've designed for when I have a home of my own," I say, "a place I can stay."

"We don't offer design classes in the summer. Just core cur-
riculum—math, English, history, and science."

"That's okay. I would like your opinion on the design."

His office phone rings. His head jerks toward it. He hesitates
then strides up to the model, bends over, scans closely. "I don't
know, this, um—" he looks over at the ringing phone. I turn
the model for another view. His nose wrinkles and he covers it.
"Rawhide? This makes no… I mean…this shows no feeling for
living in a house. Is it a joke?"He looks at me. "Oh, dear, um,
look. Let's see if we can't arrange for you to start next week.
Why wait for summer? Huh?"

"No," I say. "I'm going to a school in San Francisco."

"That right? Okay! Great schools there. Will you excuse
me?"

He lunges back for his office, snaps up the receiver. "Hello?"
His voice catching, "Oh honey, oh you..."

Everything goes quiet. In the silence, time stops up. In me.
Cramped in my belly. Classroom after classroom, this is any
school I have attended. Kept in tight, no one allowed in or out.
Toilet or not. Around the corner, I collide with a uniform. His
long limbs steady my model. The uniform says, "Hallway pass."
The uniform shows no feeling for living. I ask the uniform to
please step aside so I can go to the toilet.

Women's is Out of Order.

I push through the Men's and would duck into a stall, but
the door is jammed. A wheeled bucket full of water blocks the
only other stall.

Caution. Wet Floor.

I step over the bucket and kick open the stall door, accidentally whapping it against the guy standing behind it. He whirls
around like someone caught. On the wall, written in pink: *It
sickened me to be part of family picnics*——————————

"Damn, baby girl, look what you made me do!" McFate
drops his big pink marker. He yanks a rag from denims that
hardly hold to his skinny hips and squirts ammoniac fluid. He
rubs where the last word ran off, and says, "What? I need to

keep myself in a job. Supplemental graffiti. Better Bukowski than the vanilla these kids scrawl." He looks back at me and his rodent eyes soften. "You look greased up for the fryer pan. I know that kind of sweat. It's bowl friendly. Let me lighten your load." He lifts the model out of my hands and backs out of the way. "Go ahead, heave ho."

I slide to my knees before the bowl. The walls are lousy with the sound of how hot. Someone bangs on the stall door. They can bang all they want. Bang until the door drops, the walls cave, the whole stinking building falls in.

McFate strokes my hair, dabs my forehead with toilet paper. Outside the bell clangs and students pound out of classrooms. I drop back against the stall. McFate flushes the toilet. He leans against the opposite wall, staring down at my house. "There is a beautiful idea," he says, "even though it stinks." He sniffs it.

I slide to my feet, lift the house out of his hands, kick him in the shin and walk out of the stall. His yowls follow me down the hallway. So does the uniform. I spin round like nothing special and walk fast to the other end of the hallway. Now I am running down the stairwell to the exit.

Somehow McFate stands at the bottom of the stairs. He leaps and catches me. The house slams against his chest. Behind us at the top of the stairs the uniform hollers but stays put, like a dog that has scared you off its yard.

McFate slips his hand into mine. I could pull out of that hand. His hold is not tight. He starts running and I run with him. He stops to look at me. "Coming? Coming with?"

Then, only then, do I feel time again. The schoolyard air funnels into my chest and I am jolted electric. My legs kick out beneath me and I speed. But McFate yanks me back. "Heel, baby!" He reroutes me to the parking lot. "The car. The car."

He swings open the passenger door of his lowrider, scoots across the bench and up behind the wheel to screw in one key out of a key-thick-chain into the starter, all while not letting go my hand. He draws the passenger door closed behind me. "No going back now, lady." He pulls out of the lot.

"Let's go then," I say. "Let's go."

Behind me, smaller and smaller, is the school I did not begin, even though it had begun its work on me. Imagine pretending to know the first thing about a home. But I know one thing now, maybe always knew. Home requires sacrifice, as any household spirit will tell you. Look at Jack. He slaughters just to get himself a housedog.

"Baby girl, listen up, listen up." McFate watches me, not the road. "I'm going to do you like a rock to you." The hairs above his lip spring up like baby chicks. "My rock is mighty and it's going right up against your head. Bam. Out you go like a closet. 'Cause that's how I like 'em, tight and ribbon wrapped out cold. Hear that, lady, my lady-girl? Rock, rock, rock you a little night."

If McFate had a tail, it would be swinging. He is dog happy.

"You will be screaming for it," McFate is saying. "My personal guarantee. Aaaaaaaah-ooooooh. Ah-ah-oh-oh. Rock me, baby. Rock me in you, umph, umph, all night long. What I can do with you. What can I do?" He says to look out my window. Far off, socked in yellow, the mountains fold into forever. McFate says he can drive into those mountains, way past the Griffith Park Observatory, and have his way with me. See how the city skyline chops up the smog? See that tall silvering building? Up on the top floor they let you hang girls upside down so you see what is happening under the skirts. McFate says, "Do you hear me, lady? You listening? This is your captain speaking."

"Pease stop the vulgar talk," I say.

"What vulgar talk?"

"I'm just a girl."

McFate's eyes drop off and wander back onto the road, kicking a tin can down the lane. Won't look at me now, which for better or worse provides a good view of his profile. His face is all Toucan. His chest burns coral bright along the edges of his wifebeater. McFate can talk. This is something he can do. If his talk were not so vulgar, he could be a man of the pulpit. With talk like his, he must hear often of its failure. He is not alone in practicing his art, in disregard of the opinion of others, and he is not alone in the hurt it pays out of him. But the things that McFate does, beneath all the talk, for puppies and for girls hurling up in toilet stalls, are kind.

The windows are all down. The wind whaps in the lowrider solid as bed sheets. I imagine the house model that rests now atop my thighs spinning out of my hands on a twister. The number of cars has increased on the freeway, but so has the speed, a floor of swift flaring metal. I lift up the model, figuring if it will fit through the window. I shove it through. The wind snatches the house from my hands. The rear windshield gives a good view of the flight of the house. First it twirls in uncanny multiples then it hits the concrete spitting rawhide shrapnel. Cars swerve. McFate swerves too. Everything hits the doors. He slows down to stare out the rear windshield. His mouth hovers over words, but nothing comes out—until it does. "That was a bit of Bukowski you booted!"

I toss the airline liquor bottle into his lap, wishing I had kept his sister's gift of a window frame too.

His fingers close around the bottle and raise it to his ear, smiling at the saltshaker ping of toenail parings. He stores the bottle in his front pocket. "But why chuck your beautiful idea?"

"The administrator told me the house was a joke."

McFate shrugs. "Where to now?"

"Don't care," I say. "I'm never coming back. Screw school."

"There you go. A little insult and it's cut and run time."

"Hey, you're just the driver here."

"But can you swim?"

McFate pulls into a parking lot with the shortest line to the beach. Impatient skateboards carve around our car. The line moves up. McFate honks at a blanketed man operating a grocery cart filled with knotted plastic bags. The long-shanked dog tied to the cart barks at McFate. Dudes with bright torsos balance surfboards above their heads. A man and a woman hustle coin, washing the windows of the cars in line.

McFate points to a group of girls spread across towels near the lot.

Yes, there is much flesh on display, but I wonder what drives McFate in his endless spill of words. He is not the only one. Jack also likes his talk. So did the administrator at school. Talk, talk, talk. Bird does not talk. Maybe Bird sings now and again. But song is all feeling. Bird was not singing when Jack shoved him into the closet this morning. I should get back home. But instead I cut and run, like McFate says.

Clunk.

A rubbery bucket slops water on the hood of McFate's lowrider. McFate's grin fades. He swivels round, outraged. The man with the bucket squirts liquid at McFate's windshield. McFate cranks down his window to curse the hustlers off when the woman reaches into view, her breasts pillowing the wet screen as she guides a squeegee along the glass. Little bubbles pop at her lips, her necklaces throb at her neck. McFate quiets. He eases into his seat to take in the show. All at once I am very cold. Then I am hot. The seat vinyl gets slippery under me. Do not look at the two at the window. Something pushes down my shoulders, fixing me to the seat. The man's thick black braid smears the window. His body clunks against the door. They are the same man and woman from the park, the ones that used Mom's car like it was theirs. Now they wash McFate's windows without asking. Already the man rubs the windshield dry with his hundred hands.

The hot powder of her mouth shouting at my face. *What are you looking at?*

I reach for McFate.

He says, "Like to watch?"

Clunk. Clunk. The man's fist raps the hood. "What's it worth to you?"

McFate tosses a quarter out the window. The man ignores the quarter. He whips his braid, not budging out of our way. McFate lays on his useless horn. Cars cut in front of the lowrider, flooding the pay booth.

I roll down and down my window and stare up into the woman's eyes. I dig out from my coat the emergency money Jack gave me and I hand it to the woman. She snatches the bill and unfolds it with ritual attention.

She waves the twenty at the man.

The man steps out of the way of our car. This man and this woman with nowhere else to be. The windows stay open as McFate parks. The salt in my sweat dries and diamonds in the ocean air.

The waves run up to greet us. The water noses my feet. Now it curls around my heels. I kneel down before it.

"What's it called?"

"What is what called?"

"This?" I say, cupping the seawater up to McFate.

"The Pacific, baby. Pacific!"

"Your name really McFate?"

"Zanzibar Buck-Buck McFate."

McFate's shirt is coming off, now his pants. He is down to jockeys, patterned with license plates, which flap around his goose legs. Oh, he is skinny in this sun. On his chest is what started out as a tattoo, B̶u̶k̶. Crossed out now.

"Who is Bukowski?"

"You *are* fucking with me." He points at me. "Take those clothes off your bones. It's skin time!"

The weather here is fluky as McFate, freezing last night and steaming today. Lounging under umbrellas striped every color, people cover their hides in thick sunblock. Before I unzip my coat, McFate drags it off my shoulders. "Do you have a permit to wear this? Yow! It bites!" He chucks my coat on the sand and starts on my shirt, but I knock his mitts off and undo the buttons myself.

He says, "You're the kind that doesn't think you're too good looking but, lady, you're okay."

He catches my shirt and rolls it into a ball and throws, but the wind catches the shirt and flies it into his face. He stumbles

around, snapping it off. He is good for a laugh. McFate lunges
forward and drags off my pants, and I dig my fingers into my
underpants to keep them up. His hands clamp on my butt, and
his face presses into my underpants. I do not look at the top
of his head. I do not look back at the people staring out from
under umbrellas. The elastic lace of my underpants is buckling,
and I hold it where it should be. McFate pulls me to the water.

"No, no," I say. He pulls me in and pulls me in. Water, water,
everywhere.

He says, "Stop rattling your teeth."

He says, "Just let go, lady. I got you."

He says, "Turning blue on purpose?"

I am flapping at water, not such a pretty bird. Things float
by on the foam. Shadows of passing sea creatures. Seaweed,
plastic bottles, me. Water fills my mouth, fountain-wise. The
water slips over my head.

He grabs me, this boy. He pulls my head above the waves.
"Can't swim, can you?"

I kick him off, but this is what he does. He unfolds me.
Holds me straight on his arms, and he keeps his arms there. I
let him, though he struggles to stay above the waves, flat out
himself.

He says, "Okay, so listen up. I'm going to take my arms away.
You read me? Here goes one arm. Ah-ha! See, still floating. The
babe is still floating. Nice. Now the other one. Just the other
little arm, okay, girly-whirly? Got to do it. Can't float for the two
of us. Not in the books. Here's the beauty of it. Don't need to.
Are you fucking taking this in? I don't need to float for the two
of us because you can float for yourself. Yes, you too can float
like the next piece of garbage. Because it so happens that you
are not *just* a girl. You are Aphrodite. You cruise the sea foam."

He slips his other arm out from under me.

"Give it up, Aphrodite. The waves may hit, but you go with
the roll."

He winds my arms over my head. "Stay," he says.

We lift and drop down with the waves, our hands holding

us head to head. The only holding of any kind we do. Floating on the surface of all this weighty water. There is a place for the body, giving up, giving in, and just because you cannot swim does not mean you cannot float.

Sun prints my lids. Kids yodel on the shore as mothers swing their babies above the break. Mom dipped me into the vacancy pool. I kicked and squirmed in her hands. She held tighter. The terror in her face terrifying. The pool stretched before me in aquamarine adventure. She held so tight I couldn't breathe. She was that scared I would drown.

"Hey!" McFate yells from the break. From the place where I let go and let him float off. From where I flipped over and did what I could in the way of swimming to shore.

My shirt sticks to my wet bra and the buttons stick to the salt on my fingers. McFate stomps up the sand and grabs my wrist and pulls me into the cave of his chest. "I thought you'd fucking sunk," he says, his heart thumping at my knuckles, his eyes fleeing mine. He, too, is scared.

21

A hand rolls over my shoulder to stop me from running, but I am not running. I am trying to sit up. "You weren't at school!" Jack squats beside me. His irises flare in the overhead porch light. "I've been up and down Riverside looking for you." He flings his arm out toward his truck parked aslant in the driveway, door ajar, headlights on. "Not easy with a cop on your ass." He says, "Fuck it. You came back."

"I was never leaving," I say. I scratch at sand in my scalp. Jack's grip eases. His hand moves under my arm. "One, two—" he says, "this includes you." We go up. Like this we walk into his house. "That's right, damn it. Time you stay, mother or not. Go take a bath. Dinner'll be ready before you are."

McFate punched his number into my cell and dropped me off a block early, but there was no reason to duck out. Jack's house was dark, the doors locked. I felt in my pockets for the key and came up with grains of sand. Mom is the one who leaves keys to vacancies. Jack has never given me a key to his house. I tried the windows. All locked. I might have broken one, anything to get in—but a cruiser had started circling. I leaned up close to the front door, hidden behind a hedge. Safe in the knowledge this house is my place to be. Without McFate's talk, the night quieted. So quiet I started thinking about talk. Not just McFate's, but my talk too. How I have been doing a lot of it. Crowing about how I have talked myself into a place to stay. But was the only reason I was still here because I kept my mouth shut around Mom and Jack?

Last night, I apologized to McFate for speaking ill of his family. His parents cherish McFate, and what child wouldn't wish for that? I told him I was trying to commit to what had shaped up to be my family. If that was what it took.

McFate said, *If you're going to try, go all the way. Otherwise don't even start.*

   — *Bukowski.*

Hot water pumps into the bathtub. Jack said I could stay.

Dirty towels pile up the laundry basket. Jack said I could stay.

I pull my suitcase from the closet, set it on the bed, and open it. I unpack every single thing in inside. I fold the clothes into the drawers of the bureau. Jack said I could stay.

Jack has dressed up lamb in herbs and white onions. Some cooking. He pulls up a chair beside mine and sits cowboy style. Bird sniffs at Jack's plate but Jack lets him. Jack says, "Something special for your first day at school."

"I didn't go to school," I say. "I went to sea with a crazy boy."

"To sea with a crazy boy. That's always an education."

Education is right. I learned that I liked the feel of my hands in McFate's hands. But does that mean joining my fingers with his across the stirring water is the thing forbidden me? I spied on McFate touching himself in his car. He peeped in on me in my bedroom. But McFate and I are no longer spying when we touch now. Is that the missing part to complete my image of the world? Watching that man and woman rubbing each other against Mom's car in Griffith Park, watching Jack touch Mom, but watching without spying, because now I know the difference. What has been missing is a place to look from that is mine.

Jack stares down at his lamb. "I know what I asked of you. You're not yet enrolled in school, I know. But I needed the appearance of status quo." He picks up a fork. "Cops are very neutralized by status quo." He stabs a chop. "I had an unexpected day too," he says. "Once I got back home, I had words with the officer tailing me, then went inside to run that dog through basic commands, and did I do it?" He thumbs over at Bird.

Bird sprawls across the heating vent, lazy boy. His eyes switch over to us. His tail lifts off, *thwack, thwack.*

Jack picks up his plate. He takes mine too. Look, neither of us is eating. He says, "Don't ask me what happened to me. I look at that dog and all I see is a pet." Jack sets the plates back down and sits again. He runs the flat of his wide palm down Bird's belly. Bird's eyelids go heavy with the stroking; this is the first time Jack has shown simple affection to his dog in my company. *The Dog Encyclopedia* says canines are culturally sanctioned receptacles for male affection.

"That's not entirely true. I know what happened." Jack looks up. "You happened."

The table is not near enough space between us. I push out of the chair with my plate.

"You said I should trust Bird." Jack goes on. "Well, Bird didn't trust, either. Then you showed up. Bird bonded with you and he proved it by protecting you, at a cost." Jack rises and shuffles to the counter to scrape lamb chops into the bin. Bird trots up to be of assistance. "I've been too busy retrieving him. Your mother calls it rescuing, but it's more of a retrieval. Anyway, that's a problem of mine, retrieving. Maybe that's why you came along. I don't mean you came along to point out that Bird and I were having a failure of confidence, though I'm grateful you did. I mean that when you came, you came to stay."

Grrrrrr. Bird's growls echo along the walls of the rubbish bin. His head rises, whiskers greased. He trots out the kitchen, shoulders braced, ears perked. Red and blue cruiser lights swirl the hallway walls around him.

Jack drops the dishtowel and rushes after Bird, catching his collar and wheeling him back into the kitchen. Bird swivels his head in the muzzle Jack straps on. "Olya," Jack says, "we got to figure this out. Not just this situation with the dog. I need to move on, I mean forward, I mean family. Get your mom back—"

"Mom's lived in this house—I mean before me?"

"Yeah. So?"

"And after you got home from the war, did she come then?"

"What? Probably, sometimes," he says. "Take it easy. She never stayed in my house long. We're pretty hit or miss, your mom and I, here or there, hot or bother."

"You ever ask where I was?" I say. "You ever ask her that?"

Jack tightens the straps on Bird's muzzle. He stares at the dog. He says quietly, "Not enough."

A short sharp rap on the door.

He does not look at the door. He looks at me. "We could do this over, you know. Be a family, regular."

"Us, family?"

Bird puffs barks. His ribs flare like gills. But the effort is shadowy, dull. Maybe *The Dog Encyclopedia* has advice on canine fatigue.

"Bird, too, a regular pet."

"Jack?" From the other side of the front door a woman calls. "You going to open?"

Jack backs Bird into the closet. "My old partner. Pay no mind."

"You shot her dog!" I say.

"She'll sell it that way." Jack shrugs. "But it won't right an unrequited love."

"Did you say *love*?"

"Answer the goddamn door, Olya." His whisper is a hiss. "Don't let her in. Whatever she points at you."

Officer Barbara Ross stands on the threshold. "You still here?" She holds in her arms a bulky garbage bag that juts at wrong angles. She offers up the black bag like something sad to show you. Sweat rolls into the cave of her eye. "Get Jack." She tilts to look into the house. "This is heavy, let me tell you."

"Want to put it down?" I say.

"You bet I do." She pushes the bag at me, like she will let me take a turn holding. I reach out for the bag. But that is not it at all. Barbara pulls the bag out of my arms and pushes in at the same time. From behind, Jack draws me aside and shoves Barbara back onto the stoop.

"You need a search warrant to enter," he says.

"Don't need a warrant to give you a present," she says. She

lays the black bag on the stoop. A tuft of fur chunks out from a tear in the bag. Her fingers shake as she loosens the knot at the top. The knot fights her. Jack leans against the door jam, watching, no offer of help. At last, Barbara coaxes the plastic out of itself and the bag drops open. A pair of flies shoot out. She draws back the plastic. The dog inside is hard, the skin sucked to the ribs. Its eyes are open, and maybe Barbara just notices because she places thumb and forefinger on the eyelids to draw them down. Crouched over like this, her knee rubs against the dog's neck where the bullet entered. She looks up at Jack. "You did this," she says. "He was shot with your rifle, a .30-06, 220 solid-grain bullet. I don't need ballistics to say it."

"Why would I do something like that? Wasn't it your thirtieth?"

"No one remembers you at my party. Until right before the incident. In army fatigues. What was up with that?"

"Does anyone remember seeing you at your party?" Jack says. "Nobody can quite drink like an officer of the peace." Jack nudges the dog's shrunken belly with the toe of his boot. "Get it off my steps."

Barbara looks down at her dog. She looks at Jack. "I want your dog."

Jack's eyebrows fly up his forehead. "Are you referring to police property? If so, please take proper procedures."

"I've contacted Lackland AFB, the 37th Training Wing," she says. "Find out what happened over there. I got in touch with Bird's handler. A guy named Poughkeepsie—"

"Bird's fine."

"Bird is not...*right*." She points to her head. "Health is declining. PTSD."

"Dogs don't get —"

"It's not for you to fix, Jack. Bird can't be trained." Barbara steps over her dog's body. She reaches up to Jack's head and guides it to her chest. Because of his height and her lack of it, he has to bend his knees. "Oh, Jack," Barbara says. "Why not just kill me?" She pats his head, like he is her crying child, but she is the one. Tears run out her eyes. "Don't make me beg," she says.

Jack places a hand on her shoulder. It seems he means to reassure but instead he uses her shoulder to leverage away. She tugs his head harder to her chest.

"Barbara. Don't embarrass yourself before the kid."

Her nails dig in. Blood dots his scalp, the sutures there. Her fist punches his back.

I grab her arm.

"You've caused enough trouble," she says, shaking me off. "This man's gone off the rails since you. You're just lucky I intervened before Nurse Fenton got to Child Protective Services."

Jack's hand comes out and guides me back into the house. "Go on," he gasps. Jack's hand swings back and slams Barbara in the spine. Her arms spring open. His head is free. Barbara wheels off the stoop but catches herself at the bottom step.

Jack walks the lady cop back to her cruiser, his arms loaded with her dog wound up in the black garbage bag. She holds to Jack's arm as the trunk of the cruiser rises. Jack sets the dog inside. Barbara eases down the trunk.

Will Barbara's dog be enough sacrifice to appease this house? Maybe, but more likely her dog is just the beginning. The rear lights of the cruiser trail down the street. Or is it burn? *I would have poured my heart out to you...*

Jack switches on the hallway light, passing me without a word. The hallway closet creaks open. "There, boy," Jack says. "There, there."

A body hits the floor. Jack is rolling the dog onto his forearms when I come up. Bird's eyes drift in their sockets. Only the tip of his tail flicks as I kneel beside him.

"He just dropped," Jack says.

"No air in that closet. No light. That's why."

Jack shakes his head. His fingers tap the visible ribs.

"Barbara didn't feed him enough," I say.

Jack says nothing. Only the sound of a dog's tail. *Donk,*

donk, donk. The hallway shines against the night in Bird's eyes. Jack sits back on his heels. "Barbara feeds dogs like kings. It's Bird, which turned up his nose to her kibbles. Dogs will hunger strike. It's not Barbara's fault he missed me." We both know this isn't true about Bird missing Jack. On the other hand, what ails is not PTSD either. Bird is surely a holy idiot for God. Does he not sing His praises?

Jack probes his back where Barbara punched him. "Did she hit you in the same spot?"

"She'll keep punching until she makes a hole big enough to crawl into." At that, Bird rises, tail swinging low. He nuzzles my hand. Jack eyes Bird and with tenderness. He says, "Olya, you look a little grilled around the greens yourself."

I take Jack's hand and guide him to his bedroom, helping him into a chair. Clean sheets are still where Nurse Fenton folded them into a drawer. The sheet unfurls across the mattress. One by one, I fold the edges into tight corners. I turn around for the top sheet, and there is Jack, the sheet open over his arms. He crawls into the bed still in his boots and pulls the sheet over him. "C'mon, you two." He pats the space beside him.

Bird leaps onto the mattress and curls against Jack's chest. I crawl in beside Bird. Jack's forehead touches mine, Bird's snout snuffling up between. Jack takes my hand then rests it on Bird's shoulder.

"Don't hold so hard," I say. "I'm not going anywhere."

Jack pats my cheek. His legs jump. Sleep has him.

I watch Jack's face. His lids slant oblong under a high forehead. His long nose skews right over crooked lips. He is gap-toothed and big chinned. He is so long his boots hang off the bed. Up to now I am not sure I could have picked Jack out of a police lineup. And Jack makes an impression. Describing a person requires taking them in, the bad with the good. Mom has known Jack, known him longer and more often than I thought. Something between them, more than cousins between them, but whatever it is they don't say, and maybe I don't want to know. Jack said I will not like the answers, the answers will beat the living dickens out of me. Jack also said we could be family, but does being a family mean getting the living dickens beaten out of you? This is likely how family feels to Mom, a lot of bad before you get to the good, if good there is. No wonder a house is so much safer than the family inside it.

Jack breathes in deep waves. I let go of his hand but I do not go. I stay beside him. What I know now is that not holding on is staying.

22

One coos, another garbles. Bird snores against my arm. All these songs before my eyes open. I drop my legs over the side of the bed. Bird's head pops up but he stays stretched out across the otherwise empty bed.

Jack is gone already.

Fog rolls in from the open window, snapping static in the air. Songs in the valley below, calls in the higher tree line, croaking, a tussle in the leaf litter. Woods run up against Jack's yard. Since when all these trees? Airplanes rumble up the clouds; a dog yips in the street; water dribbles in a fountain; kids high-five; the catch and creak of a porch swing in the wind; a door slams; a car putters; a piano goes *dum-di-dum*; someone says, "A dime a dozen"—all wrapped up in the chimes clonking above the porch rail on the house next door. Have these songs been here all along? Why has the life in this house only now come alive to me?

Jack's house is not grand, the walls could use new paint, but unlike a vacancy, Jack's house is filled. The more I stay, the more it fills me. My bones, the blood in my veins, the saliva in my mouth, the moist stuff in my eyes, the noise in my ears—my skin is the holding wall. My body houses me.

And I tell you endure the house and you will come home.

Bird eases off the bed. He scratches the door with his paw. He trails me down the hallway through the kitchen and past the fridge with Jack's note: *Buying bacon. May stop at hardware for screen.*

Bird cannot get out the back door and into the yard fast enough. His leg lifts and he sprays the plastic leg of the patio chair, where Mom sits under the open umbrella pearled with water droplets. She lifts her sunglasses and grins. "Look what a cat drags in."

Pretty is everything: curled hair tied in a green scarf, green dress, green eyes, the tilt of her head. Mom has come home. "Where is hug?"

I jump into her arms, happy.

She says, "Jack?"

"Buying bacon."

"Good. Hurry now. We must go."

"Jack said to stay." I say it into her neck to hide my smile. She throws her head back and laughs big. She is edgy after being away. She expects nothing to change while she is gone. Usually nothing does. "Mom," I say. "Did the ballet corps take you? Do we go to San Francisco? We can go together now. All of us."

"This is not a big family adventure, Olya. This is art. But this only a Russian understands. Director of San Francisco corps say he is looking for talent but how will he see without talent himself?" Her eyes shift to the door. "Get your suitcase," she says.

"No."

"What?"

"I mean, I need to pack."

"Pack? Since when you unpack?" Bird noses my thigh. Mom's eyes walk Bird's spine. "Never mind suitcase," she says. "I buy us new stuff. I got nursing job." She sighs.

"Okay," I say. "It doesn't matter where we stay."

"This is new," Mom says. "A home was very big deal to you."

"I had things the wrong way." I collect her cool fine fingers in mine. "Jack wants us together, Mom."

Her fingers close over mine. "Why is a cop parked outside the house?"

"It's probably better if we clear out. Jack kind of has to."

"What did Jack do now?"

I yank out my hand. She does not let loose. Bird's head roots between our knees. Mom looks down at Bird, really looks. "What is this doing here?"

"We got Bird back," I say. "Jack and I."

"You stole it?"

"What if we did?"

"Very good. Now you make big crimes with Jack…and bigger friends. What was I thinking leaving you here?"

"You want a home on the stage. You went for it. I want a home too. You tried to get me one. That's all," I say.

Mom straightens, like she wants to grab at those words but will not allow herself. Instead, she turns on Bird. "I know you," she whispers to him. "I was not sure before. You all alike."

I draw Bird to me. "You don't know Bird."

"I know since Jack trained him in Afghanistan," she says.

"Bird was never in any war," I say.

"Look in the ear. Q-106…something like that. They give to all dogs in war."

I kneel beside Bird. "I know every inch of this dog. No number," I lie.

"Jack wants a problem with the law, I will give him big problem."

"The cops already know Jack took the dog," I say.

Mom says, "Do they know he take you?"

"Really, Mom?" I say it gently. "You're the one who took off."

Mom pulls me off the patio with her. "We go!"

"Go where?"

"Wherever there is vacancy."

"The vacancies are filled. See?" I punch her off my arm. Bird lunges for Mom's leg. My hand shoots in to block him. Bird bites my wrist.

23

The hospital cafeteria chowder is flavored with bottom dwellers. Fish morsels lump the surface. I pitch my fork in the bowl—what a splash! But nobody notices. Good thing. Mom said, "Do not invite eyes." She said this after the doctor sewed up my wrist and released me from Emergency. But I stayed in hospital to wait for Mom's shift to end. The first time I have waited in hospital and not in a vacancy.

The bite on my wrist was serious. No cause for delay, no saying goodbye to Jack, again.

Mom gave me a choice: ride alone in an ambulance or ride with her to San Bernardino Hospital. She was headed there anyway for work. She gave me another choice: say goodbye to Bird or hand Bird over to the cop parked on the street.

"Be good," I whispered into Bird's ear before leaving him safe in Jack's yard.

Mom waved to the cop in the cruiser as we walked past. The green scarf she tied around my wrist had already soaked to black. It was blocks to her car. As usual, Mom parked streets away.

"Glad to finally get out of Jack's house?" Mom asked but she did not require an answer. She knew I was better at keeping promises to her than I was to myself.

Red lights swirl at the cafeteria's windows. Across the street, people carry signs: *Band-Aid Measures* and *Pull the SCABS!* San Bernardino Hospital is jumpy with workers on strike.

"You could use an ice cream cone." Nurse Fenton stands before me, vanilla pooling her thumb.

Nurse Fenton is a happy surprise, but I shrug and look away. Mom said I was to attract no attention. That probably includes Nurse Fenton. She scoots in beside me anyway. "I asked for chocolate, by the way." She bites into the cold white cream.

"Some don't like how we crossed the line. They're loyal to the nurses on staff and get back at you how they can." Fenton wears burgundy scrubs, like the scrubs Mom pulled on before reminding me not to invite eyes. Then Mom rushed off. Going, but for the first time, not leaving me behind. All I have ever wanted. But. If it was so easy to bring me along, why not bring me before?

Nurse Fenton catches my eyes on her scrubs. "Normally I don't work hospitals. But on account of the strike, San Bernardino is frenzied for relief. Hiring anybody, even nurses *nobody* hires." Fenton is not one of those, she makes clear. Since this woman is the nearest person I have to Jack, I reach for the other ice cream cone.

Fenton nods toward the bandage around my wrist.

"Bird," I say.

"Knew it!"

Before Fenton can start with the questions, I start with my own. "Why would nobody hire a nurse? I mean what would she have done?"

"Hospitals cut nurses loads of slack. The only way to become a no-hire is to show how you are. How much you don't give a piss." As Fenton talks, she starts licking fast. "Nobody hires a nurse whose judgment is lousy."

"How do you know if someone is a no-hire?"

She smiles. Ice cream smears her teeth. "Well...they get fired a lot."

Mom has work at this hospital. That's all that matters. But what was so important about this job, this time, that we had to leave Jack's right away? Mom has had a hundred nursing jobs. Because sooner or later. She is fired.

"Do you talk to God, Nurse Fenton?"

"What, do you talk to him?"

"I asked him to take me away from Jack's house."

"I wanted to help you. I tried—"

"No. God told me I had to stay."

Sun flares, rimming the crown of Fenton's hair. "Did you?"

I contemplate the soup, those things sunk to the bottom. "It's always questions with you," I say.

She leans in. "Think it's contagious?" She says, "Ever figure out what happened to your dad and Bird in Afghanistan?"

I take a casual lick off the cone. "Did Jack tell you that Bird was with him in Afghanistan?"

Fenton thinks about it. "No, it was just there between them. Some old habit of blood."

Bird's ears folded back when I said goodbye. Inked against his ear's outer white, Q-107. Mom had been off by one number.

"Glad you got out," Fenton says, gliding toward a bin, tossing the cone. "That house does not deserve you."

The signs on every wall in every corridor implore families to treat the hospital as their home. And use the sterile wipes dispenser. Early evening in the pediatric playroom, I kick around kiddy cabins rigged with kitchenettes. Someone has shoved a pooped diaper up a couch cushion in the waiting room. I sit on the cold floor, stare up at the TV. What would Nurse Fenton say I deserved if she knew the truth about me? If she knew that the mom who chaperoned us at the museum, the mom I named Hot Legs on account of her glossy boots spread open on her calves in the bus aisle, was the same mom who had opened her home to me? After the class trip, Hot Legs took back her offer to live at her home. I was not the kid she had in mind. That door closing on her home made me sore. I thought it was owing to what I had spied out. But now I know that Hot Legs's nice family home was not the home I had in mind, either.

Midnight and the waiting room is a Frigidaire. Too bad I left behind my warm orange coat. Mom rushes in with a sweater for me. She complains of the other nurses. Her voice is jokey, but she does not smile. A look comes over her. How hurt she is by it all. She walks me to a room with vacant beds. "Is too much, being in hospital. Too much for anybody with eyes in her head." She says, "Sleep." Metal balls rattle the runner as she drags the curtain around the bed, hiding me from sight. Don't invite eyes, she says, not long now, she says. She goes.

This bed smells of bleach and flowers rotting in a jar. To the distant beeps of a monitor, I count pinholes in the ceiling. The pinholes squiggle question marks in the wily corkboard. The curtain rattles. Mom slips in, eyes blinking. "You awake?" A muscle twitches in her cheek. Her fingers pinch at my pillow. "What happened?" I say. "Did someone see me?"

Her green eyes beetle across my sheet. She says, "Give me your cell phone." The cell is deep inside my pants pocket. She claws at my hands for it.

"Where's your cell, Mom?"

"I sent you link to audition in San Francisco," she says, ignoring my question. "Everyone in ICU asking to see it." Her hands shake but she manages to get the audition to play. As we watch the screen, Mom breathes fast, a soundtrack to her feet flicking the boards, dotting and dabbing, cricket weight, springing and soaring—

Mom presses pause. She hesitates then says, "I am good, no?"

"Shouldn't you be working now, Mom?"

She points at the frozen screen. Judges sit at a long table before a bank of mirrors in the audition studio. "See how they argue? They are arguing over me. You wait," she says. "I may still get a call." But the cool faces of the judges are unreadable. No one argues. Mom's eyes burn into me, daring me to doubt.

Beyond the curtain comes the sound of running down the corridor, stopping, running. Mom peers through a crack. She throws a smile and slips out through curtain. She did not take the phone to show the others. Through the crack, I see Mom stopped by another nurse. "Everyone is looking for you. Doctor Alvaro is freaking," the nurse says, her amazed eyes thick with liner.

Mom walks around the nurse, but the woman shifts and blocks again. "I know your kid's in there." She points at the curtain.

Mom shakes off the woman and goes.

"No wonder nobody hires you," the woman hollers after Mom. She looks back at the curtain and catches my eye. I duck. She curses softly and walks out. The curtain shifts a little and settles.

✦

I slide into a thin morning. The sink beside the bed trickles cold. I splash the water onto my face, but Mom cuts the tap. "Olya, what you doing? We must go." She uses the bedsheet to pat my face dry. "Baryshnikov in town tonight! The show was sold out long time ago. I found tickets." She glances over her shoulder at the empty corridor. "Hurry."

"Forget ballet," I say. "Just do your job!"

"I would not have to do this job if I had met with Misha that night, but I am too stupid. Who is safe in parking lot full of coyotes and drunks?" She slips her arm around me and laughs sad. "You would not last long in Russia, Olechka. Moms and dads drunk since breakfast."

"We're not in Russia, Mom." I crawl out from under her arm. "Where is my breakfast?"

She sits beside me on the bed. "You are tired. Was long night."

"That nurse said nobody would hire you. How long since nobody would?"

She flexes her feet. "Years."

"Years? But…where did you go? If you weren't going to work?"

"Where else? Tonight. Only *one* night. Misha dances better than God. Can your little child mind understand? Ballet company makes committee decision. Baryshnikov will give company in San Francisco eyes to see what I dance. He will do this for me."

"Why, Mom? Why will he do that for you?"

As if in answer, Mikhail Baryshnikov soars over the dividing curtain, without rattling a metal ball. He hangs in the air to land *en pointe* between us. He bows, this danseur, and snatches up

Mom. They dance on the narrow, curtained stage, feet rising and roaming the rumpled sheets. He raises her up and spins, a blur of burgundy scrubs. Now I know why we left Jack the way we did, why she risked her new job by sneaking me in here, why the trouble in Griffith Park messed things up, why this must be happening now. I figured it out, like Jack said I would. Baryshnikov. Mom has been saving up to tell me that the great Mikhail Baryshnikov is my father.

"I know, Mom," I say. "Finally, I know. Baryshnikov is my dad."

She hardly looks at me. "That would be nice," she says. "But Jack is your dad."

24

Mikhail Baryshnikov's heart is hooked up to a tiny wire monitor. The beat of his heart is pumped through speakers so that all can hear. This Baryshnikov on stage is no figment soaring over the dividing curtain of a hospital bed. He is real muscle and bone dancing to the beats of his heart. Not much to dance to at first. Just *bum. bum. bum.* Baryshnikov finds something though. He needs so little, this dancer, to dance. His legs too. Slow, dragging feet, light leaps, stops and starts. *bum. bum. bum.* His heart pumps quicker through the speakers. More to do now. The dance takes over more of the stage. Dancing does not get in the way of how you feel. What Baryshnikov feels is his heart and he is dancing it. *Bum. bum. bum. bum.* Running and turning the air and landings. Such landings. The more he dances, the faster the heart beats, the faster the dancer must dance. How to catch up to the beating of his own heart? More music than he knows the dance for. Was that a skip? Did his heart skip? Skip a beat? The beat of the heart, held between beats. Uncertain what he will do next. Except one certain thing. He is my dad.

Jack is my dad.

When Jack cooked stew for me, was he? When he bought the orange coat, was he? Was he when, between us, Bird leapt so high for the disc, when Jack held so tight to my hand before falling asleep, was he my dad? All along I must have known that he was, but it was how I knew him that changed. I came to know that Jack could be that, a dad, not just a room in a house.

Baryshnikov's arms settle at his sides, his thighs twitch until still. But not the beat of his heart. It is a one-man band booming under the din of all of us clapping. On his face is surprise. Shock even. Even Baryshnikov does not quite know what he has done. Does not want to know what his heart is capable of.

Mom told me Jack was my dad from the go. If I knew all along, why not say it? What good is my talk if I do not tell it all?

The audience is on its feet. The tears on Mom's cheeks grab the stage lights. She looks over at me and her eyes go wide. She shovels through the layers of her handbag, hitting on a tissue printed with lipstick. Thanks just the same, I will dry my own tears.

The women's restroom is all hollow gold and mirrors. I turn on the spigot and the water howls into the bowl. I shove my face in the water. It spills down my cheeks, my cheeks the main occupants of my face, mother's face. The girl standing before the mirror has her mother's build, narrow ribcage, hips. We could be twins, say the men behind the vacancy front desks. So why believe he is my father? A lot of men have loved Mom. Any one of those men could be my dad. Mom has made a mistake. She is almost certainly wrong about Jack. He is not my father. If he were, he would be in this face in the mirror.

Mom will be wondering what is taking so long. I should go. But I stay.

True, my arms are not as fine as Mom's, and longer. Already I am as tall as she is and will surely pass her in height. Jack is tall. Mom's eyes are emerald and miles away. Disorderliness sparks my eyes. My smile chipmunks my cheeks. Jack's face juts out, set for laughing. The gap between my front teeth is the gap between Jack's teeth. He has been there all along, his face in mine. But I had only seen in my face what I lacked in Mom's.

Not Jack. He could see the resemblance, and he did not tell.

No wonder I could talk my way into a place to stay but I could not keep it. I could not see the house for the home it was. But Jack could see and he did not tell. He hid. Even when he took me in, he kept me out.

Applause rushes up from the auditorium. The restroom door swings wide. Mom flies in, looks around, a panic. Our eyes meet in the mirror. "Hurry. We will miss him!"

I push past her into the empty lobby. Mom swoops to the glass doors. But she stops on the threshold, ears cocked to the dying applause from the auditorium. "Where was he?" I say. "All that time while we were in vacancies, where was Jack?"

She eyes the first few people clearing out of the auditorium. "Jack left me for Afghanistan. Abandoned us." She reaches out her hand.

I take her hand. She navigates us around the squares of longing sea grass that line the exterior of the performing arts hall. The rear of the building lets out into a loading area beside a small parking lot, cordoned off. Before a door marked Deliveries a dozen people hold playbills, notepads, bouquets of carnations. Mom maneuvers us to the front of the crowd. "I know Misha." She shrugs as if this is obvious. "We went to same school in St. Petersburg—"

"Vaganova's," I say.

"Misha will help me to dance in corps de ballet. The best. San Francisco."

The small crowd hoots as the door bangs open and security guards march out, arms thrust against the press of people. Mom smooths the brave strands of hair that have broken free of her bun. She rises on her toes. Baryshnikov slips out the door. He is dressed in a sweater and jeans, a red gym bag slung over his shoulder. His head down like a bull in a ring. He is shorter and fiercer than he appeared under the lights, his face lined and almost kind. A woman and a man in shiny black suits walk at his heels.

Mom clamps a cold hand on my shoulder and pushes right up to the black suit nearest Baryshnikov. In a high, thin voice she says, *"Misha, ya tozhe uchilas v Vaganovskoj shkole! Ya ballerina. U nas odna istoriya. Ty dolzhen mne pomoch. Pomogi, Mishenka, ya tebya umolyayou!"*

Baryshnikov hears Mom. He veers toward her, dodging the suit. He reaches for Mom's hand and regards her closely. He smiles. Mom smiles too, grasping his hand to her as her other hand fumbles inside her purse. The woman in the shiny suit taps Baryshnikov's shoulder. He nods, then tugs his hand out from Mom's. Security hustles him through an opening in the crowd toward a chauffeured limousine idling in the lot. A red-gloved hand waves from the backseat. "Misha," Mom screams, holding up the business card she fished out. "Misha!" The dancer glances over his shoulder, right through us, folding into the bright pitch dark of the limousine's interior. Mom's hand drops, her torso bent weird with what she never expected. She comes up with this terrible smile for the retreating limousine.

I stand and stare at her, heart pounding at my ears. My feet skip beneath me, propelling. I dash across the lot, rush for the limousine, colliding with the door, banging black glass in the instant before it pulls onto the street. "Don't leave her!" I shout at him behind the glass. "You cannot abandon her!"

The window stays closed. The limousine glides out into traffic.

When there is nowhere else to go, you go to a vacancy. I told Mom I had left them, but she said they haven't left you. It's motel, she said, not vacancy. We trudged into the room. Mom opened her suitcase and pulled on her old nightgown, hauled back the papery sheets, crawled in and closed up like a daisy.

The room's only chair is where I sit and flip through a real-estate magazine featuring houses tricked out with infinity pools and turrets, houses built like tree forts, like silos, like UFOs. My wrist throbs from banging the window of Baryshnikov's limo. The doctor had told Mom to change my bandage daily. I will ask her to change it when she wakes up. Did Jack finally get those stitches out?

"I never should have left Russia," Mom says into her pillow, awake after all. "I could have danced at Kirov, had my own apartment in St. Petersburg. Maybe a dacha on Baltic Sea."

"We have a house to live in here."

"Yes," she says, quietly. She says, "You are right. Go to Jack. Take taxi. Take money from my purse. What do you want with me? I am without talent. No ballerina. Not since I was kicked out of school. Is a lie and I am telling it to myself all day. Is a lie and it is you who have been taken in more than anyone by this lie. I'm sorry, Olechka. You not deserve. Thanks god you find a friendship with Jack. Go to him, Olechka. Go to Jack."

She curls up tiny. Something born before its day. I throw down the magazine. Cross the few steps to the bed. I drop beside her and wrap my arm around her. "No, Mama," I say. "I'll stay." She folds my hand into hers and closes her eyes.

Think about houses. Think about home. Smudge a form against the wall of the mind. A figure walks among the rooms. Jack. I am in Jack's house. Not the house I would design—no matter, this house has designs on me. Memories all the way down to the basement, where God spoke through a crack. Where Jack stored the kid's bed, pictures too. Pictures of me.

"Why did you ask Jack to keep the baby stuff?" I say.

"I do not ask," she says. "I told."

"Are you and Jack married or something?"

She laughs into her pillow. "Something."

"After he joined the army, you saw him, right?"

She yawns, like it's obvious.

"How much. I mean, when you left me alone, was it to go to work or to Jack?"

"I had to work." She is getting sore at all the questions but too worn out to stop them.

"You never held on to enough work to go to," I say. "Did you have to see Jack, I mean, without me?"

She reaches for the lamp crouching on the table, but she does not turn the switch. "Think I was not scared to leave you?" Now she switches it off. "It scared me even more to take you."

"Why?"

She does not answer.

"Did you ever think about how scared I was?" I ask though she is done answering questions.

But after headlights from the parking lot circle the walls above our head, she whispers into the dark, "When I was left home by myself as a kid, it was relief."

I tuck the bedspread around me, the oregano of sweat and sex and disinfectant rising from the nylon fibers like flames from a hearth. "You had a home," I say.

The mattress bumps atop the corners of the room. I climb out the window behind the bed, jumping through red berries to Jack. He wears hip boots and holds his rifle above the water. The house is up to the roof in water. Bird is on the roof and will not come down.

Mom throws off the sheet. The lamp switches on. I open my eyes, in the vacancy again. I do not lift my head from the pillow, just watch her pull pins out of her bun. The pins scatter willy nilly as she leaps off the mattress and light-foots it into the chair. Sitting princess straight, she picks up her cell phone and scans the messages.

"Any news?" I say. We didn't leave a note, nothing for Jack.

"Not from director of San Francisco ballet anyway." She knocks aside a strand of hair. "He said it could take few days to persuade judges to reconsider."

"Mom," I say. "What happened to Jack in Afghanistan?"

She drops the cell onto her lap. "Is not Afghanistan. It is that dog." She studies her nails. The fingers fold into a fist. "He ever tell you how it went over there? How a lot of soldiers got shot and killed in a cave? It only happened because of Bird singing. Jack believed it was his own fault soldiers die. When Bird ran off, Jack kind of broke. He went after the dog. But got lost in desert. No one knows how long he was wandering under that sun. Until Jack got caught trying to steal Bird from a village or something and put in Afghan jail. Goddamn Bird. Bird, Bird, Bird. All he cares about. Not me, not you. He does not want you there. He does not want anybody."

"Jack said I could stay," I say. "Mom or not."

Mom is always in motion. Even when she is not, some part of her gnaws at movement. But in this moment, she goes still. One eye wanders off me. One eye. "He did not, Olechka," she says. "Don't lie...or he lies." She lifts a hank of hair off her neck. The pulse throbs. She picks up her cell. I turn off the lamp. Mom just brings the phone closer, seeing into the stingy light.

"Don't you want a home, Mom?"

"Sure, having a house is nice."

"A family. I guess, that's what I'm talking about."

Mom smiles at me like a polite child and sets down the phone. She slumps over the armrest. I cover my ears against the panic thump of her heart.

25

Mom is not sleeping beside me when I wake up. She is not sitting in the chair. But someone is. That someone is Officer Barbara Ross.

"Hungry?" Barbara hands me a bag from a donut shop. She adjusts the gun belt jugging at her hips before settling back in the chair. The plastic window curtain behind Barbara burns orange. Not yet nine, says the nicked alarm clock on the bedside table.

"Where's Mom?"

Barbara makes a big show of looking around the room then throws up her hands.

"How did you get in?" I say.

"Put down three months advance on a room, and they give you the key." She points to a plastic key card on the table, the only key card. "It's yours," she says, crossing her ankles. "On one condition. Mom stays away from Jack."

I head into the bathroom. "My mom would not go to Jack's without me."

In the bathroom mirror I can still see Barbara but now I can see her trying not to smile. I turn on the taps. Barbara strides to the door, leans on the jamb as I brush my teeth. "You know all about Jack," she says, "don't you?" I spit out the backwash and push past her into the room.

"Bird was Jack's dog in Afghanistan," she says.

"The name of Jack's dog there was Daed."

"Short for Daedalus. But after he flew out of a tree, he was all Bird."

I shake out the bedsheet, launching the bag of donuts. Fat chance I'm telling Barbara that I always knew Jack's story about Bird did not add up.

"Don't be sore. You're not the only one he's lied to. Jack

conned us all." She picks up the bag, dropping back into the chair. "Thanks to the other handler on base, Lieutenant Poughkeepsie, Jack's trick is up."

She pulls out a cruller from the bag, bites off a hunk. "Bird disappeared into the desert for a long time. When he finally wandered back into base, the army retired him like any piece of military equipment not up to par."

"Why? At least Bird made it out of the wilderness."

"Ah, his identification rate for IEDs had slipped." She wets her index finger and taps the sugar on her lips. "Bird was put up for adoption. Law enforcement agencies have second dibs."

"Who has first?"

"Handlers. They can put in a request for WMDs. A Bad Conduct Discharge ruled that out for Jack. Ironic, huh, since it was refusing to give up on Bird that blighted his military record. When Jack learned Riverside PD had adopted Bird into our K-9 unit, he tricked us into hiring him as a handler."

"It's no trick, Officer Ross. Jack will never give up on Bird."

"One more signature and I get Bird. I'm getting the dog." She stuffs the rest of the cruller into her mouth. "The guys want to take it by force, but I tossed them another bone."

"Jack says Bird might not be good police dog material," I say. "Called him a loner."

"How can Jack want a woman like that?" Now the words are out, Officer Ross's mouth drops open. She has so surprised herself. "That dog," she says. "That dog is army gone on PTSD."

"Do you think," I say, "that taking Bird out of Jack's life will get you in?"

Barbara pushes up to her feet. The bag drops to the empty carpet. She kicks it and heads for the door, straddling the threshold. Her cruiser in view at the curb, chrome casting queer orange light.

"I've done my checking. What comes up on your mom is, well… You've been left alone in cars. Taken into custody by officers, placed in foster care. Testimonials from motel owners of abandonment." She looks up at the room number hanging crooked on the door and fixes it. "Child Protective Services can be kept away only so long."

The real-estate magazine seems to jump into my hand. The thin pages sting like nettles.

"When Mom does come back," she says, "you tell her the deal: stay away from Jack and this room is hers. Guaranteed."

"We don't want your guarantees." I wing the magazine at her head.

Barbara ducks but the magazine cuffs her chin and drops to her feet. She stares at it. She bends her knees, ladylike, to pick it up. She looks up at me, all along rolling up the magazine to a baton. "It's your safety I'm after. Get it. Safe. Me." She runs at me, one hand swinging the magazine baton, the other clamping my throat to shove me at the wall. She whacks the magazine at the wall and shouts in my ear, "Not her, you. No room for you anywhere!"

Was that a skip? Did my heart skip? "In this wilderness," I say at the hand at my neck, "we are tested, and our faith is strengthened."

The real-estate magazine undoes in the officer's hand. In her hand a UFO. She hands the magazine to me and goes.

The roar of the cruiser's engine improves a little on the silence of the vacancy. I drop into the only chair to listen for the engine's fade. My cell phone has a message. The text is from Mom. Last night she wrote: *Ballet is the only family for ballerina if want to survive but is that living? Now I am not sure. Clever Olya what you think?*

What do I think? I think of my toes. Toes up. Toes down. Heels up. Feet tap. Tap to the skip of my heart. What I'm thinking, what is starting to get through, is that too much wanting, and especially wanting to be safe, is a lot more of a lock on a door than room in a house for others.

Mom's phone buzzes against the table. She forgot it. Mom does not forget her phone. She is calling to check in. Or to find her phone. Or it is Jack, trying to find us.

"Hello?"

A man on the other end says his name. I only hear San Francisco Ballet.

"She was expecting your call," I say. Not what Mom would want me to say but then she should be here to answer her phone.

"Yes," he says, "may I speak with Irina?"

"Not available."

"Yes," he says. "Please give this message—I'd hoped to tell her myself…"

I wait.

"Yes. Please inform her that she is to start on Monday."

"Mom's in?"

"Yes," he says. "We are delighted to welcome Irina to our little company."

I hang up. The cell phone blinks off. The black screen mirrors the orange sun on the curtains. The vacancy still and ticking. Mom is dragging her feet. She should be here to tell the man she is ready to dance. Be here to tell the news to every hospital that won't have her. She should be here to tell off the mouthy cop who will pay her to stay away from Jack. Mom is not here.

She goes.

Always goes.

All those times she left. Just left. Left me to—

The UFO house.

The UFO house over the real estate magazine. Hovering cylindrical steel. Plaster cascades from the ceiling. Gold flecks! I rise up on the rumbling heat of the only chair. The floor kicks away. The whole room aloft. A journey to unknown lands. Pray.

The chair drops.

Ceiling dust trickles down the walls. The tipped table rolls one more turn. Car alarms blare in the lot. People shout from adjacent rooms. "Earthquake!" shouting, "You there?" shouting, "Not over."

The ground bowling and heating under me, I sway through the door. Broken glass flashes on the stoop. People point at sidewalk they swear jumped a foot in the air. Telephone wires necklace over ticking cars. Popped transformers flash. A guy with an emerald green parrot stumbling drunkenly on his shoulder asks if I'm okay.

"Are you?" says the parrot. "Okay?"

Someone says the epicenter of the quake is in Riverside. Jack's house is in Riverside. Jack's house is on a fault. That's why the crack in the foundation. A shaking house would scare Bird. Bird might hide—

Beside Jack's front door. Four numbers in ascending order. 2229 or 2929? The name of his street will not rise up, either. The Good Book will show the way to Jack's. 22:29. *And the LORD opened the mouth of the donkey, and she said unto Balaam, What have I done unto thee, that thou has smitten me these three times?* The donkey reminds Balaam that he has ridden her day in and day out, that she never failed in her duty to him. Balaam claims the donkey disobeyed and mocked him. He raises his sword to kill her. Now the angel of the Lord opens Balaam's ears. Know this, Balaam: *Thy way is perverse.*

In Balaam, the Lord has encountered one such as Jack before. Jack would bend a beast of burden to his knee. Jack claimed his dog mocked him. Jack's ways are perverse. Now Jack wants family. His home will require great sacrifice for such belated wants. Bird under the house.

The bald man behind the front desk puffs cigarette smoke at his computer. News anchors talk Richter scales. Images of damaged homes, their wagon wheels pitched.

"How much to ride the bus to Riverside?" I say.

His thumb and forefinger take up the cowboy hat resting on the keyboard and set it on his head. "Isn't it a buck-fifty?" he says. "About another buck-fifty for to transfer."

"Three dollars," I say.

"Three dollars."

"I will take three dollars for this." I set the Gideon's on the counter, having no further need of it.

"You don't sell a man's items back to him." He puts the book in a drawer.

"I didn't take it from here," I say.

"Take one from any, take one from all."

"Please give my mom this message: I went back." I hopscotch all the walkway cracks out the door.

"Buses ain't running after a quake," the vacancy man hollers.

I have no need of a bus. I have a friend. Under *Z* in my cell, Zanzibar Buck-Buck McFate.

26

He says, "Family is not for everyone."

He says, "Family takes a toll on the heart, on the nails, on the hair."

He lifts the hair off my neck. "Your locks have lost a lot of luster."

"Not a peep out of you!" he says. "Got so needful I hung out with Captain Canine. That man is a downer. Totally undone by military combat. Seen it firsthand. Pap was in Iraq."

McFate drives past an apartment building where people shift cinder blocks that used to be a wall. The orange air coughs on all the dust. McFate fiddles with the tuner. *Delia, oh, Delia, Delia all my life, if I hadn't have shot poor Delia, I'd have had her for my wife.* A report about a collapsed parking garage interrupts the song.

McFate looks me up and down. "Your 'hood is on the fault. What do you expect?"

"Faster," I say.

He is driving fast, and smart, navigating all the closed-off streets, until we hit Jack's neighborhood. A car parked askew at a curb looks like Mom's car. But then we turn the corner. At the top of the street sits Jack's house. McFate pulls into the driveway.

"The house held," I say.

"Sure, if you're cool with a crack down the middle!" McFate gapes at me.

It is true. Jack's house is split, from top to bottom. The right half of the house sits lower than the left—not one book leaning against another, but books standing side by side, except on different shelves. But the house still held.

McFate grabs my hand. "Hear this: I'm leaving. I don't mean now. I mean forever. Will you hurl into the abyss *avec moi?*"

"I'm thirteen. I'm too young to hurl into the abyss."

"We can sleep on the beach?"

"I just want to make sure Bird is okay." I slam the door.

Bird's howls are loud, though I heard them from the car. I heard the howls a couple blocks away. I heard his howls from the vacancy. The concrete by the gate has erupted. I scan the shrubs lining the house for red berries. The gate slams shut behind me. Bird's howls are dismal. I picture him pinned beneath piled cement. But Bird is not under the house. He is in his yellow doghouse.

"Here boy. Sweet dog." I call him beauty; I call him mine. I kneel before him. Might as well kneel to a ghost. He is pasted together, dull-faced. Has Jack finally given up on Bird? Without Jack to fight, has Bird just given up? A damp blanket lines the boards of the doghouse. Bird needs to be warm.

The house stares at me crooked. I push through the rear screen door and on through the kitchen, where cupboards hang dumbly open. Groceries coated in flour thaw on the linoleum. Spilled kibbles make for slow going down the hall. Glass snaps underfoot. Jack's commendations askew on hooks. The piano has rolled out the doorway. *Dah-dah-dah-dah.* Mom's purse lies sideways on the lid.

The bed in Jack's room is made. A lamp upright on the floor. The room empty with relief. I have come for the orange coat. Bird needs this warm coat more than I do now. Something insists though, some premonition, calls me. A last missing part. The coat hangs still in the closet in my bedroom. Bird is howling again. I pull the coat off the hanger, setting off the other hangers on the dowel. The floor rumbles. Something knocks the wall of the closet. I grab the doorframe, brace for aftershock. When laughter demolishes the air. More laughter swings up from the room on the other side of the closet, the room where Mom stayed when she did stay.

The doorknob to her room sticks in my hand. *You not allowed in.*

I push open the door. The door collides with a pile of

clothes, rolls a high heel. She is on the camp bed, naked body open to him. Beneath her, fixing his hand on her hand on her boob, holding her to him, saying something into her ear that makes her laugh again, holding her laughing, again, in his arms, again.

Do they see?

Dirty little spy.

Anyway. The laughter stops.

Now you've done it. Now you'll have to pay.

The house pops out all around me. Walls unfold, a hundred rooms in one. I am in all of them and I am in none. The screen door to the backyard slams my back. I cannot say which side of the door I am on. But sundown glances off the roof of the yellow doghouse, and I am outside again.

Whap, whap. Bird's tail pounds the doghouse.

"Olya."

Someone standing on the other side of the screen door wears Jack's bathrobe. It is hard to make her out in there, but who else would it be? I do not answer. Mom steps back into the house.

Shouting starts, a noisy finger pointing ricocheting off walls. Bird's tail whaps the doghouse boards. All their shouting is nothing to the voice booming out the crack that splits the house. As if that crack in the foundation stretched and reached until it came into the light, if that is what it took to be heard. From top to bottom, the house bellows, *Endure the house and you will come home.*

"There is no house. Look at you. Broken," I say.

There is family.

"Family?" I say. "You mean the doings of a man and a woman?"

I mean those two in there.

"Those two? Sneaking around—in their own home. I'm not the one spying. They're the ones. They're—"

They are your parents.

"What kind of parents leave their kid alone?"

All kinds.

"Is that how family is, only happy if someone is left out?"

Happy, no.

"But safe?"

A hand on my neck. "Alive! Standing there like freaking stone. That's some ghoulish shit, Olya." McFate takes the orange coat from my hands. "Here, stinky." He hooks his fingers into Bird's armpits and drags him out of the doghouse onto the coat. In the shelter of the orange, wrapping it around. Bird's leash is buried. At least he had enough in him to shit on it. Even for someone McFate's size, Bird is still a lot of dog to carry. At the gate, I kick more than it needs kicking. The gate jangles open to let us out.

McFate lays Bird on the backseat of his car and scoots in beside him. The interior is dark on account of the purple-tinted windows so McFate probes with his hands for why Bird is in such shape. He unscrews a jug of water. The liquid seeps at Bird's lips. "Dehydration," he says, stroking Bird's snout. Bird's tail wags between my palms. "The way you folks treat dogs," he says.

"Jack didn't do this," I say. "Bird did. Jack just stopped trying to stop him."

"That's interesting. In my house, we take them to the vet."

I let go of Bird's tail and stand on the driveway. The sun sits on the backs of the houses across the street. Chipped stucco, broken windows, a wagon wheel down. But nobody is out of their house. The birds are silent. Over the brown hood of McFate's car, I can see the front door on Jack's house. The holed-up screen is gone, the entire frame taken off. Was Jack finally aiming to repair? On the other side of the door, Mom and Jack shout my name at each other. Their blowup is a lot louder than on the first night we came. Those are my parents.

I reach in and grab McFate's arm. "Yes! Take him to a vet. We'll get him patched up and go away, like you said. You, me, and Bird hurling into the abyss."

McFate's eyes bead. He wriggles his arm out from my hand,

then makes as if he is making Bird more comfortable. "But damn does this dog have an odor," he says. "On the other hand, a McFate stands by his dog." He backs out of his car, shoves his hands into the hacked-off sleeves of his shirt. "Is that what you want, to cut and run?"

I say, "I don't know what I want."

"Yeah," he says. "How about we just take Bird to the vet and take it from there—crap!"

A cruiser is turning into Jack's driveway. The K-9 Riverside Police unit parks behind McFate's car, blocking on purpose.

McFate jogs up to the cruiser and pantomimes rolling down the window. The driver obliges. "Mind?" McFate says. "Sick dog on board."

The cop swings open his door without warning so McFate has to hop back quick. Both uniforms unfold from the vehicle. Doors slam. The younger of the two walks up to McFate's lowrider and peers in. He covers his nose. "That dog needs medical attention."

McFate says, "I knew you would understand, sir. Now moto."

The cop smirks at McFate. "Soon as we've had a word with members of this household." They march across the long grass, between them a dog that might once have been Bird.

The cops hesitate before the stoop, discussing the crack that splits the house. The older one shouts at the front door, "Riverside Police."

"Look at those kittens," McFate says. "Scared a house will fall on them. We got to get Bird out." I follow McFate up the walk. He skirts the cops and jogs up the steps to bang on the front door. He yells, "Hey, you two, bring your beef to the yard. Men here to talk to you."

The raised voices inside cut. The front door opens. Jack, wearing the bathrobe now, his hand cupping a smoke. He looks McFate up and down, looks at the cops, then his eyes land on me. He frowns at the bandage unraveling at my wrist. He is still looking at it when he up and runs down the steps, blowing smoke at the cops' chests.

Both men step back, hands on belts. "Jack Marea," the older says, "we're here to—"

"Good!" Mom shouts from the door, finger wagging at Jack. "I have restraining order against this man."

"Which you're in violation of," Jack says, marching back up the steps at her. "In *my* house."

Her small fists pound Jack's chest. Jack dodges her hits, and she clasps him to her. "Happy now?" she mumbles to Jack. "Olya see how her mother and father do?"

"She knows what she's dealing with," Jack says.

Behind Mom's head the sun implodes on the roofs of the neighboring houses, and it is once again the middle of the night that we arrived. Bird watches me from the street. That night I would have taken anything, so long as it was a place to stay. Bird fought that black dog for a scrap of meat dragged from the garbage and Bird won. Then he dropped the meat on the ground and never looked back. Bird knew there was no reason to cling to a scrap. Jack was right. You could learn from that dog.

"Jack Marea," the older cop says, "we're here to—"

"Take the damn dog," Jack says.

"Dog?" he says, yanking on his own dog's lead. "We don't know about a dog. We're here for a Ms. Irina—"

"What's Irina done—" Jack laughs. "Now?"

"She's wanted on grounds of child neglect and endangerment."

Mom turns to me. A quick vanishing look of shame in her eyes. She steps to the front door and slips into the house. The door hangs ajar behind her.

Jack glances at me. I follow Mom to the door.

"Take me," Jack says to the men. "I'm the one to go."

From the doorway I can see the kitchen go light in the littlest way. The screen door opening and letting out through the other side of the house. Mom, stealing out the back door. Mom thinking no one will notice. I look over at the cops. They do not notice.

"We have orders to take you in as well, Jack," the older cop says. "You are in violation of a restraining order placed by—"

"Irina?"

"Affirmative."

"Barbara put you up to this?" Jack says, on to something.

The cop repeats, "We're here for Ms. Irina Volk—"

"She's not here," Jack says.

The cop looks at Jack, like give me a break.

The younger says, "We'd like to verify that?"

Jack points at their canine. "Wouldn't that nose be of more use to folks buried under shopping mall lots?"

The cops follow Jack to the door. I scoot out of the way. Jack says, "Just keep off the grass, boys." The faintest hesitation, they cross the threshold. The moment they do, the older cop lets the dog off the leash.

Jack says to me, his eyes marking the progress of the canine trotting in and out of rooms as the cops trail after, "When'd you last eat?"

I just laugh.

"I'll get something started in the kitchen." He looks at me then goes.

Mom will be coming out from the rear of the house about now. I could follow Jack into the kitchen, or I could intercept Mom at her car, parked for a quick getaway. But I loiter on the threshold. Going and not going, not knowing where not to go—

The cops shuffle back up the hallway, hands high in the air, their gun belts missing. Jack scoots 'round them to brace open the door. In his other hand he holds a gun. "Thanks for stopping by," Jack says.

Hands still high, the older cop's belly nudges the younger cop through the doorway. They both turn around at the stoop. "Stop being such an asshole, Jack," the older says.

"C'mon in." Jack is talking to me.

I step back inside the house just as the cops' canine leaps out from the parlor, its teeth flying at me. Jack knocks me against the door. He steps in the dog's path. "Halt."

The dog freezes midair. It drops to all fours and stares up at Jack, stockstill.

"Sit," Jack says. The dog sits. "Stay."

Not a muscle flicks on the dog, except the muscles that shut jaws.

"You don't tell another handler's dog what to do," says the older cop, his belly thumping on each word, his hands sinking down.

Jack looks back at the vexed faces of the men. "Hands in the sky," Jack says. "About face. To your car. March!"

"We'll just come right back," the younger says. "More of us."

"Need an escort?" Jack glances at the dog.

"Fuck you, Jack," the older one says. "Coots is not your canine."

"Show them to the car, Coots," Jack says. The dog rises to all fours. Head lowered, eyes high, the dog creeps toward its handlers. It will use teeth to guide them should they delay.

"Halt, Coots!" the older cop hollers. The dog does not halt. The cops whirl around, scrambling from their dog. "Get in your vehicle," Jack says. "Touch firearms and I shoot."

Jack tracks the cops to the cruiser, holding the passenger door open for Coots. On command, the dog vaults over the young officer's lap. Jack steps backwards up the driveway. He makes the sign for rolling down the windows and shouts, "All hands out the windows. Drive with your knee." This is how they drive away.

McFate sits on the trunk of his lowrider. He thrusts out a hand to high-five Jack. Jack walks past McFate without a look. McFate drops off the trunk and eases back behind the wheel, revving the engine and flagging like mad at me through the windshield.

Jack pushes me back into the house, closes the door, locks it. "What is that criminal up to?"

"Bird needs to go to the vet, Jack."

"Quit interfering with that dog. Is evidence still insufficient that I'm doing what I know?"

I want to say that it is true, I did not believe enough in what he could do with a dog that had learned the stay. But Jack is in no mood. He tosses the cop's gun from one hand to the other, his eyes roving the walls. Truer still, I am in no mood either to talk about what my father has chosen to reveal about himself—and not reveal.

He points the nose of the gun down the hallway. "Your suitcase is where you left it."

"Mom?"

"She's coming with us. Go, go, go." Mom must still be here, just hiding.

The soft toot of a horn outside. McFate.

Out of patience, Jack pushes past me into the room where I stayed, where Bird whined for me under the floor at night. Jack wings my suitcase over the bed, snapping open the clasps to pitch in clothes, his gun taut in the other hand.

"Where's your coat?" he says. "You left that here, too, after you lit out —"

"We had to use the coat for Bird—"

Beeeeeeeep. McFate lays on the horn.

Jack's head turns toward the street. He sidles up to the window, tips the gun to the edge of the curtain, lifts, looks out. Shaking his head. "Tell the crazy boy to take off," he says, "or I will."

I'm heading out to McFate when something scratches up the boards under my feet. How is this? Bird under the house again? McFate let him out? Why would he? I drop to my knees, listen at the boards.

"You lost your meat?" Nothing in Jack's eyes says what he will do next.

His chin lifts. He hears the scratching too. "Goddamn mother fucking dog." He points the gun at the floor. "This will make you stay."

Jack's face is lit. Like old times. Bird getting up to tricks; Jack letting him just try. Nobody backing down. Hope wings me to my feet. There is life in Bird yet. *Bang. Bang. Bang.* The boards jump. The house catches and sucks. Jack shoots. Holes pop inches from his toes. A voice rises up under the floor. "What have I done to you to make you treat me so?" The Lord has opened Bird's mouth. Verses 22:29. Jack's showdown with the holy.

Jack answers. "You have made a mockery of me."

Open Jack's ears, Oh Lord, for his way is perverse.

Jack is deaf to the cries. The cries rising already from below.

Pounding now on the front door. "Open up! Olya?" McFate yells from the other side.

This is no apparition. That is not— "Not Bird," I whisper to Jack.

No yelps. No whines. Not a song. A woman screaming.

"Do you not hear her?"

Jack hears. His hand snatches the gun from himself and hurls it at the wall. "Oh, my baby." He drops on the floor, drops his mouth on a bullet hole in mad resuscitation. He pounds the boards, like he can pound to the place under the house where Mom hid from the cops, thinking herself safe.

I pull at Jack's robe, but Jack will not get off his hands and his knees.

I slam against the rear screen door and race across the yard to where Bird went under. Mom is already coming up from under the house, fisting red berries to pull to standing. Blood pumps from her knee. Her arms *en haut*, she stumbles upright, hauling the leg after her. Hop, stumble, drag, a kind of dance. *Bum-bum. Bum-bum. Bum-bum.* She trips and slides down. I kneel beside her and lightly set my hand on the hurt leg. "Mom, are you okay?"

She reaches past her knee for my hand and lifts the bandaging that has come undone on my wrist. Her fingers tremble over the stiches. "Olya," she says, "your bandage is dirty."

I snatch my hand away. "I know. I'm sorry—"

"No, no, I didn't make change. Some nurse I am." She looks up. Her eyes shine. "Sorry, Olya."

"Oh, Mom. Let's get you up."

"Not with that wrist you don't. I can myself." But she cannot get up on her own now and she knows it. I think of her good news, how the San Francisco corps said yes. But how can I tell her this now? I ask instead if her knee hurts a lot.

"Eh, I've seen worse." She winks. "I will heal. And dance better than before."

"Olya," Jack calls, striding down the front steps, the house cheerful and secretive behind him. "Help me with your mother."

But McFate has already stepped up. Jack's eyes meet McFate's. "One, two, three!" They lift Mom to her feet. Her head hangs down, rocking between them as they walk her to the house. Sure, there has been a failure of confidence, not enough trust going around. But could we start over, be a family, like Jack said? The Lord desires mercy not sacrifice. There is also in this world grace, so if there is to be shelter, let it be us.

The cops have come back, like they said they would. The two from before and more cruisers packing up the driveway behind McFate's car, the sun careening and dousing the street in robes of silver and gold.

All the dogs of the neighborhood have trotted onto the street. One lets off a nervous bark. The others take up the cry, collectively raising their heads to yowl. A white utility van puffs up the street and parks behind a cruiser. A large man with a flaming red beard climbs out. He stands beside his van, taking in the scene. McFate's dad sees me, and he waves. We meet at the rear door of McFate's lowrider. "My son sent an SOS," his dad says. He leans in and murmurs to Bird. He peers over his shoulder at me. "You take the rear." I hold part of the orange coat, so it forms a stretcher under Bird.

"He a goner, Pap?" McFate says, coming up.

"Nah," he says, "with luck this one's just starting out."

McFate throws his arms under Bird so we can all move quick. His dad instructs me to open the rear doors of the van. The two lay Bird on a dog bed. Bird sits up, licking his chops, the yellow eyes catching light.

McFate squeezes in beside Bird and waves.

The van pulls away.

Cops mince around the lawn, no one getting too close. Except the young cop from before. A quake-hit home don't stop him. Canine at his knee, cuffs ready, he tracks me along the dead grass to Jack and Mom huddled on the stoop.

Jack tells the young cop to call an ambulance. "Then please get off my lawn," he says, flashing me a smile. He hikes up his bathrobe and draws Mom's leg onto his knee. Her blood smears his thigh.

Mom says, "Put down my leg, Jack."

Jack saying her leg must be elevated. For her own good. When all at once the house reshuffles. A drumming up from the bottom. Walls squeal free of a beam. Half the house drops another lifetime into the earth. Light pours in and air sweeps through. Dust crowns the heads of the two on the stoop.

"What are you looking at?" Jack says to the young cop held up and undone by a sort of fool's stare. "Go home. Go to your own damn hole. Take a look at that."

Jack shifts himself over, patting the stoop for me to sit.

Even though Jack and Mom sit on the level half of the house, the whole set-up is clearly not safe. But my bones are strong and there is room for me now, so I sit beside them on the stoop.

"Lucky for us, Ira," Jack says, "our daughter has joined us."

"Family is bad times," I say, "and good."